The

Pulsar

Files

Iain Cameron

DEDICATION

For Roger, a man whose love of books knows
no bounds.

Homeland Security Agency (HSA)

HSA is a fictitious organisation established by the Home Office, the brainchild of minister Sir Raymond Deacon. Its unofficial motto is: 'Fight Fire with Fire,' and it is staffed by agents operating under similar rules of engagement as the UK military.

It was set up to combat the changing threat faced by UK security forces from terrorists, criminal gangs, ruthless organisations and individuals. Terrorists who no longer appear in the open, but integrate themselves into local communities; criminal gangs who use open borders and the web to traffic guns, drugs and people; and rich organisations and individuals who believe they are above the law.

The headquarters of the agency is located at a secret address in London. There are other HSA offices at various centres around the UK.

Chapter 1

The boots of the man with the backpack made little sound. It helped that the twigs and leaves lying underfoot were wet from earlier rain. He'd parked in a track off Ladder Hill, and now was striding with purpose down a narrow path between a thick line of trees that jutted into a large field. It would take a keen eye to spot him as he wore a black fleece with black trousers and the copse produced its own dark shadow. If this didn't give him confidence at not being seen, he knew few people would be awake at this early hour of the morning, and even fewer wanted to gaze over this featureless Oxfordshire countryside.

He found a good place halfway along with a clear view of the area and placed his backpack on the ground. He opened it and removed a flask and a cup. He unscrewed the top of the flask and poured the strong, aromatic coffee into the cup. He returned the flask to the backpack and stood looking at the landscape, the cup not far from his lips.

The fields on both sides of the tree line had once grown wheat, he guessed from the stalks lying over the earth, but the crop had been harvested many months before, giving the land a barren feel. The only other landmarks on the immediate horizon were a derelict stone tower and giant electricity pylons, black high-tension cables strung between them.

Five minutes later, the coffee gone, he spotted a hot air balloon in the distance. He reached into the backpack and pulled out a pair of military grade binoculars. Raising them to his eyes, he brought the balloon into focus. He now had a good view of the occupants of the basket. Standing beside the grizzly old owner of Hewton's Balloon Tours, were Mom, Pop and two teenage kids, one girl and one boy. He smiled, revealing two prominent incisors, a noticeable gap between them.

He bent down and removed the stock, body, barrel and ammunition magazine from the backpack. In seconds, a process he could perform in the dark, as he often had to, he screwed the sniper's rifle together. With a final satisfying *click*, he slotted the magazine home.

From a protective leather case he removed the optical sight and screwed it to the top of the rifle. Lying down on the grass he focussed the crosshairs on the tip of the nearest electricity pylon, which he knew to be a distance of one hundred and ten metres, as he'd paced it earlier. Satisfied, he allowed the rifle to rest in his arms. He lit a cigarette while he waited.

The balloon made slow, steady progress towards him, the bulging red- and yellow-coloured envelope providing a splash of colour against a bleak landscape. He could make out the old man, his hand on the burner control, giving the lever an occasional tweak to increase the height, sufficient to clear the electricity cables now in their path. He extinguished the cigarette he had been smoking, and threw the butt into the bushes. He lifted the rifle and focussed on a point about ten metres above the nearest pylon.

In seconds, the livery of Hewton's Balloon Tours filled his view. He began to count. On reaching twenty, he fired a single shot. The hollow-point bullet pierced the skin of the balloon, like a hot knife through butter. It created a neat incision in one side and would tear a hole the size of an industrial dustbin in the other.

The balloon began to lose height and was now at the mercy of prevailing winds. At this time of day, the winds were predominately light and easterly. As expected, they blew the balloon towards him until it struck a 400,000 volt cable.

Chapter 2

'What time is it?' the otherwise lifeless body beside him asked.

'Four-forty. Go back to sleep. I told you last night...'

Matt Flynn glanced over at Emma and decided not to finish the sentence. She had gone back to sleep. Her deep slumber was a characteristic he longed to emulate as he had to make do with four or five hours of restless turning that often saw him banished to the spare room.

Flynn, an agent with HSA, Homeland Security Agency, he didn't have the excuse of a tough job, as his girlfriend, Emma Davis, had one herself: Detective Inspector with the Metropolitan Police. His poor sleeping habit was an inherited trait from a restless mother, his 'Duracell Bunny' as he often called her. He hoped the serial philandering that became the backdrop to his teenage years, and the lung cancer that killed her, weren't hereditary traits as well.

He eased himself out of bed and walked quietly towards the bathroom, although 'quiet' wasn't a word normally associated with this house. It was an old place that had been renovated before they'd bought it. Even then, the floorboards creaked, the water pipes groaned and clanked and, due to insufficient water pressure upstairs, a noisy pump started up as soon as the hot water tap was turned on.

The pump clattered now as he switched on the shower, but Emma wouldn't have to suffer a second helping when he filled a basin with hot water for a shave. His job often required him to go undercover. This usually meant growing facial hair to make him appear scruffy, trendy or like a jihadi sympathiser. For this morning, and most of the previous two weeks, the razor had sat motionless and unused on its stand.

Fifteen minutes later, Matt walked out to the car. The morning felt chilly, still dark with the rising sun struggling to make an appearance behind a thick layer of cloud. It wasn't so cold he needed to scrape ice from the windscreen, but it did require running the fan at maximum for a minute or so to clear the windows.

Neighbours living close to their house in Ingatestone in Essex would describe Matt and Emma as quiet. If asked to take a guess where they both worked, they would say he looked like a manual worker, and she a schoolteacher. It would be a fair description of him as for the last few weeks he'd left the house early in the morning, his hair unbrushed and wearing dirty clothes.

He had joined a gang demolishing a former rope-making factory in East Ham. He didn't need the money or a trip down memory lane, but he needed to ingratiate himself with a group of Armenian workers, suspected of bringing shedloads of heroin into the country from Afghanistan.

HSA didn't routinely investigate drug cases, leaving them to the larger and more capable units within the police, like the place where his partner worked. However, researchers in HSA and SIS, as MI6 was now known, believed the profits of their lucrative drug running operation were being channelled to fund terrorist activities in Europe.

He started the engine, drove along Stock Lane and approached its junction with the High Street. At this time of the morning he could turn without stopping. During the day, he would sit there for several minutes as a succession of delivery vans, shoppers and those like him today, motorists heading for the A12, filed past. He drove along the High Street. The restaurants, pubs, and shops were all closed, their bins of rubbish standing outside awaiting the arrival of the refuse lorry in a couple of hours' time.

Speeding up on the slip road, he joined the A12. On reaching the speed limit, he sat back and tried to relax for the rest of the journey. He was trying to forget the difficulty he was having building trust with his taciturn co-workers. A few minutes later, his phone rang.

'Morning Matt.'

'Morning Rosie, you're up early.'

'I need to be for the busy day I've got planned.'

'Good luck with that.'

'It includes you too.'

'What do you mean? Aren't you forgetting something? The Armenians at the building site?'

'Matt, I regret to say, you need to can the building site visits for the foreseeable.'

'For fuck's sake, Rosie. It's taken me weeks just to sit on the same bench as these people in a break.'

'I'm sure Gill appreciates your hard work, and if we close this new one quickly, maybe you could go back.'

'Don't be daft.'

'You could tell them you'd been arrested for selling drugs, or you needed to take care of a sick relative.'

'I don't think selling drugs would wash with these characters, but at least I can walk the talk about looking after a sick relative.'

'Don't be so touchy, but something family-orientated might appeal to their better nature.'

'Words like better nature aren't part of their vocabulary, especially when it concerns an outsider like me.' He sighed at the thought of all his hard work and early-morning starts floating down the Swanee. 'What's the big panic?'

'I can't talk about it on the phone. Pick me up at my place and I'll fill you in.'

'You got it, but it better be good.'

The M25 at that time of the morning was three lanes of slow-moving metal, a clearer illustration of Britain's twenty-four-hour culture he couldn't imagine. However, when he arrived in the Church Langley district of Harlow, less than an hour later, the curtains of most of the houses were closed.

Fellow HSA agent, Rosie Fox, didn't like living there as the demands of the job meant she couldn't keep regular hours and found it difficult getting to know her neighbours. She only lived there because her partner, Andrew Milner, was a pilot, and he was required to live no more than forty minutes away from Stansted Airport.

Matt was about to get out of the car and ring the bell, when Rosie came out of the house and strode towards him.

'Morning Matt,' she said as she opened the car door and got in. 'My God, you look a mess.'

'Morning. When you work on a building site, you've got to look the part.'

'I just hope you don't smell, it's a long way to go with the windows open.'

'How long is a long way?'

'Dover.'

'Dover? Why the hell are we going there?'

'You drive, I'll talk.'

He weaved through a warren of new houses with the strange-sounding street names so beloved of modern town planners and baffling to everyone else, Pennymead, Challinor and Momples. He headed towards the M11. On reaching the motorway, the sleepy, comforting veil of suburbia left behind, he asked, 'What's the story? Why are we going to Dover?'

'Gill called me last night,' Rosie said. 'What do you know about the war between Serbia and its neighbours?'

'C'mon, it was before my time. Plus, it's too early in the morning for a history lesson.'

'It's before my time too, but you read newspapers, don't you?'

'Your point is?'

'In the early 90s Yugoslavia fell apart, for reasons we don't need to get into. Serbia had plans to create a greater Serbia, a new Yugoslavia centred around the needs of the Serbian people, and went to war with

8

most of its neighbours, including Croatia and Bosnia. Are you still with me?'

'I think so, coffee would help.'

'You can have your fix when we get there. In this ugly and violent urban war which even now makes uncomfortable reading, numerous snipers were deployed.'

'Some infamously in Sarajevo, targeting Bosnian civilians as they queued to buy bread.'

'Ah, so you are awake.'

'Only just.'

'Some of those snipers went back to their day jobs as bakers and building site workers, while others like Dejan Katić didn't. They became guns for hire.'

'I know that name. Isn't he suspected of being involved in several high-profile assassinations?'

'Got it in one. Now one of our agents–'

'Who?'

'Joseph.'

Matt nodded.

'One of Joseph's contacts told him that Katić had been spotted hanging out with his former Serbian buddies in London. He's been trying to locate him.'

Matt sat up. 'Katić is over here?'

'We think so.'

'This is bad news for someone. So, we're driving to Dover to do what?'

'To look through CCTV pictures and verify if and when our man entered the UK, and try to get a handle on his vehicle.'

'Here's me thinking I quite fancied a day in France. Why doesn't Joseph pick up car details and everything else by conducting a surveillance operation?'

'Joseph hasn't been able to find him, and even Katić's Serbian buddies say they haven't seen him for a few days.'

'So, either he's gone back to Serbia after enjoying a few beers and a bit of reminiscing with his old army buddies, or he's out there doing something nasty that someone is paying him big bucks for.'

'The latter, Gill thinks, and the reason we need to find him fast.'

Chapter 3

The car stopped at traffic lights. What other motorists made of the two occupants of the BMW on a sunny February morning like this, Chris Anderson couldn't guess. The stony face of the driver, Chris's Uncle Kevin, was pale, emphasising his acned, scarred and pock-marked face, the souvenir of a misspent youth. It gave him more the appearance of a gangster than the businessman he purported to be.

In the passenger seat, Chris looked the archetypal teenager in a hoodie, moody and introverted, staring out of the window as if bored with the world and ignorant of its beauty. The only difference, not obvious through dark, tinted windows, were the red marks around both men's eyes.

They drove down Ladder Hill. If they hadn't known the location of the crash site on this quiet, country road to the south of the village of Wheatley in Oxfordshire, they could now see it easily enough. At a break in the perimeter fence surrounding a large field stood a police van. Following a line of trees running perpendicular to the field, Chris saw a sizeable collection of equipment and people. From a distance the gathering could be mistaken for a country fair or a travellers' camp, but on closer inspection the television satellite-equipped television vans and the numerous Day-Glo police vehicles revealed its true purpose.

They drove through the open farmer's gate, up the track and past a gaggle of curious reporters. The hacks turned and craned their necks to look at the occupants of the BMW, but on not seeing anyone they recognised, they lost interest and turned away. Closer to the crash site, they approached a police cordon where they were brought to a halt by a policeman, his hand in the air. Kevin stopped the car and wound down the window.

'This is an accident scene, sir. What business have you here?'

'Kevin and Chris Anderson; we're here for a meeting with Superintendent Cousins.'

The officer lifted his radio and, after listening to the response, gave them directions.

Kevin parked beside a large vehicle, looking more like a mobile home than anything the police would use, with the words Mobile Incident Unit etched along one side. He switched off the engine. For a moment, all Chris could hear was silence before his ears tuned into the ambient noise: the movement of vehicles, a shout, occasional laughter, the scraping of metal on metal.

'Are you ready to do this, Chris?' Kevin said. 'You don't need to, if you don't want to.'

Uncle Kevin didn't do empathy. Chris often wondered how he managed to run the family company, all those people with their petty issues and problems. He'd never seen him cry, not even when he received news of his only brother's death, and the one time he'd put an arm around Chris's shoulders, he hadn't looked or sounded comfortable doing so.

'Don't worry, I want to.'

Chris opened the car door and got out. The air smelled fresh and pungent. It was a welcome relief from the suffocating heat and atmosphere of Uncle Kevin's house where he'd been holed up for the last few days.

Not that he'd wanted to go out and be confronted by all the reporters standing in the road shouting their stupid questions. Kevin had to be counselled by his wife before he ventured out. His legendary temper was on a shorter fuse than normal, and she didn't want his picture ending up in a newspaper with his fist in some poor hack's face.

'Chris, come on,' Uncle Kevin said in a tetchy voice, misinterpreting Chris's slow pace for reluctance or the slothful walk of a teenager.

A few minutes later, they were seated in what passed for a lounge in the Mobile Incident Unit. The settee was U-shaped, taking up one end of the vehicle. Kevin and Chris were sitting along one arm and facing Superintendent Ed Cousins and his colleague, Inspector Barry Fisk on the other.

'Thanks for coming to see me again, Chris. You too, Mr Anderson. Let me again offer my sincerest condolences for your loss.'

'Thank you,' Kevin said.

'After we finish up here, I'll take you both down to the crash site as you requested.'

'That'll be grand, Superintendent,' Kevin said.

'Now that two days have elapsed since the crash, I will try to bring you up to date with everything we now know. The balloon ride took place early on a Sunday morning, so there were few people awake, never mind witnesses. Those we did find, a farmer and a dog-walker, were only able to report seeing the balloon in flight and not the accident itself. We've made an appeal for any witnesses to the balloon's final moments to come forward, but with the incident happening so early in the morning and in such a remote location, I'm not hopeful. Ten or fifteen minutes later, they would have been flying over the Oxford colleges and then it would have been a different story.'

Chris sniffed, holding back tears.

'Having a few witnesses would certainly have made our job easier,' Superintendent Cousins continued, 'but we can only work with what we're given. There are three possibilities for the cause of the crash, all of which we're investigating. Firstly, that the pilot, Mr Gerard Hewton, fell ill or suffered a heart attack. A post-mortem examination on all victims will take place today and I'm confident this issue will be clarified. Even though Mr Hewton wasn't a young man, at sixty-nine, his wife said he hadn't taken a day off work for sickness since he started the hot-air balloon business over twenty years ago.'

Chris moved to lessen the ache in his back. The seats looked comfortable, but the upright sitting position felt unnatural.

'The second area to consider is if anything within the balloon malfunctioned. The burner itself has been damaged both by fire and from smashing into the ground. Piecing it back together is a painstaking process.'

'We do it all the time in our business,' Kevin said in his usual brusque voice. 'Customers send back faulty equipment, and we take it apart to find out why it failed.'

'This is the defence components company you run, formerly in partnership with Stephen, Chris's father.'

'Aye. Galleon Electronics it's called. Although now, there's only me. The loss of my brother leaves a big hole.'

'I can only imagine, which is why we are working hard to try to establish the cause of the accident.'

'We appreciate all your efforts, Superintendent.'

'Good. Now, the third line of enquiry we are pursuing is pilot error. Even the best pilots make mistakes and this is why an eyewitness to the balloon's final moments would prove invaluable. I don't want you to think we are sitting around waiting for someone to call, we are talking to staff at the balloon company and Mr Hewton's family and friends. This, in an attempt to fill in the gaps in our knowledge and to find out his mental state.'

'What, to see if Mr Hewton suffered from mental illness or something?' Chris said.

'Yes, or something less severe like a temporary loss of memory or blackout.'

'What kind of bloke would commit suicide and tear the heart out of a decent, hard-working family like ours?' Kevin said.

'Let's not jump to any conclusions so soon, Mr Anderson. As I said, this is only one line of enquiry. We don't know if the pilot suffered from any such malady, not yet.'

'Fair enough. A man's innocent until proven otherwise, right?'

'Yes. Now when I spoke to you earlier, Chris, you couldn't remember why your parents, your sister and her friend undertook the balloon ride. Did anything in the meantime jog your memory? It's a small point, but one I'd like to clear up.'

'I told you why I didn't go.'

'Yes, and I understand your reasons.'

'Yeah, but that's not what some papers are saying, is it? They make it sound like I had something to do with it.' He couldn't help it, but tears welled in his eyes, tears he vowed would never shed in public.

'Chris, I can assure you there's no question in my mind or any member of my team, the Accident Investigation Branch or anyone connected with this accident, about you being somehow involved. To say so is preposterous and while I think newspapers are wrong to speculate, speculate they will. My advice to you is not to read any more newspapers until this story no longer interests them.'

'I think I can be of some help here,' Kevin said. 'Stephen's secretary remembers Stephen receiving an invitation in the mail from a supplier.'

'Does this kind of thing often happen?'

Kevin smiled, but it resembled the grin of a rattlesnake before it struck. 'We're in the defence business, it happens all the time. Mind you, more often than not it's us treating the big boys, but sometimes they invite us into their hospitality tent at the races or the rugby. If it's an invite to something they're not hosting, like the theatre or a balloon ride, tickets are usually given to us by a rep or sent in the post.'

'Do you know if Stephen's secretary remembers from which company they were sent?'

'I asked her, but she doesn't. Does it matter?'

'No, I don't suppose it does.'

The Superintendent looked at the Inspector and then at Chris and Kevin. 'We don't have anything more to add. Do you have any questions you'd like to ask, gentlemen?'

'When will the bodies be released for burial?' Kevin asked.

'As soon as the post-mortems are finished,' Inspector Fisk said, 'and the coroner is satisfied by the findings. I expect this will be completed around midday the day after tomorrow.'

'Why is the coroner involved? Don't they get called in for murders and the like?'

'No, the Coroner's Office investigates any unexplained death. It's a legal formality, nothing more. We'll call you when they're released. Is there anything else?'

Chris and Kevin shook their heads.

'Right gentlemen, can I suggest we move outside?'

Chapter 4

The wind at Dover Ferry Terminal was so strong. Matt Flynn thought it signalled the coming of a storm, but it didn't seem to bother the cigarette-puffing Border Force guy, Alan, beside him. Matt didn't smoke; why would he after his mother died after puffing her way through thirty-odd a day? Rosie liked to joke that he didn't smoke so he could run away from the bad guys. In his defence, the job made such physical demands on both of them that having any sort of impediment could get them killed.

He came outside as he fancied some fresh air. The temperature in the Portakabin where they were reviewing CCTV pictures varied between chilly cold to sweaty hot, depending on if the big heater in the corner was blowing or not. When it switched off, they soon froze and when it came on, it sucked all the moisture out of the atmosphere, leaving it dry and encouraging him to drink more of their crappy coffee.

From where they were standing, the terminal looked too big to be man-made, a giant metal structure in an otherwise serene landscape of white cliffs and churning gun-metal-coloured sea. Everything here looked to be on a grand scale. This, from the size of the signs to make sure drivers proceeded in the right direction, the cranes lifting cargo from ships, to the huge dimensions of the cross-channel ferries themselves. He knew there were many places along the south coast where a traveller could enter the UK: The Channel Tunnel, Newhaven Port and Southampton, but their intel suggested the Serb had come through here. He didn't mind having his hair blow-dried and his clothes fumigated of the last vestiges of cement and plaster dust, as long as he and Rosie came away with a result.

Working with snippets of information was a common occurrence in their line of work. Police and other law enforcement organisations could only move against criminals when they had a strong body of evidence. HSA agents could take action on less, apprehending criminals while they were selecting targets and stopping terrorists who were in the process of planning bombing attacks.

'How long have you worked here?' Matt asked his companion.

'Seven years now. I used to be at Heathrow, pulling in the likes of Nigerians and Jamaicans for a bag and body search. I could shock you with some of the things we found. I didn't mind the job, but I hated living so close to the airport. Had to live there because of the early starts and sometimes a late-night finish, but it was too bloody noisy and a hassle to go out anywhere. Our local road was the car park they call the M25.'

'I don't live near an airport, but I seem to spend half my life driving on busy motorways.'

'Now that I'm based at Dover, I own a pretty little house in a cul-de-sac near the centre of town. The sea is to the front, about two hundred metres away. Behind the house, a ten-minute drive or so, and I'm out in the countryside. A bit further west around Eastbourne you reach the South Downs, and for people who enjoy walking as much as me and the wife do, it's fantastic.'

'It must be hard working here with the huge volume of cars and lorries coming through the terminal every day. How do you spot the real bootleggers, traffickers and criminals from the folks trying to sneak in with an antique or half a dozen bottles of whisky?'

'Too bloody true it's hard, and the reason why we depend on intelligence from people like your lot and the other parts of the security services. Thing is, we're so focussed on drugs and the war on terror, me and some of the bosses around here think too many other scumbags are getting through. I'm talking about the likes of gunrunners, people smugglers, and small traders filling up their vans with loads of booze and fags and selling them at a street market. Now, if we had another fifty staff—'

'Matt!' Rosie shouted, her voice easily penetrating the thin walls of the Portakabin despite the absence of open windows. 'Come and see this.'

Matt nodded to Alan who shrugged and continued his smoke. Matt opened the door and walked inside, his body temperature rising at least five degrees now he had come out of the chilling wind. The one-storey Portakabin, looking minuscule beside the gigantic ferry terminal, was kitted out with multiple video screens. It also possessed all the equipment necessary to view historical CCTV pictures from the dozens of cameras operated by the Port of Dover Authority and UK Border Force. His companion, Alan the smoker, had said it: HSA passed on more intelligence to Border Force than the other way around. It felt good to be in receipt of their hospitality for a change.

He pulled up a seat beside Rosie, now operating the joystick controls. She had short blonde hair which bobbed up and down as she tapped the screen or the desk, emphasising a point. The only information they had to work with was Katić's approximate entry date into the UK, based on what Joseph's contact had told him. Using clever software, every individual arriving in the UK that day had been narrowed down to only those carrying a Serbian passport.

'You said to me, Mr Flynn, if our man Katić used a false passport we'd be stuffed. Agreed?'

'Why do I feel I'm about to eat my words?'

'Because you are, you non-believer. False passport or not, there he is,' Rosie said pointing at one of the screens. 'I should have put money on it.'

'If you'd put money on it, you'd lose. We both know what a terrible gambler you are. The only person who bets on a favourite, only for it to come in last.'

'My one and only time betting money on a horse. You're never going to let me forget it, are you?'

'C'mon, shift over and let me take a closer look.'

Rosie moved her chair to one side. The pictures looked clear, taken outside on a bright day, the driver standing beside his car while officials conducted a routine search. His hair was longer than the photo the HSA agents carried, and he now sported a natty goatee beard, like a portrait artist or a fashion designer. Despite the cosmetic changes, the aquiline nose and prominent front teeth, a gap between the central incisors, were clearly visible. He was reluctant to call his eyes evil or black, common enough descriptions of wicked men, as if what was in their heart or mind could be reflected in their eyes. However, he did have the cold and unfeeling look of a killer.

Of the many jobs attributed to Katić, the assassination of numerous businessmen, unfaithful wives and politicians from various African and Asian states, none had produced incontrovertible evidence of his direct involvement. This didn't make him a 'ghost' of the type beloved by thriller writers and movie makers, but instead, smart and resourceful. However, he needed to be on his game every time he carried out a job. One false move or one little mistake and a whole host of security agencies, HSA, Interpol, FBI and Europol would put him away for good.

'Well done, Rosie,' Matt said. 'It's our man all right. What's he driving?'

She looked up and pointed to another screen in a bank of eight. The view from a CCTV camera facing the front of the car displayed a Nissan mini SUV with Katić standing to one side, smoking a cigarette.

'The car is a Nissan Qashqai, on hire from a company in Belgium.'

'You're on fire today, Fox. Now, from the picture of him standing beside the car, we can surmise Border Force searched it. They obviously didn't find anything, or they would have arrested him.'

'Maybe the weapons he needed were delivered here by a confederate or sourced locally.'

'Yep, or maybe it was hidden in a secret compartment which I admit is doubtful in a hire, but what if the weapon was broken down and secreted all over the car? Anyone finding a piece would think it was a spare part for something else. Alan, the smoker I was talking to outside, told me a few minutes back, when they search a car, they're looking for drugs or known terrorists, not for pieces of metal that might make up a sniper's rifle.'

'If the dog doesn't get excited, they wouldn't have a reason to pull the car apart?'

Matt shook his head. 'Nope.'

'Okay, so we've established he arrived in the UK five days ago and maybe he travelled with a weapon or picked one up later. We know the car he's driving and its reg. If Joseph lost track of him in London three days ago, our next move, the only move as far as I can see, is to use ANPR to try and locate the car.'

Using a range of fixed cameras at roadsides and mobile cameras mounted in police vehicles, Automatic Number Plate Recognition reads and records ever car number plate that passes. It can read multiple number plates in seconds and will flash a warning to nearby patrol cars if a car has been flagged as a vehicle of interest.

'If he's still in London we'll pick him up in minutes, but if he's moved to somewhere in the sticks, then we are well and truly stuffed.'

Chapter 5

Chris and Kevin Anderson, Superintendent Cousins and Inspector Fisk left the Mobile Incident Unit where they had been talking. They headed in the direction of the balloon accident.

'Have you decided to go back to university, Chris, or are you thinking about taking a break for a while?' Superintendent Cousins asked as he walked beside him.

'I'm not sure at this stage.'

'I understand, you need some time to arrange your things in some semblance of order. What subject are you studying?'

'Computer Science.'

'Do you like it?'

'Yep, it's what I always wanted to do.'

'Would you consider joining Galleon Electronics when you graduate?'

'I don't have any qualms about the work they do, if that's what you mean. I've grown up with it.'

'I didn't intend to sound judgemental. I realise in the past there have been some protests outside the factory gates, but it's to be expected in the armaments business.'

The Superintendent stopped and turned to the small group. 'It's best if you wait here. Give me a moment until I can locate someone from the Air Accidents Investigation Branch. They will explain what they're doing and what they believe happened.'

They were standing in the middle of an enormous field, the hubbub of the police cars, incident caravans and television crews far away behind them. In front, behind a long expanse of police tape, the wreckage of the balloon with a low-loader parked nearby.

Chris turned to look around. Close to the road, a double line of trees jutted into the field. It was the only other interruption in this bleak, desolate landscape, save for hedgerows and giant metal pylons, striding across the fields like enormous aliens. It was a bare, featureless place to die and at variance with the people in the balloon.

His father, funny, smart, always ready to retort with a quick witticism about Chris's stupid haircut or the way he walked. His mother, wild and enigmatic, from the colourful dresses she wore to the strange cartoons she drew. Sophia, his sister, bubbly and cheerful with a smile to light up a dismal afternoon in December. Kamal, Sophia's boyfriend, a wizard on the guitar and with a voice so rich, it could make listeners weep.

The Superintendent walked towards them accompanied by a small, balding man wearing black-framed glasses.

'I'd like to introduce you to George Hamlin of the Air Accidents Investigation Branch. Mr Hamlin will try to explain how his experts are approaching their investigation of this accident and what they are doing today. George, this is Chris, son of Stephen and Laura

Anderson and brother to Sophia. This is Kevin, brother of Stephen Anderson.'

'Pleased to meet you,' George Hamlin said, shaking their hands. 'I hope I can be of some help.'

'We just want to find out what happened,' Kevin said. 'Give myself and the lad here some form of closure, if you know what I mean. We've only read what's been in the papers, so if you can give us some more detailed information, we would appreciate it.'

'I understand.' He turned and pointed into the air. 'If we can all face in this direction. The balloon took off from the company's base in Worton, to the north-west of Oxford. The route they followed which was more or less as planned, was over the north of Oxford and the colleges, the Oxford Golf Club and Slade Park, and back towards us here in this field. If not for the accident, they would have flown over our heads,' he said, turning, 'and with luck and a fair wind, landed in one of the fields behind us over there.'

'Aye this is what I remember Stephen telling me,' Kevin said. 'Sophia was keen to fly over the colleges as she was thinking of going to university there.'

Chris felt a lump in his throat at another dream now shattered. She'd set her heart on Magdalen College and told him her aim was to captain the University Challenge television quiz team. He'd told her that was a geeky ambition, but he knew she was smart enough to achieve it.

'They approached here,' he said, with a sweep of his hand, 'and as the Superintendent has no doubt told you, we're not sure yet if they suffered a mechanical fault. I think it's unlikely as these burners are pretty reliable and there's not much else on a balloon to go wrong. They would need to climb up around here,' he said pointing into the sky, 'between the two pylons to clear the electricity cables and then, perhaps due to a strong gust of wind or insufficient height, whatever the reason, they weren't high enough and struck the cables. The balloon tipped, lost air and crashed to the ground where the balloon itself was consumed by fire, fuelled by the burner's propane tanks.'

'Were they electrocuted?' Chris asked, fearing the worst.

'No. In my opinion, they died from the impact of the fall, not from the fire or being electrocuted by the power cables.'

'I don't understand.'

'Have you ever seen birds perched on electricity cables?'

'Yes, plenty of times.'

'They aren't electrocuted because touching only one cable doesn't complete the circuit. If a really large bird sat on one and spread its wings and managed to touch another cable at the same time, it would complete a circuit and be electrocuted.'

This made sense as he'd once read a story on the web about an owl knocking out the power in Aberdeenshire when it stretched its wings, but at the time he assumed it to be an urban legend. For some reason, believing they hadn't been electrocuted made him feel better. Whichever way he looked at it, his family died in a tragic accident, but he took some comfort in knowing that despite their bodies being broken, they were otherwise intact. If they had been killed by the fire or electrocuted, they would have been blackened and shrivelled by fire or fried to a crisp on the high voltage power lines.

'I think the order of events went like this: they hit the cable, there would have been sparks, if not a bang, but hitting the obstacle upended the basket. As the basket tumbled, it tipped the occupants out, and the burners along with perhaps sparks from the cable, set the balloon material on fire. I'm sorry to sound so blunt but I don't know how else to say it.'

'Don't you worry about us, Mr Hamlin,' Kevin said. 'We'd rather face the facts than make our own assumptions,'

Hamlin nodded and turned to face the low-loader. 'As you can see over there,' Hamlin continued, pointing at the wreckage beside the low-loader, 'we are now removing the remains of the balloon from the site. What we have here is the remains of the burner and a section of the basket, which will all be taken back to our laboratory for further analysis.' He took off his glasses and wiped them. 'I imagine between what you've been told by me and your earlier discussion with the Superintendent, you've heard a lot today and perhaps are finding it hard to take it all in. If there are any questions you'd like to ask me, ask away.'

'How long does an accident investigation take?' Kevin asked.

'In this particular case, I imagine we should be finished in about a week; two tops.'

Hamlin looked at their faces, inviting further questions, but Chris had seen and heard enough. He now wanted to go home, well not really *home*, Uncle Kevin and Aunt Hannah's house. The big house in Witney where Chris called home and where he grew up, lay cold and empty, waiting for a family who would never return. He'd gone back to his old room once, to pick up some clothes and his laptop. He'd left pictures on the wall of the bands he liked, footballers he admired, women he lusted after, and selfies of him and his mates. Perhaps, this was his way of saying, I will be coming back.

'Well, if there's nothing else I can help you with,' Hamlin said, 'I'll go back to supervising the loading. It was good meeting you both,' he said shaking the hands of Chris and Kevin. 'I'm sorry for your loss.'

'Thank you for sparing the time, Mr Hamlin,' Superintendent Cousins said. Hamlin nodded and walked back to the crash scene, being watched all the time by the low-load driver, standing at the side of his vehicle puffing a cigarette.

'I trust the meeting with Mr Hamlin helped?' the Superintendent said, turning to face Chris and Kevin.

Chris nodded.

'It did. Thanks for arranging it, Superintendent,' Kevin said.

'No problem. Come, I'll walk you both back to your car.'

Again, the Superintendent and Chris walked together, but this time at Chris's bidding.

'Can I ask you something, Superintendent?'

'Ask away, Chris.'

'Is there any way this crash might have been deliberate?'

'I think we dealt with the suicide theory earlier.'

'I'm not thinking of suicide.'

He shook his head. 'You heard Mr Hamlin, everyone believes what happened was an accident; tragic for causing the death of five people, but an accident nevertheless.'

Chris's face betrayed his scepticism.

'What's on your mind?'

'My dad's business. Galleon makes the electronic releases for a range of rockets and bombs being used by fighter planes on duty in the Middle East. A lot of antis would like to see it closed down.'

'I understand, especially in a place like Oxford which has so many charities and pressure groups, but why kill the owner's wife and family? I don't know who will inherit the business, but I imagine it will continue making defence equipment.'

Chris didn't feel reassured. Yes, he wanted to believe it had been an accident, but something inside, something like an itch that longed to be scratched, wouldn't let him.

Chapter 6

A small group of generals, commodores and air-marshals scanned the sky with high-powered binoculars. The conditions were near-perfect, with only a light south-easterly breeze and blue skies with some low-lying cloud. Not a hint of precipitation; the wet weather and bad visibility testing would come later.

Alex Livingstone, Senior Manager - Fixed-Wing Procurement at the Ministry of Defence, didn't feel overawed to be in such august company. To those with no knowledge of his position, he was a civil servant, mocked in his local pub for his gold-encrusted pension provision, his Harry Potter glasses and the paper-pushing antics of his colleagues. Here, in this little wooden hut, he was a god. The uniforms with medals on their chests and pips on their epaulettes treated him with respect because if he didn't buy any toys, they didn't get to play.

'Here she comes,' Lieutenant General Brian Souther muttered to no one in particular, 'bearing south-west.'

Livingstone panned the sky until he found the source of their interest: a small black object getting larger and larger as it sped towards them. Soon it would become recognisable as a helicopter, but not one in the accepted sense of the word. The sleek, aerodynamic shape, looked more like the fuselage of a plane with a large rotor blade on top.

It wouldn't sound much like a helicopter either as it didn't emit the characteristic clatter of blades, the result of years of research and the use of many new materials and techniques. This alone would get the vote of many conservative MP's, those who were also part of the landed gentry. They could no longer complain about noisy sorties interrupting their garden party or polo match, and from a military standpoint, it could sneak up behind jihadi terrorists before they had time to pick up their Stinger missiles.

'Pulsar', as the makers, Dragon Technologies, called this new and revolutionary helicopter, advanced towards them with resolve and purpose, like the true death machine everyone in the hut believed it to be. Pulsar was here in Boscombe Down in deepest Wiltshire, to give the assembled military top brass a demonstration of its fourth major innovation, the Arrow Battlefield System. This, after stealth technology, anti-missile protection and quiet blades. ABS was so accurate it could kill a person with a single round from over a mile distant and destroy an armoured vehicle with a two-second burst.

This improvement in accuracy wiped the floor with comparable armament systems, and the high initial cost of the helicopter would be partly offset by the savings made in ammunition costs. In the US, where Pulsar was made and used by the US Military, this increased firing precision forced them to make major adjustments to their logistics. So wedded were they to the principle of 'spray and pray', which required them to lug container loads of ammunition to every battlefield.

Livingstone and his companions were standing in a little observation hut, like a group of twitchers awaiting the arrival of a Willow Warbler or a Tree Pipit from Africa. The intercom crackled, informing them the pilot would reach the mile mark in ten-seconds. A countdown started around him, three-star generals and battle-hardened war veterans chanting like pre-school infants.

On reaching zero, Livingstone heard a rush of air and their enemy guards, two stuffed models set several metres apart and filled with red liquid, exploded in a sea of crimson spray. Its diffusion, thankfully, some distance away from their hut. Seconds later, another short *whoosh*, this time using different ammunition, and the mid-section of a Scimitar armoured vehicle became riddled with big holes before erupting in a ball of flames.

All watched in rapt attention as the black machine flew towards the destroyed targets, like a good soldier checking a lifeless corpse. It flipped round with the grace of a ballerina and turned to face them. Livingstone had attended many equipment demonstrations in the past and often had guns pointed at him. He'd never felt scared, until now.

From the front, Pulsar looked a ferocious beast, its low aerodynamic shape, the landing wheels tucked away and twin gun barrels looking like eyes; a hungry predator about to pounce. The noise from an ordinary helicopter hovering so close would be deafening, requiring him to shout to make himself heard by others in the hut. Due to Pulsar's revolutionary fuel/electric hybrid propulsion system, everyone could all talk at normal volume. Not that he felt like talking.

ABS consisted of two ten-barrelled weapons on either side of the fuselage and two heat-seeking missiles slung underneath. Each of the ten barrels could be fired independently, all controlled by sophisticated target-seeking and aiming AI software.

At the morning briefing, Pulsar's chief ABS designer, Randi Lenahan, nearly caused a riot when he said the system would learn the type of targets the pilot was searching for and could locate and fire at them without intervention. He calmed the subsequent rabble by suggesting he had forgotten to say the word 'almost' and assured the angry military heads that the pilot always had the power of veto.

The pilot looked inscrutable in his black, full-face helmet and black visor. It matched the colour of his machine, which rocked a little in the wind as if purring, a big cat sizing up its prey. The pilot, the sole occupant of the cockpit, operated the helicopter using fly-by-wire, which in turn was governed by a sophisticated flight-management system. If the pilot allowed the system to take over, it could land the machine on the moving deck of an aircraft carrier more accurately than any human.

With the systems on board and by utilising voice control, the pilot could destroy the building where their little group was located, or single out a specific individual for assassination. Major General John

Tasker, a tall and broad-chested senior soldier, currently seconded to NATO, was standing in front of him. Livingstone was watching the hovering beast around the general's pip-embossed shoulder. However, if Pulsar possessed the capability of pulverising a human from over a mile distant, no way would Tasker's generous bulk save him from immediate annihilation.

Pulsar faced them for what felt like minutes, when in fact it barely lasted thirty seconds. Then, the helicopter, with all the finesse of a posh waiter delivering an expensive bottle of wine, made two neat bows, flipped to the side and zipped away in the direction it had come. The small group cheered and clapped. In Livingstone's case with some relief, but he doubted if any of the gung-ho military types had broken sweat.

The rear door of the hut opened. 'The demonstration over for the day, folks,' Brad, their host said. 'I hope you enjoyed it. Dragon Technologies is grateful for your attendance here today. If you could make your way over to the cars, they'll take you back to our base. When you arrive, we will serve refreshments and tell you all about the exciting day we've lined up for you tomorrow. This way, please.'

They all made their way to a fleet of shining limousines, kept some distance away in case Pulsar mistook them for a target. It would be an unforgivable error and set the programme back years, not to mention giving this august group of military men, hardware buyers, and suppliers a problem getting back to base, but hey, what a hoot to tell his friends.

'Pulsar is a formidable beast,' Major General Tasker said, as he climbed into the rear seat of the limo beside him.

'It is. I'm sure our armed forces could find a use for it in the Middle East.'

'For sure, but in a land war in central Europe...'

The general was off, fighting the Russians again. Livingstone knew many military heads, and they all hated the enemy they faced in Iraq and Syria. Insurgents hiding in the houses of civilians, only to pop up at the appearance of a passing patrol to shoot soldiers in the back. They wanted a return to the plains of central Europe commanding a long line of tanks, battalions of men, and, in the air, the support of fast fighter jets.

In fact, much of the kit delivered to the military over the last ten years: large aircraft carriers, frigates and stealth bombers, were about as useful in desert warfare as a eunuch at an orgy. No way could a three-billion-pound aircraft carrier equipped with the latest infra-red missiles hit the said insurgent if they didn't know his location. How could a fighter-bomber flying at over two thousand miles an hour ever hope to spot him? He and others had been telling their masters for years about the error of their strategic thinking, but would they listen?

'What's your recommendation, Alex? Will the MOD buy it?' Tasker asked.

He had been daydreaming. He was unaware Tasker was no longer talking about his spectacular advance across the plains of central Europe and on to Putin's palace to give those upstart Ruskies a bloody nose, but addressing him.

'It's a fantastic machine, but we can acquire two and a half Apaches for the same money.'

'Yes, but we'll lose less Pulsars in battle due to its stealth capabilities and those whisper-quiet blades. You saw yourself how accurate ABS is.'

'I agree, but you know how the MOD works. Nobody looks at trade-offs, only the price and on this score Pulsar is expensive.'

Livingstone was spinning the company line. He didn't want to display too much interest and encourage the military top brass. They might storm into the MOD offices in Whitehall, demanding to know delivery dates, or he could be reading newspaper articles suggesting a decision was about to be made.

'Are you staying with Dragon for the full duration of the programme?' Tasker asked.

'Somebody's got to,' he said smiling. 'Tomorrow we're due to go over the running costs, repairs, spares, all the rest of the boring stuff. It looks a nice hotel they've put us up in.'

'Hotel?' he snorted. 'It's not what I'd call it, more like a knocking shop.'

'How do you mean?'

'When I was in the US a few weeks back, I met a few guys who do your job at the Pentagon. They tell me their standards of hospitality are the stuff of legend.'

'Are they?'

'Yes. They often take you to remote locations, like this spa hotel where we're billeted. Not for them the flashy resorts of the Caribbean or Hawaii where reporters and tourists might be around with their camera phones. In your room, you'll find bottles of all kinds of booze. The dinner in the evening will include as much drink as you can handle, there are drugs in another room, for those who do those sorts of things, and pretty girls wall-to-wall. When you return to your room, you'll find something like a commemorative Rolex or a gold money clip on the pillow. For an important fellow like yourself, it will also include one or two of the aforementioned ladies to warm your bed.'

Chapter 7

Matt reached for his coffee cup, but realised he'd drained it ten minutes before. The job had taught him patience but this stake-out was pushing even his levels of endurance.

Joseph Teller and Matt Flynn were sitting in a coffee house in London. They were looking out the window at the café across the road, a known hangout for former soldiers of the Serbian expansion wars of the early 90s. It was a long shot, but Border Force had assured them that Dejan Katić, the gun for hire they were seeking, hadn't left the country.

'Don't you eat cake?' Joseph asked, tucking into a slice of chocolate cake with his fork.

'I'm not hungry.'

'I think they do good paninis here if you don't want something sweet.'

'I'll stick to coffee.'

'Your mug's empty,' Joseph said. 'You want another?'

'No, you're all right, mate. When you've finished stuffing your face, I'd like to take a walk, burn off some of the caffeine.'

'What, and lose our prime position beside the window? Not to mention moving away from the delicious smells coming out of the kitchen making me want to eat something else.'

'A good view of what?' Matt said waving a hand in the general direction of the café across the road. 'A bunch of old men making a cup of coffee last for two hours.'

'They must have a lot to talk about.'

'Not the war, I hope. It was over twenty years ago.'

'Their power to reminisce and rake over old victories again and again would surprise you.'

'I'm sure you're right.'

Joseph shovelled the last forkful of cake into his mouth, but Matt couldn't wait any longer. He pushed his chair back and stood. 'C'mon Joseph, let's make a move. I need some fresh air.'

Joseph had joined HSA around the same time as Matt. He was a former murder squad detective in west London while Matt was doing a similar job in the east. A good-looking bloke with styled black hair and close-trimmed facial hair, he didn't go short of female companions. No one in the office had actually seen him with any of these girls, prompting howls of derision from fellow agents when he revealed fresh information about his love life.

They stepped out into Blenheim Crescent, a smart street full of restaurants, coffee bars and shops selling foods from various countries around the globe. The area attracted many Serbs and while Joseph had been staking out another suspect a few days before, he'd heard about the sighting of Dejan Katić. Matt trusted the information as Joseph's mother came from Eastern Europe and Joseph knew enough of the language to converse with the locals. In casual conversation with a restaurant owner, he'd confirmed the arrival of a stranger from the homeland who boasted of gangster connections.

'Not much fresh air here,' Joseph said as a bus trundled past on the Portobello Road.

'Maybe not, but when the guy in the café starts to notice the two guys sitting at the window of the café opposite, it's time to split.'

'Do you think Katić is still around? I think we're wasting our time.'

'If it was me and I came here to assassinate someone, I'd hightail it back to Belgrade as soon as the job was done. Whatever he did, no matter how careful he's been, his handiwork is bound to surface sooner or later. The longer he waits here, the greater the chance we, or some other agency will nab him.'

'I feel the same.'

'Someone's brought him over from Serbia to do a job, so the target must be high profile. Rosie talked to Border Force this morning and they don't have a record of him or his fake passport leaving the UK.'

'Maybe he's got no choice, but to stick around to collect his money. Could be, he's waiting to be told about another assignment.'

'It's a long shot, but his reputation is such that it's worth spending a bit of time looking for him. If we do spot him, we're to bring him in.'

Early afternoon, Portobello Road was busy with shoppers and kids who should have been at school. As the area was once an integral part of 'Swinging London', it attracted its fair share of tourists.

'Hey, Joseph, take a look at this,' he said jerking a thumb towards the nearest shop window. They both stopped to look at an array of second-hand phones and fancy bumpers. 'Unlock Your Phone Here' the sign said. Were they encouraging thieves to steal a phone and have the passcode unblocked, or was it something more innocent like a service to change mobile networks?

'What are we looking at?' Joseph asked. 'I'm happy with the phone I've got.'

'See the big Samsung there,' Matt said, pointing, 'the one with the silver edging? There are two guys standing talking further down the street, close to a bus stop. One's wearing a brown leather jacket, the other a green anorak. I'm sure the tall one in the leather is our target.'

'Speaking of phones,' Joseph said pulling out his as if taking a call. He swivelled around and scanned the street. 'Man, so it is. Cool, I'll catch you later.' He turned back and stared at the window. 'I see them. Yep, it's our man. What's the plan?'

'When Katić says goodbye to his pal and walks away from us, we follow. When he gets to a place a bit quieter than around here, we'll make a move on him. If he comes towards us, we'll improvise.'

'Right.'

'Whichever way this goes down, on my signal, I'll do him from the front, you do the back and the cuffs. When he's subdued, you go get the car. Okay?'

'Yep.'

Keen to make a sale, the owner of the phone shop, a fat, bald man with a thick black beard appeared in the doorway. He was about to come over and engage the two window shoppers, when Katić kissed his friend goodbye and walked in the direction of Matt and Joseph.

The two HSA agents ambled towards the Serb, both men wearing old clothes and tatty jackets and looking like plasterers or plumbers on their way back from a job. Seconds before their paths crossed, Matt nudged Joseph with one arm and rammed his other fist into Katić's stomach. Wasting no time, Joseph grabbed the arms of the winded Serb from behind and applied plastic ties.

'What the hell eeze this?' Katić said, his face red.

'Sharup, Katić, you're under arrest.'

Matt gave him a quick pat down and after locating a gun, slipped it into his pocket.

'Eet's for personal protection,' the Serb said. 'It can be dangerous here, some men they want to settle old scores, you know?'

'I can sympathise with them,' Matt said. He poked Katić in the ribs with his finger, as if holding a gun. 'Move,' he said. He chose not to pull out the real thing. It was a busy area, and he didn't want to alarm the locals.

They frogmarched him away from the main drag, down Colville Terrace. Matt spotted the back door to a shop and shoved him in the opening, face first. Joseph ran off to fetch the car.

Katić mouthed something in Serbian which Matt suspected wasn't complimentary.

'If you must say something, say it in English.'

'I want to talk to lawyer. Theese is police brutality.'

'You should be used to it where you come from, mate. Anyway, we're not police, we're Homeland Security.'

'What is theese?'

'Police with guns and the balls to use them.'

'What is going on here?' a posh English voice said.

Matt turned. A man, aged about sixty and waving a walking stick, came striding towards him.

'This is police business, sir. Move away.'

'I thought you said...Agh my arm.'

'Shut up Katić.'

'You cannot arrest this man,' walking stick man said, 'he hasn't done anything wrong. I saw you punch him, back there on the main road, and I followed you here. This is common assault of an innocent man. I demand you let him go.'

'Very public spirited of you sir, but quite unnecessary. Everything's under control.'

Matt eased the pressure on Katić's arm, but when he started struggling. He tightened it again, causing the prisoner to cry out.

'You don't look like any police I know. I demand to see your warrant card.'

'It's not possible at the moment, sir, as you can probably appreciate. Rest assured what I'm doing is legal and nothing for you to worry about. I'm a member of an undercover police team.'

Matt looked round. Where the hell was Joseph? Behind walking stick man, a small crowd gathered, swelling with every curious pedestrian who had nothing better to do this afternoon. He could disperse them with a flash of the Glock, but it would attract the attention of the boys in blue. Tension between them and the 'gun toting cowboys of the HSA,' as a former colleague in the Met described Matt's organisation, were at times, strained. A quick apology from The Director and everything would be smoothed over, but in the intervening melee, the prisoner could escape.

With an enlarged crowd egging one another on, they grew bolder with calls to release the captured man and aggressive shouts from the younger men. Some looked local, letting off some pent-up aggression while others looked East European, perhaps assessing the situation as persecution of one of their own. He was about to turn and tell them to move back when Katić made a strong attempt to escape. In an almost instinctive reaction, Matt punched him in the kidneys, eliciting an animalistic growl from the prisoner but subduing further resistance.

His action incensed the mob. They surged closer, shouting and gesticulating, some in languages he couldn't understand. Matt reached for his weapon, but before extracting it, a car careered around the corner scattering the throng on the road towards the safety of the pavement. Matt was relieved to see it was Joseph in the car and not a couple of undercover cops. He left the gun holstered.

He hauled the prisoner over to the car and when Joseph opened the rear door, he pushed him inside. He closed the door, turned and saw a fist barrelling towards him. He jerked his head to one side, avoiding direct contact, but still felt its force on the side of his cheek. Matt returned the compliment and punched his attacker in the face and shoved him backwards into the encroaching crowd. This forced them to retreat as they tried to catch the falling man or were wary of receiving a punch themselves.

Matt used the distraction to leap into the passenger seat. With hands slapping the roof and the back of the car, Joseph took off and sped down the road.

'I'm not sure if this road is a dead end,' Joseph said, his face split in a grin.

'You've a wicked sense of humour, Teller,' Matt said, rubbing his sore face, 'but if it is, it's your turn to go out and talk to them.'

Chapter 8

Matt and Rosie headed for the stairs leading down to the interview rooms. The Director of HSA, Templeton McGill, known to everyone as Gill, appeared before they reached the door.

'Congratulations Matt, I heard about the capture of Katić.'

'Not without a struggle.'

'An Inspector Harman from the Met called about a disturbance in the Portobello Road area and wondered if we were involved.'

'I assume you didn't seek to enlighten him?'

'But of course. It doesn't make sense to broadcast what we do to all and sundry. Have you spoken to Katić yet?'

'We're heading there now,' Rosie said.

'Good. Have you got anything concrete to throw at him?'

She shook her head. 'Nothing leaps out of the newspapers or the Reuter feed suggesting his involvement in any major crime. We'll be probing his reasons for being here in the UK, don't you worry.'

'If you can't nail him, Interpol will take him.'

'It doesn't surprise me to hear they're interested, the things he's been involved in.'

'You're right but you know what they're like. They'll be on the phone every couple of hours after you start questioning him. They won't let go until we hand him over.'

'It doesn't give us much time.'

'No, the clock's ticking. If we can't find out what he's been up to and throw some serious charges at him, they'll come and spirit him away, never to be seen by us again. They've got a string of stuff they want to talk to him about.'

'Whether it's us or Interpol who nail him, it's comforting to think a man like him won't be seeing daylight for a while.'

'True, but if he ends up with them, it won't be much consolation to the family or business partners of the poor bugger he's no doubt killed. Mark my words, he's not here for a week's holiday and to take in some of our ancient monuments.'

'I feel the same.'

Gill looked Rosie in the eye, a disconcerting stare for anyone. 'Find out why he's here, Rosie, and this discussion will be academic. I'll take great pleasure in telling Interpol to fuck off.'

The Director turned on his heel and strode off.

'I don't think I've seen Gill so wound up,' Rosie said as they walked downstairs.

'Me neither. He's either desperate to nail Katić or there's no love lost between him and Interpol.'

'I don't think Interpol's the problem. I seem to remember he served with the army in Bosnia.'

'Maybe his gripe isn't with Katić specifically, but with people like him who fought in the war and are guilty of war crimes.'

Rosie pushed the door of the interview room open. The room was laid out like a police interview room: a table between the subject and his inquisitors, a camera on the wall and a guard standing behind him and one at the door. The only differences a copper would notice was the room was set up primarily to record information, and all HSA staff were armed. It was equipped with audio and video recording, but the prisoner was alone, no lawyer present. HSA didn't allow them to bring or request one.

'At long last,' Katić said. 'I have been seated on my butt for many hours. I demand some food and something to drink.'

Rosie said something to Matt, and moments later, he left the room.

'So, Mr Katić, how are you?'

'I'm peessed off, if you want to know.'

'Why?'

'Because I am here in theese horrible place.'

'I don't understand why you're surprised. Entering the UK on a forged passport is a criminal offence.'

Katić banged the table with his fist. 'You sheethead, you are trying to stitch me up. I do not have a false passport, I change name.'

Rosie didn't pursue the subject even though she knew the passport owner had reported it stolen three weeks before. It would only result in a petty squabble which Katić would be happy to exploit as an excuse to refuse to talk about anything else.

Matt came into the room and passed a glass of water and a granola bar to the Serb.

'What is theese?' he said, lifting up the granola bar as if handling a piece of nuclear waste. 'We wouldn't feed theese crap to our rabbits.'

'Take it or leave it, mate,' Matt said. 'It's the best available from the vending machine.'

In a bid to be 'healthy' all the vending machines in the building had been emptied of chocolate bars and crisps, and replaced with nuts and bars made from anything that didn't include much sugar.

Katić pushed the granola bar to one side, but left the water and sat sulking with his arms folded. He was a big guy, tall and muscular with sandy coloured hair and a face rarely straying from a frown or a scowl. Perhaps if Rosie had spent her teenage years growing up with a vicious ethnic war going on around her, she would look the same, but she felt sure she would have pursued something less violent afterwards.

'What are you doing in the UK, Katić?' Rosie asked.

'I am the sales representative for Zama Tractors. I'm here to meet representatives in your excellent farming community and talk to them about distributing our fine agricultural vehicles.'

'Mr Katić,' Matt said, 'I grew up in Ireland where my grandfather owned a dairy farm. I know enough about the subject to call your bluff, but why should I waste my time when I know you're lying.'

'I told you. I am the sales representative–'

'Yeah, yeah, you've memorised an old Massey Ferguson brochure, how clever. I'll ask you one more time, what are you doing here in the UK?'

'I told you but you don't believe me.' He pushed his chair back and crossed his arms. 'I say nothing more until I see lawyer.'

'You'll be waiting a long time,' Rosie said. 'We don't allow legal representation. Now, answer the question. If you don't, I'll leave you here for a couple of hours to think it over, or I might have you locked up in a cell overnight. If you really piss us off, I'll stick you in a cell for three or four days until you change your story. How does that grab you?'

'You can't do theese. Do you think I'm some dumb Serb dragged here from the slums of Belgrade?' He tapped the table with his forefinger. 'I know the law, the police—'

Matt sighed. 'I told you before, we're not the police. We can hold you here as long as we like.'

Matt wasn't bluffing, however, there were practical issues to consider. If no charges were forthcoming, and they let the prisoner walk, he could take his story of wrongful incarceration and brutality to the newspapers. Even then, it wasn't necessarily a PR disaster. Not every account would be believed, and in the case of Katić, Rosie knew that the Serb had as much interest in keeping his face out of the media as HSA did.

Katić sighed, a sign perhaps of the message getting through. 'I'm a businessman, selling tractors, and while here in theese beautiful country, I stayed a few days to meet some old friends.'

'You're as much a businessman as my granny,' Rosie said. 'You, my friend, used to be a sniper for the

Serb Army targeting Bosnians in Sarajevo as they queued for bread or walked down the street.'

Katić's face lost its characteristic frown and displayed venomous hate. 'Theese fucking scum deserved to die. Serbia is for Serbs like me,' he said tapping his chest, 'not for Moslem pigs from Bosnia and Albania.' He shrugged. 'Nobody cares now, it is all in the past. They now live in their own little country, they are welcome to it.'

'All the information we have suggests to me you haven't changed jobs. You're still a sniper. Now you're doing it for big money. Did you come here to do a job?'

He shook his head, the shake of a teacher dealing with a dense pupil. 'I told you–'

Rosie held her palm up. 'Stop it, we're getting tired of hearing your made-up fable. Take a look at this.'

She picked two items from the file, turned them around and pushed them towards him. One was a photograph of a car taken by an ANPR camera near Oxford, the other a map of the area.

'Where did you get theese?' Katić said, looking rattled for the first time.

'Modern technology,' Matt said, 'it gets everywhere. This is your hire car, yes?' He pointed at the picture. 'And hey, look at this. Isn't this you behind the wheel?'

Katić took his time looking at the pictures, perhaps trying to remember what he had been doing there or, as Rosie suspected, constructing a cover story.

A minute or so later he said, 'Yes, theese is my car.'

'Why were you in Oxfordshire?'

'I cannot remember.' He started to smile. 'Ah yes, now I do. Lots of big fields, I went there to see customer.'

'Look at the date,' she said pointing at the date stamp on the photograph. 'Maybe, it will refresh your memory.'

'8th February?' He shrugged and shook his head.

'It shouldn't be so difficult, it's only a week ago. Do you have a diary?'

'No.'

'You're not much of a businessman, are you?'

Matt leaned over and looked into Katić's face, his finger stabbing the ANPR picture. 'You're expecting us to believe you went to see someone and talked tractors at six o'clock on a Sunday morning?'

'What can I say?' he said with a casual shrug. 'I like to leave my bed early in the morning.'

Chapter 9

Chris Anderson paced the floor of his bedroom, his head a confusing mix of anger and despair. He'd returned from a meeting with Superintendent Cousins, this time at Kidlington, the headquarters of Oxford Police, his belief undimmed that the killing of his parents, sister and her friend had been deliberate. Yet again, the policeman rebuffed him with platitudes about awaiting the results of the accident investigation and telling him that without any evidence to the contrary, they could not start an alternative inquiry.

He needed to stop pacing. Aunt Hannah was downstairs with her 'New to Oxford' people, and they didn't like being disturbed during their noisy bonding sessions, fuelled by numerous bottles of white wine. She'd established the group when her two kids, his cousins, were still at school, and despite both having grown up and moved away from home, she still continued with it.

He sat down at the desk, piled high with text books, folders and papers, all untouched since moving here from Witney, remnants of another place, another time. He'd told Superintendent Cousins he intended going back to university after Easter, and while the words sounded true at the time, he couldn't say with any sincerity he believed them.

Part of his indecision lay in the number of things he needed to sort out. Chris suspected, but didn't yet know until the family solicitor located his father's will, that he, a twenty-one-year-old university student, had now become the majority shareholder in a two-hundred-and-fifty-million-pound company. In addition, he now owned a million-pound house on the Woodstock Road in Witney, Throughout his life, his father had been a saver and not a spender. Chris knew little about the shares, property and investments he had, and there could well be a host of other stuff he knew nothing about. No wonder he felt confused.

He put his head in his hands with his eyes closed, trying to shut out the weight of responsibility he felt. The desk had been a gift to Kevin after Chris' father gained a first in Electrical Engineering. Stephen told Kevin he didn't need it as he was finished with studying, but Chris believed it was his way of dropping a hint to the unqualified Kevin that he should make a start on his own education.

'Chris! Chris!'

He opened the bedroom door and walked to the top of the stairs. Aunt Hannah was standing there looking better than many of the new mums in the lounge, some ten years her junior. Today she'd made a real effort, perhaps trying to hide her grief, with styled hair and a tight pink t-shirt he'd never seen before.

'Were you wearing headphones? I called you several times.'

'No, I think I must have been away in a world of my own.'

Her face softened. 'It's all right, you've given me the chance to get away from all the small talk for a bit. There are a couple of people here to see you. They're in the kitchen.'

'Thanks. I'll come down in a minute.'

He tucked his t-shirt into his trousers and ran a hand through his tousled hair. He owned a hairbrush, but like everything else, didn't have any idea where it might be. He walked downstairs, more irritated than curious.

If the people in the kitchen were journalists, he would tell them to get out without hearing a word. He knew what sounded like a reasonable response in an interview could look monstrous on paper depending on the angle they wanted to highlight. Given the headlines he'd seen already such as, 'The Boy Who Survived' or, in more salacious publications, 'Was Son Involved in Balloon Killing?', no way did he want to add any more fuel to those particular fires.

He guessed it stemmed from his father's reluctance to talk to journalists. They often dressed up their intentions as 'fact finding', only to find the resultant article accusing the company of raining death on innocent civilians in the Middle East. If, instead, it was a couple of police officers here to give him an update, he would listen, but he suspected they wouldn't have anything new to tell him.

He walked into the kitchen to find a slim blonde woman inspecting the coffee machine, and a large man sitting at the kitchen table with his back to him looking at something on his phone.

The woman, noticing his arrival, approached with an outstretched hand.

'Hello, Chris. My name is Rosie Fox and this is my colleague, Matt Flynn.'

Her hand felt cool and slim. He looked at the man for the first time. Flynn was tall with dark hair, a chiselled, serious face and a chin not acquainted with a razor for the last couple of days. He simply nodded.

'We're from Homeland Security,' Fox said taking a seat on a high stool beside the breakfast bar. 'You might have heard of us, your folks being in the defence business. We'd like to ask you some questions.'

'I've heard of you,' he said in voice steadier than he believed he could muster. 'Can I get you anything to drink?' he said, trying to buy some time to get his head around this.

'I'll take a coffee and so will Matt. He doesn't say much until he's had a few shots of caffeine. Milk, no sugar for both.'

He set the coffee machine gurgling, the same one they had at Woodstock Road. It felt cold, indicating Aunt Hannah and her chums had now switched to wine. He removed cups from the cupboard in an automatic motion, his mind racing. Why the hell were HSA, the bad-asses of law enforcement, here to see him? He studied Computer Science at university and had been involved with a hacking group for several years, but they knew how to cover their tracks. Had he slipped up? Were GCHQ smarter than he and his on-line friends believed?

He knew all about HSA because of his dad's business. They had powers more like the army than the police. They could hold suspects without charge for weeks, carried guns and didn't have to explain themselves when weapons were drawn and people shot. Christ! Guns in Aunt Hannah's house? What would the 'New to Oxford' women think if they found out? They would soon become the 'Never Moving to Oxford' women.

'Is this where you're living now, with your aunt and uncle?' Fox asked.

'You've heard about the balloon accident, I take it?'

She nodded. 'I'm sorry for your loss, Chris. We won't make this meeting any harder for you than it needs to be.'

'Thanks. Yeah, I'm staying here, but I don't know for how long. The house on Woodstock Road where... the place where I used to live is much too big for me and...and the psychologist I'm seeing said I shouldn't be on my own.'

'Good advice, in my opinion.'

Chris made the drinks and placed them on the table, took a deep breath and sat down.

'Thanks,' Fox said.

'You're probably wondering why we're here,' Flynn said.

It was the first time Flynn had spoken. The voice belied the rough exterior as it sounded smooth and articulate, London with a hint of Irish.

'Yes, I am.'

'Based on information in our possession, we're investigating every major incident in the Oxford area on Sunday 8th February. It may surprise you to hear, but the people of Oxford on this day were largely law-abiding. We've identified four serious incidents: a robbery at a newsagent in Cowley, a domestic murder with a shotgun at Slade Park, a car-jacking outside the John Ratcliffe Hospital, and the balloon accident involving your family.'

'Why is the balloon accident included? The other three are crimes and the police told me what happened was an accident.'

'I'm being slightly evasive here, Chris, as I don't want to panic anyone, but the robbery, domestic murder or the car-jacking make the grade. The only incident of any significance is the downing of the balloon. We're here to find out more and see if the incident might have involved any criminal activity.'

'We appreciate our approach may come as a shock to you Chris,' Fox said. 'We would have preferred in the first instance to talk to your uncle, but unfortunately he wasn't in the office when we called.'

'No, it's fine, I'm not worried about hearing this. I don't know if the Oxford police mentioned to you, but I raised the same subject with them.'

Fox shook her head.

'I even went down to Kidlington to see them this morning.'

'To tell them what, that you suspect there might be criminal involvement in the downing of the balloon?'

'Yeah.'

'What did they say?'

'They didn't believe me. They still think it was an accident.'

'What did they say, specifically?'

'Let me think. The remains of the balloon are being investigated by the Air Accident Investigation Branch and their findings support the initial assumption of pilot error.'

'Makes sense to me. What makes you think any different?'

'My dad and Uncle Kevin own a business called Galleon Electronics, making among other things, the electronic switches for releasing missiles and bombs on fighter planes. People in Oxford hate us. They demonstrate outside the factory gates sometimes and call my dad names in letters and emails.'

'If you don't mind me saying,' Fox said, 'I don't think the work that Galleon does is so serious it would encourage someone to kill members of your family, just to make a point or get at your father. I'm sure you'll agree, it's not a big company, a small cog in a mighty military machine.'

He felt deflated; she was right. He could name a slew of bigger companies: the makers of fighter plane wings, jet engines, ammunition, and those who designed the software to guide rockets and smart bombs. If he was a protestor and decided to focus on the industry, he would go after one of them before looking at his dad's business.

'Do you have any evidence of criminal involvement, Chris?' Flynn asked. 'Or is your concern only a hunch?'

'How do you mean, evidence? Like what?'

'Did your father receive death threats before taking the balloon flight or, over the last few weeks, did he seem more nervous than usual, for example?'

He shook his head. 'No, not as far as I remember.'

'What about the relationship between your father and the workers at the factory? Did he get on with them and your Uncle Kevin?'

'He got on with everybody at the factory. There's never been a strike and Kevin and Dad always worked well together, Dad as Managing Director and Uncle Kevin as Sales Director.'

'It doesn't look like the balloon incident is worth examining after all,' Flynn said standing, his face registering nothing. 'We're done here. I guess we need to spread the net wider than Oxford.'

'Hang on, Matt,' Fox said. 'What about the balloon itself, Chris? Although I believe the technical term is 'envelope'. Did it survive the crash? Is it being analysed by the AAIB?'

'It was destroyed by fire after the propane tanks burst on impact.'

'Oh.' She frowned before reaching into her bag. She stood, walked towards him and gave him a business card. 'If you think of something else.'

'Right.'

She offered her hand, which he shook. 'Thanks for seeing us, Chris.'

He accompanied them to the door.

'The papers said you're at university,' Fox said.

'At least they got something right. Yeah, I'm at Durham.'

'What are you studying?'

'Computer Science.'

'Do you like it?'

'It's what I always wanted to do, but it'll take some time and effort to get my head back to sitting in a lecture hall. I might take a few months off to sort a few things out.'

'All the best with whatever you decide to do, and thanks again for your help. Goodbye Chris.'

Chapter 10

Matt and Rosie walked out to the car after their short and less than fruitful chat with Chris Anderson. Matt glanced over at the activity visible through the lounge window, wondering why a group of women were getting pissed at this time, early on a Monday afternoon.

No words were exchanged between the HSA agents until the car reached the end of the road.

'You took a gamble, Mr Flynn, and for once in your life it crashed and burned.'

'I hoped there might be a good old-fashioned family feud lurking somewhere in the background, or at least a few silent phone calls and death threats. I guess we need to do this the hard way.'

'Off to Slade Park,' Rosie said reaching for the satnav, 'to take a look at the domestic with a shotgun?'

'We'll make a detour first and take a look at the balloon crash site.'

Rosie gave him a look and shrugged. 'Fine by me.'

Rosie could touch-type at lightning speed and her rapid tapping of the satnav screen put his earlier efforts to shame.

'Why did we let Katić go?' he asked.

'Technically we didn't. We couldn't produce any evidence to charge him, so we were forced to hand him over to Interpol. It will curb his shooting activities for a long time, but it's the last we'll see of him.'

'Surely, we could have held them off for another couple of days? No human rights campaigner would give a toss if we took that scumbag off the streets for a bit.'

'You're a hard man to please, Matt Flynn, but as much as I like to keep people like him away from the rest of the population, he told us nothing. I trust Interpol can come up with something more substantial to throw at him.'

'I don't fancy their chances.'

'Maybe we don't need him.'

'Why not?' Matt asked.

'The person paying him should be our focus. Whichever way you look at it, the Serb is no more than a hired gun; a foot soldier following orders, or in his case, a greedy bastard chasing the money. If we find out what he did, we should have a good idea why he did it and knowing this, we should be able to identify the big fish paying him.'

'Makes sense, in theory but it would be quicker hanging Katić up by the balls until he told us all this.'

Ten minutes later, they turned down Ladder Hill.

'The crash site's up ahead,' Rosie said.

Matt slowed, searching for the spot, much to the consternation of a following driver who honked his horn in frustration at the actions of another dawdling tourist. Spotting an open gate and trampled ground,

Matt switched on the indicator and turned into the field, the sound of a revving engine and a shouted obscenity somewhere behind.

With his view no longer obscured by a line of trees, he knew they were in the right place. The location matched the photograph and map taken from a national newspaper, and remnants of blue police incident tape fluttered in the wind like birds with broken wings, scant recognition of the tragic events that had happened here.

They drove some way into the field and parked under the high-tension electricity lines that whistled softly in the light breeze. The grass in the area where the balloon came down was scorched, and the vegetation all around them flattened and trampled by hundreds of feet and the wheels of many cars and vans.

They got out of the car and Matt stood and looked around. They were in a big empty field, and all around, as far as he could see on a misty day, more fields. Above them the pylons and electricity cables looked intact, either undamaged by the falling balloon or recently repaired.

Rosie walked towards him.

'If our friend Katić came here and wanted to take down this balloon, although I can't for the life of me think why he would, the place I would choose is there,' she said pointing at the line of trees they had just driven past. 'He could wait there under cover until the balloon made its appearance.'

'I admit, there's not much cover for a sniper anywhere else, but why there?' Matt said. 'Why not over there, or there?' he said indicating a few other small thickets of trees in the opposite direction.

'My line of trees is close to the road, ideal for a quick getaway, while the trees you're pointing at, would require him to drive back across this field, exposing his presence to anyone around. Also, if someone heard a shot or saw the balloon fall to the ground, they would clock his car moving back over the field to the road.'

'Good point, and I happen to agree with you.' He lifted the map in his hand and pointed to it. Using a map printed in a newspaper, he had drawn the balloon's flight on his map. 'There's another road at the opposite end of these fields, but I think the balloon would have been too far away to give him a good shot. No, you're right. It has to be over there.'

They returned to the car and drove back across the field to the entrance. He parked close to the gate and got out. From a distance, the line of trees looked like they closely followed the curve of what he believed to be a farmer's access road, but on closer inspection a bit more haphazard. Down the centre between the trees, was a well-used bridleway.

Standing at the beginning of the bridleway, Matt said, 'You take the right side and I'll do the left.'

Rosie, never one to keep quiet if she believed she was being handed the short straw, opened her mouth to say something. When she grasped that neither side offered an advantage over the other, she closed it again and said nothing.

He walked, trying to avoid head-height brambles while looking down, searching for clues. After a few minutes, he stopped to check his progress and realised if Katić had come here, he'd picked an excellent spot.

Without exposing himself to passing cars or a farmer making his way across the field, he could take time with his preparation and take the shot without revealing his firing position. If anyone had been awake at such an early hour on a Sunday morning and heard a shot, they would have no idea where it came from and assume someone was shooting rabbits. If Katić believed his firing position to be hidden, safe and comfortable, it gave Matt confidence the gunman might have become complacent and left something behind he shouldn't have.

He looked up and realised he'd walked too far, as now a pylon would have blocked Katić's view of the progress of the balloon. He retraced his steps, walking backwards. In his mind's eye, he saw the balloon rising up towards the electricity lines, the sniper reaching for his rifle and fine-tuning the sight, waiting, waiting until the slow-moving balloon reached the spot where he wanted it to be.

When Matt located what he believed to be the optimal firing position, one he would have used himself if asked to do so, he called Rosie over. He explained his logic and she agreed.

'What now?' she asked. 'Search the undergrowth and see if we find anything like a spent bullet casing?'

'No, he's too wily to leave behind something so obvious. Maybe there's something else; a chocolate wrapper or a piece of chewing gum.'

'Yuck. I'm not picking up something like that without gloves.'

He gave her a quizzical look. 'Rosie, where's your cop training? You're not picking up anything without gloves.'

They both dropped to their knees and parted the undergrowth, looking for something that didn't belong. He realised with the area being used by walkers and horse riders, it was possible they could come across all manner of discarded detritus, but the more they moved away from the bridleway, the less they came across.

Ten minutes later and finding nothing, Matt began to feel despondent. He could deploy a forensic team who were better at doing this sort of thing than they were, but this wouldn't be straightforward. The Director would baulk at the cost of pursuing a lead on such weak evidence, and Matt would look a royal prat if they found nothing.

He stood and stretched, his back muscles groaning at the effort.

'Matt take a look at this.'

'What is it?' he said, making his way through the undergrowth in the direction of her voice.

'Look there,' she said pointing. 'The ground appears more flattened than the area around it and I can see a couple of broken branches.'

Matt moved as close as he dared without compromising the scene. 'So it is,' he said, his voice betraying his interest. 'Maybe he broke a few to improve his view.'

Matt dropped to his knees and started a fingertip search of the area. Rosie did the same. After a few minutes of fruitless searching he said, 'There's nothing here.'

'I think you're right,' she said turning round. Her eyes narrowed, 'What's the white thing over there?'

'Where?'

He followed her pointing finger and on spotting the item, parted the foliage around it. Rosie leaned down beside him and pulled out an evidence bag. She turned it inside out and, using it to cover her hand, lifted a cigarette butt. She held it up for Matt to see. A third of it remained, a cigarette break terminated before it could be completed.

'Interesting, it's not a filter tip, but plain. Few Brits smoke them nowadays,' Matt said taking the evidence bag from her. 'Is our man getting sloppy in his old age?'

'Let's hope so.'

'I can see some Cyrillic writing on the paper.'

'Oh, listen to you the linguist,' she said. 'You told me you don't speak any languages, not even the language of your grandparents.'

'This looks like Russian, but I also know Serbian can be written in Cyrillic.'

'You should be on Mastermind with such arcane knowledge of odd subject matter. But if it isn't, we can still check it out for DNA as we've got Katić's on file. I might not be good at backing horses, but how much do you want to bet we find a match?'

Chapter 11

Latif Artha smiled when he spotted signs for the motorway. He liked driving around the narrow country lanes of Wiltshire. In daylight, he would admire the big houses he passed and slow down to take in some of the breath-taking scenery. Tonight, tired after a long day's work, he was desperate to get to London, while the allure of the countryside paled in the moonlight.

He joined the M40, took his little car up to seventy-five miles and hour and relaxed for the first time today. The motorway was quiet at this time on a Friday night. With luck, he could maintain the inside lane position for some time, only moving over to the middle when he needed to overtake or until he reached the busier sections of the road around High Wycombe. It wasn't that he didn't like going fast, but his little Fiat 500, great for nipping around Swindon where he worked, didn't move so quickly. Any time he did venture away from the inside lane, a big aggressive Audi or BMW with darkened windows would come up close and harass him until he got out of the way.

He didn't intend to be travelling this late, but a developing crisis at the office had delayed him. He worked as a senior analyst for QuinTec, a military equipment testing company. At one time the UK Government owned the business, but ten years ago they were spun-off into the private sector, their shares being sold through public auction. The Ministry of Defence, which at one time accounted for over ninety per cent of their turnover, were now less than twenty percent.

With their expertise in testing all manner of battlefield weapons, from rifles all the way to tanks and helicopters, QuinTec assisted governments all over the globe. With the cost of equipping even a small army running into millions of pounds, the price of their testing regime could be saved many times over. Over the last year, Artha and his colleagues had prevented the German military from wasting money on an armoured car which was unsuitable for use in the Gulf, and the French from investing millions in an anti-aircraft missile system that lost accuracy in hail.

The office crisis centred around the Pulsar helicopter made by the big US defence company, Dragon Technologies. A former pilot with the RAF Search and Rescue Service, Artha was responsible for testing rotary-wing aircraft on behalf of the MOD, and the customer was entitled to accept or reject their findings as they saw fit. His most recent report included criticism of the Arrow Battlefield System, the advanced multi-barrel weapon which boasted that its accuracy could save over seventy per cent on ammunition costs.

He couldn't fault the weapon's accuracy, nor the claims about savings made by Dragon. However, when selecting certain sequences of barrels, for example, an armoured-piercing bullet to attack a car, and then switching to normal ammunition, and back again, the weapon would lock. If the pilot was using voice control and continued to utter the 'fire' command repeatedly, as he would in a tense battle situation, the system would suddenly switch to 'auto' mode. This ceded all control to ABS. The system would then automatically select and fire at targets determined by its learned parameters. The pilot couldn't turn it off. A complete power-down and full system re-boot back at base being the only solution.

In a busy area like a marketplace in Iraq or a city in Syria, this could have catastrophic consequences. ABS, whether attuned to the pilot's target criteria or not, would start selecting targets based on the reasoning of its artificial intelligence: the tall bearded guy with a satchel over his shoulder, the woman reaching into her burqa for money to pay a stall holder, the dark car travelling fast with four local government officials inside.

This had all been explained to Dragon. While he could understand some reluctance in trying to find such a fault in over five million lines of software code, he couldn't comprehend why they were telling him the barrel shooting sequences he selected were unrealistic. This was a smoke-screen. He had found the malfunction without a great deal of investigation. What else would be revealed if he tried a bit harder?

When the MOD first received the QuinTec report they accepted the findings and their interest in Pulsar waned. A few months later, a number of MOD personnel were invited to observe demonstrations and overnight their reluctance disappeared. They now wanted to buy Pulsar.

Not only did they want to buy it, they would not listen to any criticism of the aircraft, no matter how lofty or intelligent the person uttering it. The MOD were QuinTec's customer and, like any customer, could do whatever they liked with the QuinTec report. However, in this instance Pulsar was being purchased using UK taxpayer's money and the report would be of interest to a wider audience than a few military analysts at the MOD. Hence, the terse meeting earlier this evening where the MOD had told QuinTec they wanted Artha to rewrite his damning report.

The MOD couldn't move ahead with their purchase of the aircraft without the approval of their ministerial masters, and the UK government wouldn't give the go-ahead with the spectre of Artha's report falling into the hands of the opposition. Not only did the MOD fear a leak from within their organisation, but Artha was the author of a military blog. This was the place where he posted information about QuinTec's testing regime and occasionally some non-confidential equipment test results, several of which had found their way into national newspapers. Nothing about Pulsar had been posted yet. That's the way it would stay if he valued his job, according to QuinTec's Technical Director who collared Artha after the meeting.

To add fuel to this otherwise volatile chemical mix, he was on the way to see his boyfriend, Derek Spencer, Member of Parliament for Manchester Ashton. Derek was a backbencher and took a keen interest in defence matters. He coveted the Defence brief, at present the preserve of Simon Crosby, a lazy bugger who did little, but take full advantage of any hospitality coming his way. He also had the ear and confidence of the Prime Minister.

If Derek sensed the whiff of a cover-up, he would quiz Artha until he revealed something, and the QuinTec analyst was bound to let something slip. He felt sure the MOD were playing dirty. It was a dangerous game to play as it wasn't beyond large organisations that were put in this position to try and smear his reputation. In his nightmares, he cringed at the thought of the lurid headlines: *Gay MP In Military Slip*; *Defence Secrets Exchanged Between the Sheets*.

The Chairman of QuinTec had now become involved. He started the meeting this evening assuring his colleagues he was opposed to kowtowing to the bullying tactics of the MOD. His attitude started to soften immediately on hearing from the firm's accountants, warning of the damaging effects the loss of the MOD's business would be, and from other customers who were in their sphere of influence. Latif had been sent away for the weekend to 'consider his options', a veiled threat to fire him if he didn't re-write the report, or at the very least, tone down his criticism of Pulsar. With the level of anger he felt now, he wouldn't alter a word. He needed to meet Derek and listen to his wise counsel.

Looking around in the dark night, he realised he wasn't alone. A black vehicle in the middle lane kept pace with him. It could have been there for the last few minutes for all he knew, as his mind had been wandering. He had driven the last five miles or so on auto-pilot. He watched it more closely now. Driving at the same speed as him, the black car made no attempt to motor ahead or slip in behind him; strange behaviour as the motorway was otherwise deserted.

The same thing seemed to happen in cinema and supermarket car parks. He would park at the back, not wishing to join the scramble for a slot closer to the door, and in a sea of empty spaces, a car would park in the space next to him. Perhaps the black car was being driven by some elderly man or woman, scared to be driving on a rural motorway by themselves at this hour of the night, comforted to see another vehicle beside them.

Part of him, the part that felt compelled to help the old or infirm remove their bags from overhead lockers in planes, and donate money to Age Concern, didn't mind their presence; but the practical side of his brain did. His head was in turmoil, he needed some wriggle room if he lost concentration and the car started to wander across the carriageway. He eased his foot from the accelerator and reduced his speed to seventy. Like two cars tied together by a giant elastic band, the black car surged ahead, before pulling back and returning to its tandem position.

A few minutes later, they reached a long downhill stretch causing his car to speed up, a feat not possible on level ground. As before, his companion did the same. He was about to honk his horn in disapproval, when the black car slewed across the carriageway and bashed into his.

'What the!' he exclaimed, but the words strangled in his throat as his car shot off the motorway and hurtled into the dark, enveloping countryside.

It burst through low-lying gorse and up an embankment. The steering wheel started to spin wildly in his hand and, to his horror, he realised the ground below him had disappeared, the car sailing through the night sky as if flying. The car flipped over, nose down, fell to the earth with an ear-splitting thump and bounced high into the air. It turned upside down and smashed into a large, jagged rock, the remnants of a long-abandoned quarry.

Chapter 12

Rosie Fox yawned and stretched. She would like nothing better than to put her feet on the desk and fall asleep. Her employers were tolerant of many things, but it didn't include sleeping at desks. She'd gone to bed at a reasonable hour but her partner, Andrew, had got up at four to captain an early morning flight to Alicante. It wouldn't have been so bad if he walked around the house quietly. Instead, he stomped up and down stairs as if there were on fire, and clanked his spoon against his cereal bowl as if testing the durability of the porcelain.

The disruption would tolerable if he made her happy in other ways, but some of his habits were getting on her nerves, and were at the heart of their last few fights. Before meeting her, he'd attended boarding school and while at university, lived in catered accommodation for three years. While she didn't expect him to be adept at cooking and cleaning, she was surprised to find he was also inept at tidying-up, gardening and DIY.

She wasn't without blame. She was guilty of leaving the food shop until the cupboards and fridge were bare, or borrowing money from his car park 'change' jar and forgetting to pay it back. She had gone to university too, but lived with three girls who all took a turn at household duties. While at home during the holidays, her mother would insist she 'mucked' in. If she couldn't or wouldn't, her mother would do it. In the Harlow house, if she didn't do it, it wouldn't get done.

Matt Flynn wasn't in the office today, out doing what, she didn't know. She didn't mind as his strengths were out in the field, not stuck in the office doing paperwork and following up on any research being conducted on their behalf. She had been researching crime scenes in the county of Oxfordshire, spreading the net way beyond the boundaries of the city of Oxford, but none of the incidents uncovered required the services of a crack Serbian sniper.

She stood and looked over the partitions. She spotted Sikandar Khosa at his desk and walked over. Short and beefy and wearing a 'SlashMetal on Tour' t-shirt, a bit faded and looking as though it had been worn many times before, he was supping Coke and the empty wrappers of a couple of chocolate bars lay on his desk. He claimed they were an occasional treat, but whenever Rosie walked past, he was either eating or had just finished doing so.

'Morning Siki. Ah, you're now into Picnic bars. I used to like them when I was a kid.'

'Oh, hi Rosie,' he said in a voice a couple of octaves higher than most people expected, given his sizeable frame. 'I didn't hear your stealth-like approach. I thought they'd stopped making them, but a mate of mine put me onto a sweet shop in Tottenham Court Road. Damn addictive they are, I can tell you.'

'If you were into drugs, you'd be dead by now.'

'Chocolate is just as bad,' he said screwing the paper up into a ball and scoring a direct hit into the bin. 'What can I do for you today?'

'The cigarette butt recovered from the field in Oxford. Have you received the result yet?'

'Nope, and if I did, you'd be first on my list to tell.'

'I know Siki, but I need this. Could you check, please?' she said nodding at the phone.

He reached for it. 'How can I resist your persuasive charms? Let me call my contact.' His podgy fingers prodded the handset with surprising dexterity, entering a number from memory.

The guy on the other end of the line had to be from the same part of Pakistan as Siki, as the HSA researcher lapsed into a language she didn't understand. It included much chuckling and laughing from the guy he was calling, expressions not often associated with members of the forensics fraternity. A few minutes later, Siki screeched something into the handset which sounded like an insult to her, even though he was still smiling. He slammed the phone down, making her jump.

'My God, that man can talk. I suppose I would be the same if I only had dead bodies and tissue samples to look at all day long.'

'Aside from a discussion about your old schoolmates or whatever you guys talked about, did you get around to mentioning the cigarette butt they're supposed to be analysing?'

'Cigarette butt? Shit I forgot to ask, and he's just gone out with his kid brother for the afternoon. He won't be back in the lab for two days.'

'Siki, how could you? I need it for–'

'Gotcha!' he said pointing at her face. 'Ha, ha. You should see your expression; classic.'

'You sod,' she said, trying to give him a slap on the shoulder which he nimbly avoided.

'You don't fall for it often, Rosie, but when you do, it's hook, line and sinker.'

'Yeah, yeah. Come on now, what's the story?'

'Are you ready for this?'

'C'mon, Siki, you've had your fun.'

He took a deep breath, milking it. 'The DNA sample from the cigarette butt matches...' He drummed his hands on the desk, 'our old friend, Dejan Katić.'

'Yes!' Rosie said punching the air. 'I thought it would.'

'Does this mean he shot down the balloon with the Andersons inside? All the information we've had from the Oxfordshire police says it was a slam-dunk accident.'

'It's not conclusive, but I can't think of another good reason why someone like him would be there. It's nothing but empty fields and big electricity pylons.'

'It sounds like it was him to me, the bastard. I hope you nail him.'

'There's not much chance of that happening now. Interpol have got him.'

'At least he hasn't hightailed it back to Serbia. If he went there, we'd never get him.'

'Even if he did go back to Serbia, I'm not sure we would go to the trouble of trying to extradite him. He's just a foot soldier carrying out an order. I'm more interested in finding the people who hired him.'

'Good luck finding them.'

She made to walk away.

'Before you go,' Siki said, 'I have something else for you.'

He handed her a sheaf of papers.

'What's this?' she said, flicking through the first few pages.

'The financials of Kevin and Stephen Anderson's defence business, Galleon Electronics. There's also some personal stuff relating to Kevin. I recommend you take a look at the personal stuff first. It makes interesting reading.'

She walked back to her desk, put her papers down and headed towards the kitchen. The Director, never one to ask someone to do something that he could do himself, was in there making coffee.

She shuffled her feet, not wanting to surprise him and cause an accident. 'Afternoon Gill,' she said.

He turned. 'Afternoon Rosie.'

'Would you like a coffee?' he asked.

'Don't worry, I'll make it myself.'

'Allow me.'

'Thank you.'

'How are you getting on tracking the handiwork of our Serb shooter?'

'I feel at last we're making some progress.' She went on to explain about the DNA match of the cigarette butt, linking the Serb with the balloon crash site and the lack of a major incident in the Oxfordshire area. With the exception of this one.

'Damn! We had the swine in custody only a few days ago. If we had this, I could've stuck my fingers up at Interpol.'

She shrugged. 'These things happen. They'll hang some serious charges on him, I'm sure.'

'Maybe they will, and maybe they won't. Katić has a nasty habit of wriggling his way out of situations like this. We didn't have enough evidence at the time to hold him, but hindsight's a wonderful mistress, is she not?'

'I agree.'

He handed Rosie her coffee, lifted his own and walked out of the kitchen without saying anything else. Although she did hear the word 'damn' uttered a couple of times.

Rosie headed back to her desk, sat down and picked up the research left there a few minutes before. She spread Kevin Anderson's personal bank account statements out in front of her. Without using a calculator, or expending too much brainpower, she understood what Sikandar had been alluding to. Kevin's salary hit the credit column every month with the monotony of a dripping tap, as did a host of household bills on the opposite side.

Several large withdrawals stood out: several thousand pounds over many months. To her, it suggested either the payment for a number of big ticket-items such investments or payments to builders. It could also relate to something nefarious like a serious drug habit or the activities of a heavy gambler.

She sat back in her chair sucking the end of her pen. Drug users and gamblers often needed large sums of money in a hurry, making her think this might be pointing to a reason why Kevin would try to murder his brother. Perhaps he did it to hide his addiction, and to receive a large insurance pay-out to clear his debts. Now being in control of the business, he could milk it for all it's worth.

Chapter 13

He called the meeting to order then glanced at the minutes of the last one. Kevin Anderson was chairing the Weekly Supervisor's Meeting. Its purpose, according to his dead brother, Stephen, was to foster good communication between supervisors and managers. This, to allow them to highlight issues before they turned into problems. In his experience, it was an opportunity for some of the old gas-bags to take time out from working and blow some hot air. For the rest of them, a chance to blame another department for their shortcomings and failures.

'I can't find anything contentious in the minutes of the last meeting,' Kevin said, 'do we all accept them?' He scanned the faces of the ten people gathered around the long table in the conference room. He wondered if anyone was foolish enough to get into his bad books so early in his reign by challenging him.

'When Stephen was in the chair,' Circuit Production Manager Ed Waters said, 'he always went through the previous minutes item by item, to remind us what was discussed last time.'

'Ed, I'm running the show now and I don't want to waste time talking about stuff we did or didn't do. I want to talk about the things we are going to do, okay?' The big man was about to open his gob and say something else, but before he did, Kevin said, 'Right, what's the first item on today's agenda?'

After fifteen minutes, he was bored with their inter-department rivalries and bickering. In his role as Sales Director, he was supposed to attend this, and several other meetings, Stephen organised in a never-ending quest to keep everyone 'on the same page', as he called it. With him being out on the road most of the time, he had a ready-made excuse to avoid attending.

Back then, Kevin was jealous of his brother. All he seemed to do was issue orders, attend meetings, and write emails, all from the comfort of a large, warm office. He wasn't stuck in a traffic jam on the M5, writing up orders on a clipboard, propped up on the steering wheel, and forced to eat his lunch out of a Tupperware box. Now, with his name on the main office door, ambition curdled in his mouth like week-old milk. It tasted even more bitter with every staff meeting, banal visitor and having his ear bent by supervisors' with their personal problems.

The police had now released the bodies of Stephen, Julia, Sophia and Ben, and their funerals were scheduled to take place the following week. He encouraged Chris to contact the family solicitor and obtain a copy of his parents' will. If, as expected, Stephen's share of the business was left to Chris, his nephew had a decision to make. However, Kevin couldn't see a place for him at Galleon Electronics.

Chris's degree, if ever completed, was in Computer Science. Their IT department wasn't big, and he couldn't sack the IT Manager who had been with the company eight years, even though at times he'd like to. If Chris gained some work experience before joining the company, it would make him more employable, but it wouldn't solve Kevin's immediate problem; he wanted his old Sales Director job back.

The meeting finished and they trooped out, many with more on their plate than when they'd come in. This was the way he intended to run meetings from now on. He returned to his office and ate lunch at his desk. There was a good canteen on the premises, serving hot meals, pasta and salads. The peace of his own office was still a novelty and a welcome change from greasy service station food or a plastic-tasting sandwich eaten in a noisy lay-by.

At six-thirty he left the building and drove to a pub called The Corridor on the corner of Cowley Road and Princes Street. He ordered a pint of lager and took a seat at the back, away from the window. He used pubs around the city to meet contacts, entertain customers and talk shop with other people from the industry. Tonight, it was personal. He didn't want to be spotted, especially with so many reporters still sniffing around after the balloon accident.

If meeting his buyer of scrap metal, it would be at one of the big pubs down by the river or in town. Big Ted liked to eye up the students in their tight jeans and skimpy t-shirts. Anderson enjoyed looking at the girls too, but its main advantage was in having plenty of people about if things turned ugly. So far, Ted had been as gentle as a pussycat, but he knew enough of his violent reputation and his predilection for maiming opponents who didn't give him what he wanted, not to let his guard down.

The scrap belonged to Galleon and their customers, companies good at making the products, but clueless about what they threw in the bin. Big Ted and his brothers operated a small foundry at the back of their engineering business in Cowley. Here, they extracted nickel, copper and iridium from damaged circuit boards, faulty wiring and end-cut pipes, and paid him a tidy sum for his trouble.

To date, the scrap money had funded his gambling and shielded it from the prying eyes of Mrs A. However, the money was in decline on account of new equipment being installed by companies to generate less waste. Instead of scaling back to match the income shortfall, he'd been dipping into his salary to fund the difference.

Thinking about Big Ted, reminded him of a question Chris had asked him a few days ago. Did he know of anyone connected to the business who had the means to bring down the balloon? Kevin's first reaction was to believe his nephew had gone gaga, as everyone connected with the incident: police, Air Accident Investigation Branch, reporters, all concluded it had been an accident. To humour him, he said he'd take a look.

He didn't need to look far. Galleon Electronics operated in the defence business, their products sold to military organisations and contractors. Those organisations were staffed by ex-military types, some of whom kept weapons at home and referred to the general public as 'civilians'.

On the non-military side, their biggest customer was Chess Electronics, a manufacturer of satellite navigation devices and satellite phones. The company's owner, a former Stepney market trader, had been pictured in newspapers talking and laughing with some heavyweight criminals, despite the veneer of a gated Essex mansion and fifty-foot yacht.

On the scrap side, Big Ted ran an engineering and metal bashing business with his three brothers, any one of whom could be called 'big'. Ted was the largest and meanest of the lot. Ted's other scrap contact, Terry Dennison, owned a car dealership at Woodstock. Not only did Big Ted buy scrap metal from him, they were also involved in an insurance scam involving crashed cars. Dennison acted as an agent for dodgy lawyers who were looking for whiplash victims.

On the personal front, something never to be revealed to Chris, Kevin liked to gamble. No, he *needed* to gamble. It was the reason why he got out of bed in the morning and why, as Sales Director, he would drive sixty-thousand miles a year, or as now, sit on his arse and listen to crap all day. He didn't do online gambling or enter the tawdry den on high street bookmakers. He needed to be in the company of others and feel the frisson of risk in the air. He often attended race meetings when Stephen believed he was talking to customers, and visited a casino in Oxford when his wife assumed he was working late.

In tandem with the drop in scrap income, his losses at the casino had risen. It was nothing he couldn't handle, more so as boss of Galleon where he could award himself a salary hike, but the casino manager was starting to become twitchy and demanding he settle his account. It was an ultimatum he couldn't treat lightly. The casino was owned by the Swift brothers, the eldest of whom had been acquitted five years previously of murdering a rival.

It was a toss-up trying to decide which of the four groups might have been responsible for downing the balloon. They all possessed the capability, or knew someone who did, and none would lose much sleep over the result. Problem was, he couldn't think of a good enough reason why they would do it.

A meeting with Big Ted was scheduled for the following week. While his watchword was always 'careful,' this time he would spend more time looking and listening to the man in front of him, and less ogling the pretty girls.

He threw back the rest of his drink and stepped out from behind the table to buy another. It was then the door opened, and she walked into the pub. She was wearing a clinging cotton top that emphasised her voluptuous breasts and a pleated skirt that did much to hide her great legs but nothing to disguise a delectable rear end. She noticed him and strolled over.

'Hello gorgeous,' she said, wrapping her arms around him and giving him a warm, sloppy kiss. She eased back to look at him. 'As you are buying, make mine a gin and tonic. A double, if you please.'

She made to move towards a seat, but he held her tight, one arm around her waist and the other massaging her bottom. 'Not so fast Lucinda, I was enjoying that.'

Chapter 14

'Bravo Four calling Victor Lima One,' DI Emma Davis said. 'No sign of target vehicle. Repeat. No sign of target vehicle.'

'You have such a posh radio voice,' Jacko her driver said. 'You should be reading the news or something, not swanning around in this heap of scrap looking for deadbeats.'

'Is this the best chat-up line you can muster, Jack Harris? You need to do better or you'll never meet your ideal woman.'

'I rise when the challenge demands it.'

'Don't say something like that either, or you'll have them running for the door.'

'Can we please change the subject before I dig myself into a hole?'

'You're too late, mate.'

'Bleak this place isn't it?' Harris said. 'Reminds me of the place where I grew up.'

London lad Jack Harris grew up in Bermondsey and spoke like he had, but hated anyone reminding him of it or mocking his accent. He wasn't the most handsome man in the drug squad, with cropped short hair, a round, podgy face, dark swarthy skin betraying his Greek ancestry, and a dark beard shadow that a sharp razor couldn't remove. He wasn't the ugliest either, especially now with a large portion of his features hidden behind expensive aviator sunglasses.

This part of Tottenham looked bleak to Emma, another London sink estate full of litter, spray-painted lock-up garages, multi-ethnic children and adults with a drug- or alcohol-induced vacant look in their eyes. It sure didn't look like the place where she grew up, Lincoln, with a beautiful cathedral, mews alleyways and acres of parks. With fifteen years of working in London under her belt, she missed her home town but had no intention of moving anywhere else, especially now living with Matt Flynn.

Detective Inspector Emma Davis and Detective Sergeant Jack Harris were working in tandem with a mobile Armed Response Unit (ARU). They were searching for a big-time drug dealer that Emma's boss had been chasing for years, long before Emma joined the department.

It was often said that British bobbies weren't armed. In other parts of the UK, this was the case, but in London, due to its size and the diversity of the populace, many officers routinely carried guns. The mobile ARU which accompanied them was one of thirty such units operating in the Capital at any one time and permanently armed.

The strategy was designed to divert an ARU to a site, anywhere in London, where it was believed perpetrators were carrying weapons or undertaking a serious crime, within seven minutes of the call. The man they were seeking today, Jerome Powers, had a reputation for using guns, and so the addition of an

ARU made sense, as did the arming of Emma and Jacko.

A few minutes later they drove past the home of Tottenham Hotspur Football Club. Any minute now, Harris, an avowed Gooner, would sound off. She counted the seconds, 5-4-3...

'Beat them 3-1 last time,' he said with enthusiasm. 'Not just a beatin' but complete humiliation. It will never be forgotten by a true Arsenal fan like myself for the way we dominated the whole game, from the first whistle to the last.'

'Are you finished?'

'I know you don't like football, Em, but driving past their place is intimidating for someone like me.'

'We might be passing it a few more times in the next hour, so can you–'

'Victor Lima One, calling Bravo Four.'

'Received. What's happening Jimmy?'

'Target spotted. Heading east on White Hart Lane.'

'Follow target vehicle,' Emma said, 'but no blues and twos until I say so. Understood? We're four or five minutes away.'

'Right, sir. Received and understood.'

Jacko didn't need telling, the acceleration of the picking up before Emma had pressed 'End' on the portable handset. Both vehicles being used today were unmarked with police insignia but loaded with all the equipment of a regular police car. In addition to the weaponry, this included an ANPR unit, radio, siren and flashing lights. The anonymity of these vehicles allowed them and the boys in the ARU to follow a target vehicle without the occupants becoming alarmed.

Jacko could drive better than anyone else in the unit, one of the reasons she liked working with him, and he made easy meat of the light lunchtime traffic. In the time it took them to catch up with the ARU, the target had driven down Love Lane to pick up an accomplice, the vehicle now filled with four male occupants.

They drove past Sainsbury's on Northumberland Park, a road leading into an industrial estate, and if the target Nissan carried on driving into the estate, Emma decided she would make the 'hard stop' there. Streets would be quiet, everyone working inside the commercial units, and the officers wouldn't be eyeballed by a group of nosey parkers all reaching for their camera phones, ready to post their pictures on social media.

She relayed her thinking to the two officers in the other car, and they acknowledged. She'd worked with Jimmy and Eddie in the past and liked their no-nonsense approach. It was difficult for the people in the target vehicle to spot a following vehicle, never mind two police cars. Their vehicles resembled any other car in the street: dirty, scratched and with the paintwork fading. The four boys in the Nissan Sunny in front were laughing and joking and obviously playing loud music, as she could see their heads bobbing.

In London, it was easier following suspect cars than in many other cities. Roads were busy at all times: cars constantly turning off and joining, shoppers pulling in and out of parking places, and tourists following satnav directions. Inevitably, there was always a car in front and a car behind, the price paid for living in a busy, vibrant city. It also meant if the occupants of the car realised they were being followed and tried to shake them off, the danger factor multiplied. There were large numbers of pedestrians on the pavements, roads lined with parked cars, and drivers often turned into main roads without warning.

They turned into Marsh Lane. On the left, Osborne House, London Underground's Northumberland Park control centre, and on the other, various industrial buildings. As anticipated, little traffic and few people around.

'Victor Lima One, this is Bravo Four. Go! I repeat Go!'

The black BMW of Victor Lima One dropped two gears and shot past the target's Nissan. It pulled directly in front and braked sharply. The brake lights of the Sunny came on, the occupants in the back being thrown against the front seats as it came to a sudden stop. Realising they couldn't move forward, the heads inside the Nissan all looked to the rear. Their faces fell when Emma and Jacko's car appeared in the back window, a metre or so behind them.

Emma rushed out of the car brandishing her handgun, the two officers from the other vehicle doing the same with their more threatening Heckler and Koch carbines. Jacko, slow to move at the best of times, followed behind.

'Out of the vehicle now!' Emma shouted. 'Let me see your hands!'

The four occupants didn't move, either through fear or were considering their options. To hurry them along, it was tempting for the waiting officers to grab the door handle, but training had knocked that little trait out of their repertoire. Reaching for the car door would take one hand away from the weapon, making its use less accurate, and if the occupants inside decided to leg it, the car door could suddenly open, knocking the officer off-balance.

The back door of the Nissan on Emma's side swung open and a young man came out. He looked about seventeen. She wondered if his parents knew he was consorting with such unsavoury characters. Emma patted him down, but found nothing.

'Face down on the deck! Now!' she commanded. 'Hands behind your back!'

He did as she told him without protest. She knelt beside him and secured his wrists. She heard Jacko doing the same with the other rear seat passenger. All the time they were apprehending the two rear seat passengers, Jimmy and Eddie from Victor Lima One were still training their weapons on the two passengers in the front of the vehicle who hadn't yet made a move.

The passenger shrugged and out he came; all attitude and bravura. Jimmy and Eddie were right to be cautious.

'Get Down!' Jimmy shouted.

'Hey man,' the scumbag said, 'I ain't gonna dirty my new threads on this filthy pavement.'

'I said, get down!' Jimmy bawled.

'Hey man I don't wanna. I only just bought 'em.'

'Down on the fucking deck!'

Emma's attention was diverted when the driver's door opened. Out came Jerome Powers in the flesh, exhibiting the same swagger and cool as his mate.

'No, I ain't gonna,' Jimmy's prisoner whined.

Eddie took a step towards Powers. Emma watched the scene through two sets of dirty windows in the Nissan.

The driver's hand slid into his jacket pocket in a practised movement and something black and rough-looking emerged.

Eddie's gun spat twice and Jerome Powers fell to the ground; dead.

Chapter 15

'Ah, here's the coffee. We'll take a ten-minute break.' The Superintendent rose from his seat and, almost as if performing a pre-arranged ballet, many of his fellow officers around the conference table rose in unison.

Matt Flynn stretched tired muscles. He'd gone to the gym the previous night, the first time for several weeks, and completed a heavy-duty work-out with loose weights. While apprehending a drug shipment at a remote beach in Suffolk six months before, one of the Lithuanians on board a rusty freighter, suspected of carrying a large consignment, let rip with an Uzi.

With a short barrel and the trigger finger of the shooter not letting up until the magazine had emptied, it could never be classed as an accurate weapon. Its main use was as a deterrent. With bullets zipping everywhere, it didn't come as a surprise when one ricocheted off a rock and hit someone; Matt, in the thigh. What did come as a surprise was the damage it did and how long it took for him to get over it.

Matt stood and walked over to the table at the back of the conference room, now set out with coffee and pastries. He and Rosie were ensconced in a meeting within the headquarters of Thames Valley police at Kidlington. They were listening to Superintendent

Cousins and his team brief them about the balloon incident at Ladder Hill and their subsequent investigation.

The HSA Agents wouldn't tell him about the presence of the Serbian sniper or the cigarette butt found close to the crash site. He wouldn't tell, not because they were the boys in blue and not CID, but the evidence as yet was circumstantial. In any case, incidents involving Serbian hitmen were the concern of HSA and not the local plod.

'Are you tempted by a Danish, Matt?' Inspector Barry Fisk asked.

'I think I might. It's been a long afternoon.'

'Aye, but we've covered a lot of ground.'

'Have you been to see Chris?' Matt asked.

'That I have. He's a nice lad, confused and a bit frightened, but a good lad all the same.'

'What do you make of his uncle?'

'Kevin? He's a rough character and no mistake. All the same, he must have something. You should see his missus, a right belter, she is.'

'I thought Chief Constables were trying to stamp out sexism in the force,' Rosie said, butting in. Matt noticed she didn't have a Danish or any of the chocolate biscuits. True to form, Rosie didn't even have a plate.

'Get away, Rosie, that's not being sexist. I stated a fact: Kevin is married to an attractive woman.'

'At the risk of being sidetracked,' Matt said, 'we'll park this discussion for some other time. Barry, you were saying about Kevin?'

'He's a rough looking character and sharp with his tongue, but maybe you need to be like that in the defence business. Chris seems to get along with him just fine. Mind you, what choice does the boy have with all his family gone?'

'It's not going to be easy for him,' Rosie said, 'that's for sure.'

'What about Galleon Electronics? Do we know if Chris inherits his father's share?'

'Yes, he does. Kevin said he remembered Stephen, Chris's father, making out a will in which he left his share of the business split between his daughter and his son. With her being killed in the accident as well, it all falls to Chris. The family solicitor confirmed it a few days ago.'

'Does this mean he's not going back to uni and staying here to take up a position in the business?' Rosie asked.

'He's not sure if he wants to work there or not. I suspect they don't have a place for him until he gets some experience under his belt.'

'Unless he's willing to start at the bottom,' Rosie said.

'Barry!'

The inspector turned to see Superintendent Cousins calling him over.

'Excuse me folks,' Barry said. 'God calls.'

'Learn anything new today, Rosie?' Matt asked, as he helped himself to another Danish. It probably negated many of the benefits of his trip to the gym, but custard-filled pastries were a personal favourite.

'I've learned that you can be a greedy pig when you set your mind to it.'

'C'mon, I didn't have much at breakfast and I went to the gym last night.'

'You going to the gym is to give your leg some physiotherapy, not so you can eat all the pastries.'

'You want me to put this one back?'

'Don't you dare. I've also learned there's not one iota of suspicion about the balloon accident among the assembled bodies here, even after Cousins placed a call to the Air Accidents Investigation Branch this morning. Are we missing something obvious?'

'What, you think it's a coincidence that we track a Serb sniper's car to a remote part of Oxfordshire, early on a Sunday morning. Then, we find a cigarette butt belonging to him close to the site where a balloon crashed, killing five people? I call it pretty damn conclusive, me.'

'I don't think it's a coincidence, and even Katić can't claim to be a rubbernecker as the date stamp on the CCTV puts him there in the morning before anyone knew about the accident. But even with his DNA, we still don't have a lot to go on. It doesn't tell us why, or who's behind it.'

'It's enough to get him convicted in a court of law.'

Matt received one of Rosie's cynical looks. 'Since when were you so concerned about courts of law? You joined HSA, you said, to get away from all the bureaucracy.'

'I did.'

'Given time, our Serbian hitman could think up a host of excuses for his presence there, enough to fool a jury: he's a birdwatcher, he likes hot-air balloons, he's a voyeur and went there hoping to catch some couple having a shag in the field.'

'Very good, Rosie, you're convincing me.' He took a drink of coffee to wash down the Danish. 'The reason I think we can't say why he shot down the Anderson balloon is because Chris Anderson isn't telling us everything he knows.'

'Where did you get that gem from?'

'Let's accept the sniper-for-hire theory for a moment.'

'Okay.'

'Who would have the motivation and the money to pay for someone like him to come here and shoot the balloon down? That's the question we need to answer, and I think Chris knows.'

'It wouldn't be his uncle or anyone connected with the business. We said when we met Chris, they're small fry in the defence world. Plus, if the antis of Oxford are behind it, killing Chris's father and his family won't stop the business working on defence contracts.'

'No, not even if the killer now lines up Uncle Kevin as next in line for the chop.'

'You do have an elegant turn of phrase, Mr Flynn.'

'So Emma says.'

'When you're doing what, may I ask?'

'Rosie, you don't want to know.'

'What about Kevin Anderson's large withdrawals from his bank account? If he's in hock to some Chinese gambling syndicate or a violent drug dealer, he might be desperate to lay his hands on some ready cash. If he takes over the business, he can take whatever he wants from its bank account, or Stephen might be covered by a big insurance policy with Kevin the main beneficiary.'

'Some top people in business are covered by special insurance policies,' Matt said. 'They are designed to pay out if a key employee falls ill, or they're incapacitated in an accident. It's a good point. I'll ask Siki to check if one exists. If Kevin's a big-time drug user, I still don't think the withdrawals are of sufficient magnitude to encourage someone to kill his brother and his family.'

'You're right, as he's probably earning a good salary to cover anything he needs. What if he wants to take control of the business so he can milk it long-term? Then, he could gamble, buy drugs, play the stock market; do what the hell he likes.'

'I understand your logic but I still don't think it stacks up. Kevin knew the contents of the will and knew Chris would inherit his father's share. It doesn't matter how much Kevin's in debt, Chris takes over from Stephen.'

'Chris can't step into Stephen's shoes right away, can he? While he's learning his craft, there's no one looking over Kevin's shoulder to stop him doing what he likes.'

'Killing his brother and his niece just to hide a few bad habits?' Matt shook his head. 'I don't see it. The solution is way out of magnitude to the problem.' He leaned closer, his voice quiet. 'What if the target wasn't Stephen Anderson or anyone else aboard that balloon, but Chris? From a distance, Ben, the guy who joined them on the flight after Chris bowed out, may have made the killer think the whole Anderson family were aboard.'

'How do you work that one out, clever clogs? He's a second-year student of computer science at Durham uni, not a cryptanalyst at GCHQ or a Middle East expert at SIS. Why would anyone want to kill him?'

'It's standard detective procedure, if you can remember that far back. When you've looked at all the possibilities and they don't work out, the one that seems impossible or improbable must be the solution.'

'I must have fallen asleep when I attended that one, but I'm listening.'

'Let's go through the facts: he's good at IT.' Matt looked up. 'Oh, hi, Barry. My, you looked flustered.'

'I've just run back here from the other side of the building, I'm puffed. Right, I think the Super's ready to go again. Shall we re-take our seats?'

Chapter 16

Matt returned home from Oxford at seven in the evening. He was surprised to find the house tidy and Emma sitting in a chair in the lounge. She had a magazine on her lap and a glass of wine in her hand.

'Hi there,' he said leaning over the back of the chair to give her a kiss. 'How come you're home so early? Did they finally decide the fight against illegal drugs is no place for a woman and gave you the heave-ho?'

'I didn't know I was living with a misogynist dinosaur. You hide it well. There's beer in the fridge if you want one.'

He went into the kitchen looking for a bite to eat. Finding nothing in the cupboard, he settled on a banana from the fruit bowl. When finished, he took a beer from the fridge, opened the bottle and walked back into the lounge.

'Cheers,' he said as he slumped on the settee.

'Your good health,' replied Emma, not looking up from her magazine.

'What are you reading?'

'It's the story of a woman who was forever telling her husband to go to the doctor as he had a pain in the neck he couldn't get rid of. When he did, he found out he had motor neurone disease and at best, three years to live, the majority of the time in a wheelchair.'

'Bloody hell, what an uplifting read.'

'Even though it is a difficult subject I like the cheerful way this woman writes.'

Matt leaned over and picked up the wine bottle.

'You've hit this hard,' he said holding it up for her to see.

'Get away, I didn't drink all that. Don't you remember, you opened it the other night?'

'Ah, you're right, so I did. You are excused. Have you been here all afternoon?'

'I've been given a few days of garden leave, orders from the boss. Do you want to hear about it?'

'Sure.'

Stories from the drug squad were either stupefyingly dull or utterly petrifying with nothing much in between. A thirty-man team could be waiting around for most of the morning, before kicking in the door of a lock-up only to find it empty. Alternatively, a couple of officers could be knocking on the door of a known drug dealer, when the glass on the door is shattered when someone inside opens up with a sub-machine gun.

'Man, that's terrible,' Matt said when Emma had finished telling him the story of her afternoon and the killing of her department's most wanted. 'How are your lot? Did anyone get injured?'

'No, they're okay. Same with the other perps. Only Powers.'

'It's a good job you didn't stop them on their own estate. You'd have his mother and half the bloody neighbourhood trying to tear you all to bits.'

'Don't I know it.'

'Have you spoken to Eddie?'

'He's well pissed-off and not looking forward to his time in the office. Says he's been meaning to go back to Barbados for a couple of years and visit his relatives, so maybe he'll take some time off.'

'Does the shooting of a wanted drug dealer improve his reputation within the ARU or degrade it?'

'I'm sure it'll raise his standing with the lads, but not with me or the folks upstairs.'

'You're tough nut, Emma Davis. A drug dealer pulls out a gun? Eddie Johnson's got a clear cause to shoot, I know I would.'

'I've saved the best bit for last. It wasn't a gun he was reaching for, he was pulling out the stupid beanie hat he always wore. The daft bugger wouldn't be seen in public without it, even when being arrested.' She started to cry.

Matt walked over, sat on the arm of the chair and put his arm around her. 'It's okay to feel this way. It's been a tough day,' he said.

'I know, I speak to shrinks too. I don't know why I feel like this. He's the enemy, and we're doing some good in the world, so why does it make me feel so crappy?'

They sat in quiet contemplation for the next five minutes before the rumbling of Matt's stomach broke the silence.

Emma started laughing. 'Are you hungry or something?'

'I prefer the happy face,' he said. He bent over and gave her a kiss. 'After the meeting today, we pulled into a service station for something to eat, but I didn't fancy anything on offer. I'm starving.'

'Before you came in, I was about to make some lasagne but I'm finding it hard to get up from this chair. Give me a few minutes to tidy myself up and I'll make a start.'

'Nah, forget it, you've had a crappy day. Why don't we go down the pub and let them cook for a change? We'll be extra daring and leave them with the dirty dishes.'

'You make a tempting offer, but don't you think it's a bit decadent for a Monday night...ah what the hell. When someone offers to buy you dinner, it would be churlish to refuse.'

'I said I fancied going out for something to eat, I didn't say anything about paying.'

It was a short walk from Stock Lane to the High Street. From there, an Indian and a Thai restaurant were within easy walking distance, but Emma decided she wanted pub food. Matt, his hunger overriding any preferences he might have had, was happy to go along with her decision.

They walked into The Star, a place where they'd eaten several times before. To his surprise, as he expected the place to be empty, it was busy and he recognised a couple of their neighbours.

'So, is this what everybody does on a Monday night when I'm watching *Holby City*?' Emma said. 'Who would believe it?'

'You need to get out more often.'

'You need to take me.'

Twenty minutes later Emma's choice from the menu was laid in front of her: haddock and chips, the ultimate comfort food. He opted for a burger.

'I've been so wrapped up in my shooting drama I forgot to ask about your day. How did the trip to Oxford go?'

'We told the local plod we were interested in the case due to the large loss of life, public interest in the story and all that. To their credit, they didn't have a hernia, which makes a change. I think they're more concerned about getting their story straight before a big meet next week with the Chief Constable and local dignitaries. Overall, we didn't learn much other than they are convinced it was nothing other than a hellish accident.'

Her fork stopped in mid-air, about to put a large piece of fish in her mouth. 'You're doing the opposite of detective work. You're not investigating a crime, you are trying to find out if and why a crime has been committed. Is this Serbian gunman the real deal?'

'For sure. He's been implicated in the assassination of a Kuwaiti oil minister in 2004 and the killing of an American general on leave from Iraq in Cyprus in 2006. Worst of all, about six years ago, he was named as the shooter of a French helicopter which crashed into a hillside, killing all twelve anti-terrorist officers aboard who had just attended a conference in Nantes.'

'I remember the last one. I thought they put it down to bad weather and pilot error?'

'They did, but don't you think it would cause more alarm if they said the helicopter had been shot down by person or persons unknown?'

She gave him one of her sceptical looks. 'If he's so ruthless, why hasn't someone lifted him before now?'

'He's been in custody several times, but he does every job cleanly, leaving no evidence of his involvement. In fact, I hope Interpol have got something solid to throw at him, otherwise he might be walking again.'

'What makes a guy do a job like that?'

'It's a good question.' He laid his cutlery down. 'What you've got to remember is the war in the Balkans kicked off in the 1990s. It's not like World War Two that happened generations ago, and not in some far-flung desert kingdom in the Middle East either. It was here on Europe's doorstep in cities and towns like ours. Guys who were soldiers then aged nineteen or twenty are in their 40s and 50s now. Memories of all the horrors and terrifying moments will still be with them and in Katić's case, maybe he didn't stop being a soldier.'

'It's more recent than you think.'

'The thing with a modern conflict is not only do the people involved still possess all the skills they learned while they were in uniform, they're still young enough to use them and many of the weapons still work.'

'We often take guns away from street kids,' Emma said, 'and they can be traced back to wars in Africa or they've been smuggled from Iraq and Syria. The anti-terrorist guys say the same thing. What are you planning to do now? It sounds like you don't have many leads.'

'There's nothing we can do about the Serb shooter, he's with Interpol now and anyway, he told us nothing when we interviewed him. Our main focus now is finding out who hired him and why.'

'Is that what he is, a gun for hire?'

'Yep, no allegiances to anything but money.'

'How will you find the guy who paid him?'

'We need to go back to Oxford and talk again to Chris Anderson. There's something he's not telling us about his father, or something he's involved in himself.'

'Chris? He's only twenty-one. The hardest thing for a kid of his age is getting out of bed in the morning and writing a personal statement on a university application form. I can't see how he would have done anything so major it would provoke someone to hire the Serb to kill his family.'

'You sound like Rosie, but the answer to this must be there. It can't be anything else.'

'Mind you, I'm thinking about some middle-class kid whose father owns a defence business in Oxford. Many of the kids I come across are breaking into houses at fourteen and have a serious drug habit before they can legally drive. Even if they can avoid drugs, they're out boosting cars, robbing off-licenses and nicking mobile phones. If Chris has got just a small part of what they have, then maybe you'll find a motive.'

Chapter 17

It had been a long day. Kevin Anderson had spent the afternoon interviewing candidates for the Sales Director position, left vacant when he moved into the Managing Director's chair. Was he being fussy or was his heart not in it?

The last guy interviewed exuded all the confidence required to walk into a room full of uniforms and tell them what they needed to know, but where he excelled in salesmanship, he lacked in technical knowledge. Kevin now realised it could be a showstopper. He didn't have the time or the inclination to train a new person.

Kevin had never trained to be a salesman but it didn't stop him being successful. However, the nuances of his new role as Managing Director eluded him. He knew enough not to call the overweight women working in the staff canteen 'fat', or the disabled people on the shop floor testing electronic circuits 'cripples'. Nonetheless, trying to get the best out of people in a one-to-one meeting was harder than it looked.

Looking back over the completed interviews, he'd been too eager to talk about his own background, or finish sentences when the candidate couldn't think of the next word. As a result, several candidates faded from his memory as effectively as someone he'd passed in the street.

This evening, he could do with the comfort of his secretary, Lucinda. With the door closed and her beside him, ostensibly taking notes while he massaged her thigh, but she had left for home several hours before. She'd been Stephen's secretary before him, but even then, the two of them had been at it like rabbits whenever the opportunity arose.

He pushed the CVs to one side and stood. He couldn't do much more tonight and began packing up to go home. Like the optimistic salesman he'd always been, it would all look better in the morning. He turned off all the lights, a habit ingrained into all the staff by Stephen, and exiting the building after first locking the front door.

They didn't employ a doorman or feel the need for a caretaker. The company didn't operate a night shift and the nature of the work meant no member of staff needed to stay beyond the normal knocking-off time of five-thirty. Kevin had been the last one out of the building every night since assuming his new role, but he didn't do it willingly.

He walked down the stone steps at the building's entrance and then around the corner to the car park at the rear. He could see his car under the glare of the security lights and beside it another car. In all his time of doing the new job and being the last one out of the building, his car had always been the only one remaining in the car park.

He assumed a member of staff had left it before heading out to one of the pubs or restaurants nearby, but why would they? Galleon was located at the Oxford Business Park. While some of the pubs in the area were satisfactory and fine for a quick working lunch, far better bars and restaurants could be found by the river and in the city centre, both only a short drive away.

He walked to his car and as he got closer, the doors of the other car opened and two men got out. They headed towards him.

'Kevin Anderson?' the taller one said.

Kevin's heart sank; it could be cops or journalists, neither of whom he wanted to talk to right now.

'Who wants to know?'

'You need to come with us.'

'Show me your–'

A punch in the gut floored him and before he could respond, he was knocked to the floor and duct tape wrapped around his hands and his mouth. They pulled him upright and an arm grabbed him around the throat causing him to gag. They frogmarched him to their car and seconds later, hands gripped his body and threw him on the floor in the back of their car.

He didn't waste any energy struggling or trying to shout over the gag. Two against one was unfair odds. He would wait until they reached their destination and then try to do something. If they were cops, they sure hadn't been on the same interviewing course as Inspector Morse.

He could tell by the bump and sway of the car they weren't taking him out to the country. There, they would tell him to strip, and he would be forced to walk home naked. This was the sort of stunt his mate, Bob

Taylor, was likely to pull on his birthday, but today wasn't his birthday. He knew they were heading into town as he could feel the car slow and stop at various points which he assumed to be traffic lights, and swing left and right as it sailed around a succession of roundabouts.

Ten minutes later the car stopped. The door opened and they hauled him to his feet. He felt drizzle on his face and, looking around. They were parked in a back alley. They bundled him towards a door, blank without signs or insignias to say what was inside. One of the guys pressed a buzzer and a few seconds later he heard a *click* as the door lock was disengaged. He realised now would be the best time to try to escape before he disappeared into the bowels of this building. This wasn't possible, not only did his captors do a good job of trussing him up, they stood on either side him gripping his arms.

They led him up a steep, narrow staircase into what could only be described as a well-appointed office. Too red and opulent for his tastes, with thick carpets and heavy furniture, making him think he was in a room at the back of a nightclub or casino. The realisation hit him, sending a shudder through his body: casino. If tonight's strong-arm charade was about his gambling debts, it meant he was about to meet one of the Swift brothers.

Declan and Gary Swift had built up an impressive gambling empire of betting shops, on-track betting and casinos, all from the inheritance of a single betting shop in Woking fifteen years ago. The brothers were chalk and cheese; Declan the brains, Gary the brawn. He'd known several habitual gamblers who had fallen on hard times after a run of bad luck and received a visit from one of the brothers.

If Declan turned up at your workplace or home, the Swifts considered you a valuable customer. He was there to provide reassurance of your continued admittance to their gambling establishments and discuss a payment regime to reduce the outstanding debt. If Gary arrived, they wanted their money now, and he didn't care how many bones he broke or ligaments he ripped to get it.

They untied his hands and dumped him in a chair in the centre of the room. The relief was temporary as strong hands gripped his wrists and tied him to the arms of the chair. He still wore the gag and couldn't ask why he was there or what they wanted.

Five minutes later, he found out the answer when Gary Swift walked into the room. Decked out in a smart dinner suit, he looked to the punters in the casino like one of the croupiers. To Kevin, he resembled an old-fashioned gangster, clever on the outside, evil on the inside. He had a well-styled mop of black hair, perfect teeth and a handsome face, but to those on the receiving end of his bad temper, looks could be deceiving.

Swift removed his jacket and rolled up his sleeves; tattoos vied for space on muscled arms. He walked around the desk and sat on the edge looking at his prisoner. He nodded to one of his heavies who pulled the tape away from Kevin's mouth in a quick movement, making him wince.

'You are here, mate, because you owe me a lot of money.'

'I know, I know, but I can pay you back.'

He laughed, flashing those famous pearly whites. 'I hear that more times than I've busted people's arms, and that's saying something.'

The two heavies joined in the merriment but Kevin didn't find it funny.

'I can get you the money, I've got a good job.'

'Kevin, I know what you do, I know where you work, I know you and Hannah live in a nice house and your children are all grown-up and have moved away.'

He was gobsmacked. How did Swift know all this about him? Kevin was a cautious man. He worked in a tough business and routinely checked his street and car to ensure no one was watching and someone hadn't followed him home. Had the furore surrounding Stephen's untimely death: the reporters at the door, Hannah's bouts of crying and Chris in the upstairs room, distracted him? Had he become too complacent?

'The problem is how will you pay me back if I burn down your little business? I'm tempted to do it and there are many in Oxford who would thank me for doing so.'

'You wouldn't.'

'Don't underestimate me Kevin, or what I'm capable of. Maybe to make it interesting, I'll wait until all the employees, including yourself, are inside, eh? I've done a lot worse.'

It came to him in a flash; Chris was right to think the balloon had been downed deliberately. Maybe it had been done by Swift to demonstrate his reach and ruthlessness.

'Gary can I ask–'

He held his hand up. 'No, you can't ask. The time for discussion is over. I brought you here today, Kevin, to show you that we mean business. When the manager of my casino in Oxford asks you to pay back the money you owe, he shouldn't need to ask you a second time.'

Swift nodded to one of the heavies.

A fist came towards him and smacked him in the mouth. Then another, then another. Swift said something and the beating stopped.

Kevin spat out blood, then a tooth. Blood and snot dribbled on his trousers and down his white shirt. He tried to open his mouth wide, but the excruciating pain made him stop. His head felt heavy, he couldn't lift it. Someone grabbed his hair and lifted it for him; Swift.

'You will make a payment of the money you owe this week. You will make this your top priority. Do you hear me, Kevin?'

He nodded.

'Just remember, I won't ask a second time. Understand?'

He nodded again.

'Every time you look in the mirror, your damaged face and broken nose will remind you of this commitment.'

Broken nose? Too late, Swift's fist drew back and came flying towards him.

Chapter 18

The problem with living in Essex, according to Matt Flynn, wasn't the local accent or the blonde girl jokes, but that everyone he wanted to see lived in London or further west. As a result, he spent more time negotiating the M25 than many and like always, today it was choked with traffic. His phone rang.

'Hello Gill.'

'Where are you?'

'On the way to visit Sir Raymond and find out how his daughter is doing.'

'Poor girl. Give Raymond my fondest regards when you catch up with him, will you? He and I haven't talked for a while.'

'You were best friends at one time.'

'Stop fishing, Flynn, nothing's changed between us. It's difficult sometimes to find the time.'

'Tell me about it.'

'I heard about Emma's shooting incident.'

'Yeah, it's a sorry business.'

'Is she all right? The report I read said there were no other casualties other than the man they killed.'

'You would be the first to hear if anything went wrong. Your niece is fine as so is the rest of her team, but I think it's all set to get worse.'

'How do you mean?'

'I hear an organisation called Victims Against Police Aggression are planning a march this afternoon. Met analysts are predicting it could attract up to ten-thousand people, and they expect it to turn nasty when it gets dark.'

'What's your take? Should the Met pick a fight with the CPS if they decide to prosecute the ARU officer?'

'Emma says she would've done the same thing as Eddie Johnson, the ARU officer involved, and opened fire. If you wait until a perp shows you what he's got in his pocket and it's a gun, you're too late. Eddie's mistake, if I can call it such, as these things happen so fast, was not shouting a warning to Powers to keep his hands still.'

'I bow to you and your partner's more contemporary operational experience. I'll pass your comments on to the Met Commissioner when I see him and offer any help we can give. I also wanted to ask, what's the latest in trying to find out what our Serbian gunman, Dejan Katić, has been doing?'

Matt brought him up to date, including details of the research done by Sikandar Khosa. The traffic ahead of Matt's car started to speed up.

'Is Kevin Anderson out of your reckoning?'

Matt shrugged to himself. 'I think so. We've looked at the big withdrawals from his bank account and tied them to gambling debts. No way does it warrant the engagement of a Serbian sniper.'

'I agree. This leaves the Anderson boy who you believe is harbouring something?'

'We've eliminated nearly everything else and it's not something we can dismiss, despite what Rosie says. Chris is studying Computer Science at university and according to his tutor, he's a natural. What if he hacked into a company's systems and saw something he shouldn't, or messed up their system, making life difficult for serious criminals or a bad-ass gang?'

'If you remember,' Gill said, 'the guy who developed the Silk Road website on the dark web wasn't more than a teenager when he set it up, and we know the sorts of characters who inhabit that space. You might be on to something there. What I don't get is why Katić's results aren't more visible. Hits done by people like him in the past were never so subtle.'

'I understand your frustration, but maybe Katić wasn't trying to disguise it. If he did shoot down the Anderson family balloon, I think he struck lucky when the envelope hit the high-power cable and caught fire. If it didn't ignite and fell more or less intact, a bullet hole might have been spotted by AAIB investigators.'

'Maybe. Go and talk to the boy, do what you need to get the truth out of him. We're missing something and you know me, I don't like us being out of the loop. Speak to you soon.'

Forty minutes later, Matt turned off at the Windsor junction and ten minutes after that, his car crunched along the pebbled driveway of Clifton Manor, a large baronial house set in twenty acres of beautiful Surrey countryside. He loved the view here: long sweeping slopes of grass, small clumps of trees, a herd of cows in the distance, but he hated the house. It had been the family seat since the late seventeenth century, but the house always felt cold and draughty and cost its owner a fortune in utility bills and maintenance to heat and stop it falling apart.

David, Sir Raymond's personal assistant, opened the door.

'Good morning, David, how are you?' Matt asked.

'Good morning, Mr Flynn. I'm fine, thanks for asking. Here, let me take your coat.'

Matt handed him his coat and David turned to hang it.

'Let me take you through to Sir Raymond.'

Sir Raymond Deacon was the antithesis of everyone's idea of a baronial house inhabitant. He didn't wear tweed, he didn't drive a Rolls Royce, smoke cigars or speak with a plummy Oxbridge accent. He was a former Scotland Yard Assistant Commissioner, and the main architect of HSA. He also took charge of the agency when Gill received a bullet, putting him out of action for three months. Sir Raymond could shoot, didn't grumble about spending hours in a surveillance car and was a good interrogator of scumbags, some just as likely to spit on their questioner as talk to them.

'Matt, it's good to see you again,' he said throwing his newspaper down and walking over to shake Matt's hand.

'How are you?' Raymond asked. 'Come over by the fire and take a seat.'

The drawing room of dark, wood-panelled walls, traditional furniture and a large fireplace, which someone of Matt's height could walk inside, matched the exterior of the house. He took a seat on one of the settees, set either side of the fireplace and opposite the Eighth Baron of Clifton and minister at the Home Office.

'I hear good things about HSA, Matt. A few chief constables and a couple of government ministers who should know better envisioned an unwashed and bloodied Jason Bourne roaming our streets, pointing his gun at petrified passers-by. I think Gill has steered the organisation close to the original vision set out in my paper, a cross between US Homeland Security and the FBI, strong investigative skills coupled with the power and muscle to back it up. Touch wood,' he said tapping the fireplace, 'no banana skins yet.'

'Surprising given the fine line we walk.'

It was good to hear Sir Raymond's vote of confidence. Even though Matt regarded him as a friend, his department would have no compunction about shutting HSA down if the clamour of MPs and the public, alarmed at their methods or lack of success, became too great.

The door opened and David came into the room wheeling a trolley. Matt always felt spoiled whenever he visited Clifton Manor. 'Coffee and biscuits' were never less than could be found at afternoon tea in one of London's top hotels. The day following a boozy night always left him hungry. He and Emma didn't leave The Star until closing time, she drowning her sorrows at the death of a suspect and Matt joining in just to be sociable.

He filled a plate with a couple of sandwiches, a few biscuits and a slice of David's wife's signature Battenberg cake; baked nectar.

'What case are you working on at the moment, Matt?'

He explained about Katić and his suspicion about a tie-in with the balloon accident in Oxford.

'It amazes me we're still letting these people into the country.'

'A false passport and a new identity as a tractor salesman. What can we do?'

Raymond pulled out his notebook. 'I don't know but I'll damn well ask Border Force. If we can find a way of stopping these people at ports and airports, you and everyone else who are trying to make this island more secure, will find the job very much easier.'

'I can't argue with you there.'

'How's Gill?'

Matt talked to him about HSA's boss, the Director Templeton McGill, although Raymond seemed to know well enough.

'How's Lisa?' Matt asked.

A cloud passed over Raymond's usually optimistic face.

'No change since your last visit, when was it, six weeks ago?'

Matt nodded. 'I'm sorry it's been so long.'

'Don't worry, I know you're busy. She still doesn't go out, stays in her room and doesn't say much.'

'Post Traumatic Stress Disorder affects everybody in different ways. Not every reaction has been documented either.'

'The doctors say the same and I tell you Matt, I've seen enough of the men in white coats to last me a lifetime. Despite spending my entire career in the service of government, I'd resign on the spot if they ever tried transferring me to the Department of Health.'

Matt smiled and knew he wasn't joking. 'I should go up and see her. She can probably hear us talking.'

'Go on. She loves it when you come to see her.'

'Don't I remind her of what happened?'

'I asked one of the psych doctors and he said no. She rationalises the incident. You're part of the solution, not the problem.'

He climbed the stairs with some trepidation. Such a lovely girl, Lisa, but unable to leave the prison she had created for herself. Four months before, Matt had rescued her from the clutches of an Arab terrorist. His explosive device failed to detonate as the ministerial car containing the Defence Secretary arrived outside the Home Office where he was attending a meeting. He began firing at the minister's bulletproof car with an AK47, and when the bullets didn't penetrate the interior, grabbed the nearest passer-by and highjacked a car. The kidnap victim was Lisa Deacon, on her way to the Home Office to see her father.

Not content to wait until he reached heaven and received his promised gaggle of virgins, he couldn't resist Lisa's obvious charms and raped her time and again. Matt often experienced remorse at the taking of a life but not this one. Her attacker was dead before he hit the ground. He did Matt a favour by pulling out a gun. No way did he want the terrorist's ugly mug being plastered all over newspapers during a long and expensive trial which would only torment his victim one more time.

He knocked and on hearing her say, 'Come in,' he pushed open the door.

She had her back to him, writing something as she sat at the elegant mahogany bureau.

'What is it Dad?' she said in an irritated voice that teenagers reserved for talking to their parents.

When he didn't reply, she turned.

'My God! Matt, it's you!' She pushed her chair back with some force and rushed towards him. She threw her arms around him in an almost child-like gesture. If Emma was standing beside him, she would suspect something untoward was going on between them.

'It's so good to see you,' she gushed, struggling to get the words out. 'It's ages since the last time you came to see me. Come on,' she said, breaking away and taking his hand, 'sit with me at the window.'

'How have you been?'

'Same as before,' she said as her sunny disposition faded like the warmth as the sun disappeared behind a thick cloud. 'I'm still scared to go out, and I spend most of the time in this room with my laptop and diary.'

Aged twenty-three, Lisa at times spoke and acted like a teenager, as if the ordeal she'd gone through had knocked years off her age. Her reaction at not going out, not saying much, losing contact with friends was extreme, but not unusual in PTSD cases, according to many psychologists. Recovery would take time. Luckily, that wouldn't present a problem as her father was rich and could hire any professional help he cared to, if he believed their contribution would make a difference.

'The last time we met,' Matt said, 'you told me you were writing your own comments on social media instead of just reading what other people were up to.'

'That's right and now I'm getting good at it. Come and I'll show you what I've been doing.'

Chapter 19

'Chris, you don't answer my calls or emails for weeks. When you do, you tell me I'm the nastiest hack who's ever set her scaly paws on this earth,' Louise Walker said, her face red. 'Then yesterday, you ask me to drop everything and come to Oxford and talk to you. Please explain; I'd be very interested to hear what you've got to say.'

They were inside a pub called *The Head of the River*, seated close to the window. This was where Louise wanted to sit, against the wishes of Chris Anderson who said he didn't want to be visible to anyone outside. His choice of seating was in the depths of the bar, beside a continuously beeping gaming machine and within sniffing distance of the urinal, clean at this early hour of the day, but still smelling of strong chemicals. Her dad often said she could be as stubborn as a mule and he had a point. All her journalistic training told her to kowtow to the demands of a valuable source like the one in front of her, but today, she wasn't in the mood.

She'd been to Oxford three times before on the off-chance of an interview with 'the boy who survived', but each time she returned to London empty-handed. Now, at the point when Jed, a handsome colleague at the national newspaper where she worked, had finally summoned up the courage to ask her out, the call came from Chris begging her to come to Oxford.

'What can I say, Louise? I'm sorry for giving you the run-around, and to show my appreciation, I'd like to buy you a drink. What's your poison?'

'Apology accepted; a Diet Coke please.'

'I think you'll need something a bit stronger when you hear what I have to say.'

'Oh, go on then, you've twisted my arm. Make it a vodka and lime.'

'Coming up.'

He turned and walked to the bar. The barman ambled over to him with the easy manner they often reserved for quiet lunchtimes, the customer interrupting his perusal of the sports section or the pretty girls on the centre pages. Chris returned a few minutes later with her drink plus a whisky and a pint of ale for himself.

'Splashing the cash about aren't you, Chris? Are you trying to spend all your student loan before you go back to university?'

'I'm surprised you've heard of student loans, you being Scottish and all.'

'I live in London for your information, but I'm a journalist. I know all sorts of things.'

He sat down with his back to the window, glancing over his shoulder before reaching for the whisky glass and taking a gulp. 'Medicinal purposes,' he said, 'I don't often drink spirits, but I need something stronger than beer.'

'Fill your boots, lad.'

He put his drink down and leaned towards her, speaking in hushed tones. 'I asked to meet with you today because I think I know the reason why my family was murdered.'

'What? Whoever said anything about them being murdered? I'm here to talk about someone left orphaned by a tragic accident.'

'Things have changed, Louise. I'm talking about a serious investigative story here, not a feature on some five-minute celebrity. Can you handle it or do I need to be speaking to someone else?'

'Of course, I can handle it, don't you worry. I'm just a bit shocked by what you said.'

'You sure, because this is big?'

'I'm sure you're right but what makes you think they were murdered?'

'It'll make more sense if I show you.' He lifted the laptop beside him, opened the cover, tapped a few keys, and turned it round for her to see.

'Read this email.'

She scanned it, part of her mind believing this was some sort of a wind-up. Perhaps his way of getting back at her for some insult or factual error in the many articles she'd written at the time of the accident.

'Who's Daniel Leppo?'

'He's Head of International Security at Dragon Technologies.'

'International being everything outside the US?'

'Yes.'

'Who's the guy the email was sent to?'

'Latif Artha.'

'And?'

'He's a ballistics and helicopter expert at an equipment testing company called QuinTec.'

'Chris, this Q&A session would be fine if we were sitting at a press conference, but we're not. Why don't you just cut to the chase and explain to me what I'm looking at? Tell me where you got it and how it's related to the balloon accident.'

'Sorry, I'm being an idiot. You're right.'

For the next fifteen minutes her head began to fill with a host of new words, acronyms and ideas, words like Dragon, Pulsar and the Arrow Battlefield System. 'So,' she said after he stopped for a breather, 'you think people at Dragon Technologies are out to get you because you hacked into their computers?'

'I thought so at first, but it would be a bit extreme, don't you think? Companies are happy to see hackers hauled before a court and thrown in prison for a couple of years.'

'If you've annoyed them this much, did you do something more than just muck around with their systems? I'm not an expert on those things, but did you leave behind a nasty virus or wipe important files?'

'No, I would never do anything like that. It may surprise you, but there are ethics among hackers. I'm what's called a white hat hacker, not a black hat hacker, if you know the difference.'

'I don't, but I can guess. A bit like white and black witches.'

He didn't respond to her little dig and carried on. 'I think they're pissed because they know in the documents I hacked, there's enough evidence of illegality here and in the US, for the UK government and NATO to wash their hands of any interest in their new helicopter, the Pulsar. It's such a big deal, it would in all likelihood bankrupt Dragon and leave a huge hole in the finances of their US parent company.'

'If this is true...'

'Of course, it's bloody true! Do you think I'm making this up?'

He turned to look out the window again, and she noticed his hands were trembling.

'Calm down Chris, no need to attract attention to ourselves, even if it's only a small group of locals more interested in their beer than what we're doing.'

He turned back. 'Sorry, but if you don't believe it's serious, take a look at this.' He retrieved the laptop and spent a few minutes tapping the keys before handing it back. 'There are memos here written on their headed notepaper detailing payments made to UK politicians, visits to nightclubs, the use of prostitutes, trips on private yachts, the whole stinking mess.'

She scrolled down the screen at a steady pace and it didn't take her long to realise this material was something her boss would call 'prima facie' evidence. Something they could publish and withstand external scrutiny, despite the threat of litigation.

She blew out a long, slow puff of air. 'Some of the names here I recognise, MPs and senior military figures. You're right, Chris, maybe I have been a bit too cautious in not believing you at first.'

'If just a small part of this gets out, it would blow the lid off Dragon's dirty can of tricks. It would force the police to look at them for killing my family.'

'It would put the boot into a few political careers at the same time, I would think. What I need to do now is sit down for a good couple of hours or so and go through each of these documents in detail. Then, I'll send a sample over to my editor, see if he can sort the legal end out.'

'Excellent news, I think we're getting somewhere at last,' he said rubbing his hands together in obvious pleasure. 'You make a start and I'll bring over some more drinks.'

'No, no. I can't work here,' Louise said. 'I need a quiet space, free from distractions,' and pushing her half-finished drink away, 'I need to keep a clear head.'

Louise and Chris left the pub a few minutes later and climbed into Chris's car. Chris drove while Louise called her boss, Kingsley Vincent.

'Hello Kingsley, it's Louise.'

'Now if it isn't Scoop Walker. What have you got for me this time? I know, another big story about your drunken countrymen, or you need me to authorise your travel to Ibiza to chase a recalcitrant father who's holed up in a nightclub.'

'You're such a wag. Any more of this kind of talk and people will think you like me.'

'You know I do, Louise. I just hide it well.'

'Listen carefully, I think I'm about to make your week.'

'I doubt it, unless you've decided to resign.'

She tried to speak but her mouth clamped shut as a white van rocketed out of a side road and slewed across their path. Chris jammed on the brakes and stopped in time. To her horror, the doors of the van flew open and two men got out. The men ran towards their car, their faces set in stony seriousness.

Before she could scream 'road rage,' or 'drunk driver,' Chris bellowed in her ear, 'It's them Louise! You've got to do something!'

The passenger door of their car opened and a hand reached inside and grabbed her arm. Without thinking, she swung the phone in her hand, her boss still on the other end of the line, and whacked her assailant hard on the side of his temple. To her surprise, his knees buckled, and he and her phone dropped to the ground. She leapt out of the car, took one look at the stricken man, on all fours, trying to get up. She swung a foot at his wedding tackle with a ferocity she didn't know she possessed.

She ran to the front of the car where the other attacker was hauling Chris towards the van, his arm in a stranglehold around his neck

'Hit him Chris!' she shouted, but he didn't respond either because he was too frightened or couldn't hear. She looked around for a weapon, and spotted Chris's laptop lying inside the car. She ran over, grabbed it and raced towards the struggling pair. She lifted it high above her head and crashed the edge down on the back of the assailant's head. It didn't have the same debilitating effect as her phone on the other guy, but enough to slacken his grip. Chris struggled free, his arms and legs flailing in a wild panic. In the resultant melee, Chris's thumb jabbed into his assailant's eye, causing him to double over in agony.

Chris stared uncomprehending at the injured figure in front of him, and for a moment she felt sure he was about to apologise. Chris's car was unusable, jammed right up against the van and with several cars stopped close behind them. Gripping the laptop under one arm, she grabbed Chris's hand and raced across the road. They dodged through slow-moving traffic as cars tried to weave past stranded vehicles, and headed towards a waiting bus. While they waited in the queue, she stepped back to look at the scene, making sure they weren't being followed. They climbed aboard.

Through the rear window of the bus she watched the strange sight of Chris's abandoned Corsa, a large van blocking its path, and a small traffic jam lining up behind the stationary vehicles. Two heavy-set guys stood there, one rubbing his groin and the other his eye, both sporting the scowls of bad losers.

She feared the men might jump into their van and follow the bus, but the van looked boxed-in, not only by cars, but with several irate drivers standing in the road, arms gesticulating at the traffic mess all around them.

'Who the hell were they?' she hissed at Chris. He rubbed his neck, now bearing a large red mark from his assailant's arm.

'I didn't get a good look,' he replied, in a voice high on emotion. 'Did you see the guy who grabbed me? He had a bloody gun under his jacket!'

'I did, but keep your voice down. No sense in causing panic.'

'Christ, I understand it now!' he said staring at her, his eyes popping wide. 'They know I didn't go on the balloon trip and now they've sent a team after me. What am I going to do?'

'Calm down Chris,' she said taking his hand like a priest comforting the bereaved. 'Let's forget the 'I' for the moment. Remember, they tried to grab me as well.' She hoped she sounded composed and calm but inside her body her heart, adrenalin levels and overwrought brain refused to play ball.

'Where does this bus go?'

'I don't know.'

She leaned across the aisle and tapped the shoulder of a young woman playing a game on her smartphone. 'Excuse me, can you tell me where this bus goes?'

'The railway station,' she said without looking up.

Chapter 20

'I'm getting used to this journey,' Rosie said. 'We're seeing the Oxford countryside shift from winter into spring.'

'You do exaggerate,' Matt said, 'but you're right, we've done it a few times now. I'm beginning to get fed up with it too.'

'This is because of your low attention threshold.'

'Where did you retrieve this little piece of home-spun psychobabble? Are you doing an Open University course you should be telling me about?'

'No, I'm talking about my observation. I notice you get jumpy in meetings if they go beyond about half an hour. The one we did with Superintendent Cousins in Oxford earlier in the week, you were about climbing the walls.'

'If not for the coffee break, I think I would've been. I went to the gym the previous night and my muscles were starting to seize up. I don't think I would say I have a low attention threshold, but I don't tolerate fools.'

'Present company excepted.'

'Let's just say, my bullshit monitor is set to a low threshold.'

'I think my term sounded more scientific.'

The next ten minutes were spent in silence except for the radio playing at low volume, Matt itching to drive faster which the heavy traffic wouldn't allow, and Rosie looking at something on her phone.

'Something I meant to ask you,' Rosie said. 'When you spoke to Gill yesterday, did he make any comments about all the driving we're doing around the Oxfordshire countryside without a result?'

'Is this how you see it, driving around?'

'I think the case is building, bit by bit, but if I feel we're about to hit a brick wall, so will he.'

'Perhaps Gill takes the long view more than you or me. I told him we were interviewing Chris Anderson, and he said to do whatever we think is necessary to find out what he's not telling us.'

'Whoa, that gives us a fair amount of wriggle room. Chris Anderson's not by any stretch of the imagination someone you could call a seasoned criminal. Would you be happy chucking someone like him around the room?'

'You think I wouldn't, if I believed he was holding back the key to all this?'

'Matt, we're talking men against boys. Where's the fun in bashing up a middle-class university geek?'

'He might not be as innocent as you paint him.'

'True, there's a lot you can do nowadays with a laptop and a knowledge of coding, as our good friends at GCHQ will testify.'

'The answer must be there with Chris,' Matt said. 'It can't be anywhere else.'

'So you've said. Today, you're about to be proved right or wrong. I know which one my money's on.'

They arrived in Oxford at six-thirty and drove straight to Kevin Anderson's house.

'Oh, hello Matt, Rosie,' Hannah Anderson said on opening the door.

'Hello Mrs Anderson,' Rosie said. 'Is Chris around?'

'No, he's not. Come in and Kevin will explain. He knows more about it than I do.'

She guided them into the lounge.

'We're having our evening meal at the moment. Kevin will come in and see you both when he's finished. In the meantime, I'll bring in a cup of tea.' She disappeared out of the room.

Rosie took a seat on the settee while Matt wandered around the room, looking at the many photographs. Pictures of young Kevin, lithe and tanned and squinting at the sun as he stood on a white, sandy beach. Hannah and her two boys riding bikes in a forest. A staged portrait of the whole family with neatly brushed hair and wearing smart clothes. Another with Kevin standing beside his brother, Stephen.

It was taken a couple of years ago and from what Matt knew about the personalities of the two men, it captured them accurately. They were outside a bar and the heavy, solid stone construction of the building, the sweeping vista of the rolling hills behind and the dark, foreboding skies suggested Cornwall or the Lake District. Stephen displayed an easy smile, reflecting the character portrayed in newspaper biographies of an open, caring personality and a man comfortable in his own skin. Kevin wore the merest trace of a sneer, hinting at hidden ruthlessness and arrogance, or perhaps the wild rebellious streak of his youth still un-sated.

He was about to take a look through the bookcase when the door opened and Mrs Anderson walked in bearing two cups of tea and some biscuits.

'Help yourself to these. My husband will be through in a minute.'

Matt sat, although still restless after sitting in a car for two-and-a-half-hours. He was also eager to speak to Kevin and find out where Chris might be.

Half-way through his cup of tea, Matt was about to explore the Anderson lounge once again when Kevin walked in. He headed towards the armchair and put his cup down on a small table. He turned to the two HSA agents and shook their hands. He sat down heavily in the armchair.

'Did you have an accident, Mr Anderson?' Matt asked, noticing the angry, red lesions, recent bruising and the tape across his nose.

'Aye, I had a bit of a smack in the car a few days back. Lack of concentration on my part. And call me Kevin. Mr Anderson reminds me too much of work.'

Matt was intrigued. He liked cars and before coming into the house, had good look at Kevin's BMW 4 Series in the driveway. It was the 'M Sport' variant, heavily modified with darkened windows, lowered suspension and smart sports wheels. If there had been any sign of crash damage or a body-shop repair, he didn't see it. 'Was anyone else involved?'

'Nah, only me and a fence. How was your journey down to Oxford?'

'The traffic was heavy, as usual,' Matt said.

'Maybe, next time we'll come by train,' Rosie said.

'You might not fare any better there. They've been redeveloping the station and surrounding area for a few years now. There's always something going wrong and causing major disruption.'

His speech was slurred suggesting a problem with his jaw but Matt felt he'd asked enough about his injuries. It wouldn't do to give the guy a complex.

'We came to see Chris,' Rosie said, 'but we understand from your wife that he isn't around. While we've got you here, Mr Anderson, I hear the ownership of the business is settled.'

Kevin moved uncomfortably in his seat, maybe the result of a back problem to add to his list of woes.

'It is. I knew about it in any case, I just needed the legal bods to confirm. My brother left all his shares and assets to his wife, and in the event of their simultaneous demise, to be divided equally between their two children. In summary, it now means Chris is the owner of seventy per cent of the business his father started.'

'Does he intend becoming a sleeping partner or will he take up a position within the company?'

Kevin laughed, wincing at the same time. 'I'm not sure I could find anything useful for him to do. You see, defence electronics is a specialised field, especially at the technical end where we are. From a sales perspective, the area I focus on, it's all about who you know.'

Matt didn't yet have a clear picture of Kevin in his head. Research done by Sikandar Khosa discovered he had been the wild child of the family in his younger days. He'd flunked school, didn't go to university like his brother, and spent five years in Thailand where he got busted for possessing drugs.

A little thought passed through Matt's head in the middle of the night, suggesting the balloon incident had nothing to do with a teenage computer hacker and everything to do with sibling rivalry and greed. He dismissed it, despite Kevin looking like a rough character and talking as if he carried a large chip on his shoulder. Matt believed he wouldn't be averse to pocketing the odd backhander or taking a free seat at Lords during a test match. However, he didn't think him capable of engineering the death of his brother, sister-in-law and his beloved niece, just to take sole charge of a small, but profitable defence company.

'Where's Chris?' Matt asked.

'He's gone away for a few days.'

'Has he? When your wife said he wasn't here, I assumed he'd gone down the pub with his mates or gone out for something to eat. Was this a planned trip or a spur of the moment thing?'

'Spur of moment, I think. I mean he's a man now, he can do whatever the hell he wants.'

'I realise that, but did you consider he might be running away to escape some psychological trauma that he's trying to come to terms with?'

'I'm sure he is, we all are. Who can lose a large slice of their family in one fell swoop and not be affected? But, I ask you, with the best will in the world, what can I do? I'm a businessman, not a bloody psychiatrist.'

'Did he go alone or with a friend?'

'He went out this afternoon to meet a journalist and decided to get away after the meeting.'

'Did he take a car or public transport?'

'Public transport, I assume. The copper who came to the door told me I had to go along later this evening to the police compound and retrieve his car. I said to Hannah, I'm not happy doing it. Getting a car out of those sorts of places can be expensive. The bit I don't get is why Chris would leave it where it might block other traffic. He's not usually so cavalier.'

Matt was confused. 'What's this all about? Did something happen before he left Oxford?'

Kevin sighed and moved again, trying to get comfortable. 'Late this afternoon, a copper came to the door and asked if we were aware that Chris had abandoned his car on Abingdon Road in Oxford after a traffic incident.'

'What sort of incident?'

'I don't know. The copper said he wanted to speak to him, I think to test him for drink or drugs, but I told him to behave. Chris is more sensible than a lot of lads around here who drink, drive and take drugs. The copper didn't seem too concerned as the vehicles were undamaged and no one got hurt, so I wasn't bothered either.'

'Do you have any idea where he went?'

'No. He phoned about half an hour before you guys arrived and said he was fine. He said he would be back in a few days.'

'Do you know the name of the journalist he met today?' Rosie asked. 'Perhaps she knows his whereabouts.'

'No, I don't, but Hannah might. I'll go and ask her.'

Kevin gingerly got out of the chair and walked to the kitchen.

'I don't like the sound of this, Matt. We need to speak to this journalist and get some idea of his frame of mind. We should also talk to the local cops and find out what happened to his car.'

'Yeah.'

'Louise Walker,' Kevin said, walking back into the room. 'She's with one of the nationals.'

'Her name rings a bell,' Rosie said. 'I think she used to cover the crime beat when I worked at the Met.'

'She did a piece on the family a couple of days after the balloon accident,' Kevin said, resuming his seat. 'Now, the whole world knows about my conviction for possessing five ounces of grass when I was twenty-two. Bloody cheek of it. I get ribbed about it every time I meet a customer, so I tell you, I'd like to find her too and give her a piece of my mind.'

'Mr Anderson,' Matt said, 'I don't think you're treating the disappearance of your nephew seriously.'

'Why should I? He's a big boy who's buggered off to Spain or somewhere to get some peace. I just wish he'd left his bloody car in a car park like everybody else.'

'You should have called us or the police when you realised he was missing.'

'What for? He's not missing. He's gone away for a few days, nothing more. He's a grown boy, he can do what the hell he likes. When I was his age, I went backpacking to India and Thailand.'

'Maybe you're judging him by your own standards, but Chris is a different person. Has he ever done anything like this before?'

He thought for a moment. 'Now you mention it, no, but then he hasn't seen his parents killed before either, has he?'

'Does he strike you as someone who's resourceful, who could find his way around a big city like, say, London without getting lost?'

'When you put it in such bald terms, I would say no, he wouldn't know where to start. His father mollycoddled him ever since childhood, organising family holidays, helping him settle into university and fixing him up with a summer job in the holidays, the whole nine yards. I said to him, you should let the boy get on with things himself. I did with my two.'

'Let me have Chris's mobile number and if he calls you again, let me know right away,' Matt said handing him his business card. 'You might think he's all right Mr Anderson, but I think your nephew could be in grave danger.'

Chapter 21

Chris returned from the hotel buffet. On his tray, a plate bearing the Full English: sausages, eggs, beans, bacon and everything else on offer. Louise made do with a bowl of porridge.

Now and again Louise made porridge at home and would like to do so more often, as it tended to fill her up until lunchtime, but there was never enough time in the morning for cooking hot food. Filling up was an important consideration for a girl battling with her weight. In her office, someone would usually bring in doughnuts or cakes a couple of times a week. If she wasn't feeling hungry, she could show more resilience when they placed the hard-to-resist snacks on the spare desk behind her.

'I don't know where you put it,' Louise said when Chris laid his tray on the table. 'You're so skinny. All I need to do is look at a cooked breakfast and I can't get into some of my skirts.'

'Oh, is that what it is?'

'How do you mean?'

'I thought you going for the porridge was, you know, a Scottish thing.'

'How do you work that out?'

'I'm talking about all the anti-English sentiment in Scotland, newspapers banging on about independence and television programmes about the Battle of Bannockburn.'

'Am I hearing you right? You think I eat porridge and ignore food with 'English' in the title because I'm Scottish? It's the daftest thing I've ever heard. You need to get out more and spend time with other people, instead of staring at computer screens all day.'

'Ha, ha, nice one when we're holed up in this place.'

'This place' was a budget hotel in Paddington. She still wasn't sure how they'd ended up there. Chris, on paper at least, was rich and could stay anywhere he fancied, and London wasn't short of good hotels. In truth, they'd entered the first hotel they'd come across after leaving Paddington Station, the place where the Oxford train terminated. With no idea what was waiting for them back in Oxford, the Hotel Mercure was as good a place to hide as any.

'For the first time today and not for the last,' she said, 'I'm going to ask the sixty-four-million-dollar question. What are we going to do now?'

He put down his knife and fork for a moment, allowing his poor stomach a welcome rest. 'You're expecting me to say I don't have a clue, aren't you?'

'Yes.'

'Well, I've been giving the subject a great deal of thought.'

'I'm glad to hear it.'

He picked up his cutlery again and resumed eating, forcing her to listen to his ideas in between mouthfuls. Watching someone eat was not one of her top ten favourite things to do when visiting London. 'It's obvious I can't go back to Oxford or uni until...well I don't know when, because I can't be sure they're not still spying on me. Who knows, they might try to stage another kidnap attempt.'

'Okay, a sensible start.'

'We therefore need to keep moving forward, hopefully keep one step ahead of whoever is chasing us, until we find someone who can help us. Someone who believes the downing of the balloon was aimed at me, and not an accident as everybody else seems to think, and hope they can do something about it.'

'Hold it right there, I don't like the sound of us always on the move and there's too much use of the word 'hope' for my liking. To where? You need to remember, I have a job, another life.'

He nodded, but said nothing. He continued to eat.

'I saw those two gorillas back in Oxford with my own eyes,' Louise said. 'I don't want to meet them again, so in a way, I do like the idea of keeping one step ahead. What I don't understand is how a bit of bribery and corruption in a big military contract, no matter how sordid and deceitful, is enough for the folks at Dragon to try and wipe out you and your family.'

'Why not? If those documents were published, they would show Dragon up for the fraudulent company they are, and the MPs and military personnel who took the money and the holidays, as greedy, self-serving pigs. It would cause a huge stink in Parliament and the cancellation of the UK and NATO's purchase of Pulsar. It's a multi-million-dollar contract, don't forget.'

'I think you might be over egging the pudding somewhat. People have more important things to worry about than a few corrupt politicians with their paws in the honey jar. I mean, do you remember the big rumpus a few years back about some jets we sold to Saudi Arabia?'

'I thought you said you didn't know much about defence?'

'I don't. Despite working for a newspaper that often treats its employees no better than slaves, they do let us read it sometimes.'

'You're referring to the Al-Yamamah project?'

She nodded. 'Sounds about right.'

'It all started when the Saudis awarded BAE Systems a huge order for various aircraft, including Tornado jets. My dad's company, my company now, made the circuit boards for their radar.'

'I apologise for my ignorance, I'm obviously talking to an expert in the field. A stink erupted about the big bribes being paid, slush funds being set up for entertainment in night clubs and restaurants, and exotic holidays for some. A few years later, the Serious Fraud Office became involved, but the investigation was shelved. I doubt if anyone will ever be prosecuted.'

'Not bad.'

'Not bad for what? A woman or a Scottish person?'

'You're not scowling, so I don't think I've offended you. Not bad for a non-defence correspondent.'

'Thank you, but do you see my point? If it suits politicians, businessmen and the Saudis for a story like this to stay buried, then buried it stays. I don't think the general public knows too much about it, or if they do, they don't give a toss about it.'

'I suppose when you look at it like that, if the balloon accident and the attack on us are Dragon's response for me nicking a few documents, then it does look a bit extreme.' He paused for moment, thinking. 'Maybe I'm missing something; I mean I looked at this stuff around three in the morning and stopped when I spotted the names of a couple of MPs and senior military personnel that I recognised. Maybe there's more if I looked deeper.'

'There has to be something more serious going on than you've seen so far, or else we're looking in the wrong place.'

'Pushing this not insubstantial issue to one side, whatever the reason for the attacks, it doesn't make much difference to the situation we're in now, today. If we don't find someone to help us, I'll be looking over my shoulder for the rest of my life, or one day you'll find me lying dead in a skip.'

'Don't be so morose, Chris,' she said. She was tempted to add, 'Look on the bright side,' but she couldn't see any. 'Do you have any clue who we can turn to?'

'You mean, apart from the journalist sitting in front of me? No.'

'What about the policeman running the accident investigation, Superintendent Cousins?'

'What could he do?'

'He could give us protection while we try to find out more.'

'What good would that do? We need to get these documents into the public domain and shame Dragon, it's the only way I'm ever going to feel safe.'

He popped the last piece of sausage into his mouth and put down his knife and fork. 'Have you gone off the idea of having this story published in your newspaper?'

'No, but having given the issue some thought, I don't think publication is going to be as straightforward as I first assumed. If Dragon realise what we're about to do, they might take out a court injunction and try to suppress the story. They would in all likelihood succeed. Courts take a dim view of petitions based on documents obtained illegally.'

'How would Dragon find out?'

'Your guess is as good as mine. I can't know for sure until I ring the office, but how did they find out we were meeting at a pub in Oxford? If they know this much about us, they must have twigged that I'm a journalist. They may have already set the legal wheels in motion.'

'My God that would be awful,' he said wringing his hands together, a nervous trait paddling just below the surface of his easy-going persona. 'Can you call your paper and find out?'

'I will, as soon as we get back to the room, providing my boss will speak to me. I haven't spoken to him since yesterday. It was him, if you remember, I was talking to when we were attacked. I left him hanging.'

'Please talk to him soon,' he said, rising from the chair and rubbing his stomach, 'the tension is giving me indigestion.'

'That's not indigestion, it's the pain you get when you stuff your face with three sausages, two eggs, beans and a couple of black puddings. Don't your uncle and aunt feed you?'

Chapter 22

Chris and Louise returned to their room at the Hotel Mercure after breakfast. Louise watching nervously as Chris turned on his laptop. He hadn't tried using it since yesterday when used as a cudgel to bash one of their assailants on the head. She didn't feel confident it would work again.

Miracle of miracles, the laptop started its boot-up routine and didn't make any strange noises. While waiting for it to complete, she put a call through to her immediate boss, Kingsley Vincent. She couldn't call him yesterday from the bus or the train, as after smacking her assailant with the phone, she'd dropped it and didn't dare go back to retrieve it. She'd gone out this morning and bought a pay-as-you-go replacement and a charger.

'Morning Kingsley, how are you?'

'Don't come Miss Righteous with me, Walker. Where the hell have you been? You left me in limbo land yesterday and I don't like people doing this to me.'

'Get off your bloody high horse for a minute will you, and listen.'

'What! Who do you think–'

'Kingsley, listen. When I called you yesterday, I was in Chris Anderson's car. Remember Chris? The hot-air balloon accident in Oxford?'

'Yeah, yeah. Get on with it.'

'We were driving along the road as I was speaking to you. Then, a van came out of a side street and ran right across our path, nearly taking away the front of the car.'

'You expect me to believe that? You've had a couple of days to concoct a good story and this is the best you can come up with?'

'You're having me on. You must have heard the squealing of brakes and people shouting.'

'No. I gave you ten seconds to come back on the line before I hung up.'

'You can be so obtuse! Look the incident up on the feed. Abingdon Road, Oxford, yesterday. Go on take a look, I'll wait.'

She heard him tap-tapping on his computer keyboard.

'My God!' he said a few seconds later. 'This is you? I'm so sorry, Louise, I didn't realise. Were you hurt? Are you all right?'

'I'm fine. We're both fine. Chris managed to stop the car before we hit the van.'

'Have you been to hospital to be checked out? You could have whiplash.'

'Neither of us were injured, thankfully. We've got a few cuts and bruises, and this morning Chris has a sore neck, but nothing serious.'

'What happened?'

She outlined the story, details of the two men who attacked them, a taster of the documents they'd been looking at in the pub. For the next few minutes, she listened to Kingsley's response.

When at last she said goodbye, she threw her new phone on the bed in frustration. 'Damn, damn damn!' she shouted.

'What happened?' Chris asked.

'Oh nothing. The biggest story to come anywhere near my newspaper in over ten years and my chance to hit the big time as a journalist. They've both been chucked out of the window like an old fag butt.'

'How come?'

'Dragon are on to us. They threatened my paper. If we publish, they'll sue.'

'It's just an empty threat, surely?'

'Nope, my boss was persuaded after receiving a call from one of the top litigation firms in London. They gave him a summary of the complaint and demanded the immediate return of the documents.'

'Well, they would wouldn't they, but they're not having them.'

'Are you looking at them now?'

'Yep. I scrolled down to where I finished up the other night, but found nothing heavier than the stuff I told you about earlier.'

She thought for a moment trying to clear her head of the bitter disappointment. 'Why don't you look at emails sent by the Head of Security? He sounds a nasty sort. If there's any dirty dealing going on, I bet he's involved. What's his name?'

'Daniel Leppo. Good idea. Give me a couple of minutes.'

While Chris tapped away on his computer, Louise texted a friend in the office, Estelle. She told her she was fine but didn't say where she was and didn't say when she intended to return; in truth, because she didn't know. She also sent another text to her flat mate, Caitlin. She was used to Louise going away for one or two days at a time on assignment, but if this went on for a few more days, she would start to worry.

'Listen to this Louise. It's an email Leppo sent to someone who, on Leppo's instructions, escorted an employee off company premises for failing a drug test. 'Thanks for saving me the trouble. I told him at his exit interview, if he ever comes within ten yards of this building, I'll tear his balls out with my teeth.' He sounds like a right charmer.'

'Less of the frivolity and get on with some real work.'

'Yes, miss.'

A few minutes later, he said, 'I keep seeing the word, 'Renoir.' Do you think it might be a code word?'

'I dunno. Have you seen it before? It might be another name for Pulsar.'

'They often give new products a working name before they reveal its true marketing title, so you could be right.'

'I think he's a French artist from the 1800s. Maybe, they're thinking about buying a painting to brighten up the wall beside all those boring, grey pictures of planes and helicopters.'

'Yeah?'

'No, I'm only joking. I think it must be a code word; try searching with it.'

A few minutes later, she threw the hotel's in-house magazine on the floor. Working in the city, she didn't often take time out to see the sights. Now, with time to kill, she couldn't do it without looking over her shoulder, worried the bad guys might be lurking in the shadows.

'You're a bit quiet,' she said, 'I hope you're not looking at something you shouldn't.'

'No, I'm doing what you suggested. I'm using 'Renoir' to open a load of files that I ignored last time as I couldn't be bothered trying to hack the password. I now think it's the code word they use for all their dirty dealings.'

'Progress of sorts. Let me take a look.'

She shuffled on the bed beside him.

'This one's a bit opaque and talks about the need to silence Latif Artha. If you remember, his name cropped up when we looked at some emails addressed to him in the pub. He's the weapons specialist at QuinTec who's been a vocal opponent of the UK buying Pulsar.'

She nodded.

'When I looked him up in Google, it turns out he was killed about two weeks ago when his car veered off the M40 and crashed into a disused quarry.'

'How convenient for Dragon.'

'Take a look for yourself,' he said turning the laptop towards her.

She read the email once, twice and now understood what he meant by 'opaque'. It looked innocent enough on the surface, but when adding the QuinTec guy's death into the mix, the email read like an order to kill him. Her head started to spin and for a moment it felt like she had fallen into something she didn't have the capacity to deal with. She took a deep breath and tried to regroup. She'd been a journalist long enough to know making assumptions without the evidence to back them up was the work of an amateur.

'How do I get back to other 'Renoir' messages? See if something else will make this email any clearer.'

He took the laptop back, did something quickly, his fingers flashing over the keyboard, and handed it back.

'So, to view any message I just double-click on it?'

'Yeah.'

'If I want to go back, I just click on the little arrow there?' she said pointing.

'Yep, you got it.'

'This is like being inside Dragon's own system with the logo and all that.' She felt a wave of panic. 'We're not, are we?'

'Nope.'

'Thank God. I don't understand much about computers but I do know they can trace anyone looking at their system.'

'They can trace ordinary folk, but we hackers have ways of hiding ourselves from the watchers. What you've got there is an offline dump from their system, so they can't see us looking at it. There's tons of stuff in these files.'

'Right,' Louise said, 'I'm going to take my time looking through all this. You might want to find something to read.'

'I'll just lie here and work off my hearty breakfast.'

'It would take a serious workout session in the gym to make any impact on what you put away.'

Over the next hour she found emails promising monetary payments, the use of a private resort in Antigua, gifts of cars and boats, the supply of drugs and call girls. The extent of their corruption was staggering. It looked like a systemised attempt to put potential buyers securely into their pockets. When this didn't prove enticing enough, they blackmailed certain greedy or stubborn individuals with salacious videos and photographs of them sniffing coke or lying between a call girl's legs. She took careful note of the last few as they had moved their actions from pig-trough avarice to downright illegality. Louise had the bit between her teeth now and eagerly searched for more.

One email dated only two weeks before stopped her in her tracks. She nudged Chris beside her, but got no response. He didn't sound asleep but dozing. She nudged him again and, in slow motion, he pushed himself up on his elbows, his face sleepy and woozy. 'What is it?'

'This guy Leppo, yeah?'

'The security guy at Dragon?'

'So, you are awake.'

'Of course.'

'Listen to this. He's instructed someone to kill you.'

Chapter 23

Matt Flynn didn't 'do' offices. During his time in the Met as a murder squad detective, he only returned to base under sufferance. He didn't like the stuffy atmosphere, took no interest in office gossip or politics and hated long meetings. On days like today while waiting for something to happen or for their information guru, Sikandar Khosa, to work his magic, he worked from home.

In front of him, scattered over the table in the lounge-diner, lay a number of documents relating to the Anderson's. They included, financial and intelligence reports relating to Galleon Electronics, a profile of Chris compiled from social media, a report from his tutor at Durham University, bank statements and other information about Kevin. He felt confident Kevin didn't have anything to do with the shooting down of the balloon or Chris's recent disappearance, but he looked at the financials of the company nevertheless.

He didn't consider himself a skilled financial analyst, but any fool could see the turnover of the firm had been increasing steadily over the last five years, as had its profitability. The balance sheet showed a similar strong picture, with low debt and company ownership of key assets such as the building housing the business and all the machinery inside.

Kevin earned a meaty salary. In his personal life, he didn't have any loans, paid his credit card bill in full every month, and there were no other suspicious movements in or out of his current account, other than those spotted earlier by Rosie. When examined closely, they found enough payments to casinos and hospitality at racetracks to suggest he wasn't a drug addict or a stock market speculator, but a serious gambler.

If escalating and suffering large losses, such a habit could potentially have grave consequences for many of the company's workers, but in Kevin's case, his large salary and annual bonus covered it. It was possible he could have bank accounts and credit cards in other names, but Matt could only make assumptions about the information in front of him. As far as he was concerned, Kevin Anderson was no longer on his radar.

Next, he picked up the assessment written by Chris's tutor at Durham. In a class of bright computer geeks, Chris made the top three. At the age of twelve, he was writing computer games, and by fifteen, had published his own iPhone app. His tutor believed, although Chris had never admitted his involvement, that he was a member of INEXIS, a notorious hacking group involved in disrupting the activities of organisations and companies their members didn't agree with.

In common with many such groups, their members lived all around the world, using aliases in communication and sharing hacking and other software across the dark web. By deploying onion servers and bouncing their internet traffic around dozens of countries, they could disguise the location of their computers. Even experienced operators at GCHQ didn't know much about them, and their activities were almost impossible to infiltrate.

Matt couldn't help but be impressed. Chris moved up in his estimation from a simple computer geek with a silver spoon in his mouth, to a highly skilled individual. He was capable of using the tools he possessed to further the aims he believed in, no matter how misplaced or misguided they might be.

Matt walked into the kitchen, switched on the coffee machine and stood over it while it crunched and hissed and worked its magic.

'I'll take one, if you're making,' Emma said.

'I didn't hear you come in.'

She walked into the kitchen, smiling, the most relaxed Matt had seen her in weeks. She came over and gave him a hug and a kiss and didn't pull away a few moments later as she usually did.

'Cut it out, Davis. You might be on gardening leave or whatever they call it at the cop shop, but I'm not.'

'Spoilsport,' she said pulling away.

He went back to the coffee machine.

'Do you want to see what I bought?' she asked.

He could say, 'no' or 'not now', but she would be around the house for the rest of the afternoon and it wouldn't be a smart move to upset her. 'Sure.'

She held something up, cream with yellow flowers splashed over it, tightly wrapped in cellophane.

'You got me. What is it?'

'A new tablecloth.'

She reached into her bag and pulled out another similarly-wrapped item.

'By a process of deduction, I suspect new tablemats to match the tablecloth.'

'Very good darling, you're learning.'

He finished making coffee and poured it into two mugs. 'I'm going back to sit at the table, will I leave your mug here?'

'No, I'll come over and join you.'

He let out a silent groan, but he told himself it was only for a couple more days.

He sat down, opened his laptop and spotted an email from Sikander, their in-house information and computer guru. It wasn't Chris's location as he hoped, but details of the Oxford car incident in which Chris and reporter Louise Walker had been involved.

After a few minutes he called over to Emma. 'Em, take a look at this, will you? You've got more experience with RTAs than me.'

'What is it?' she said walking over.

'Photographs of a traffic accident in Oxford and the local traffic cop's report.'

She looked carefully at the photographs and skimmed through the report. 'I wouldn't call it an accident. It looks like there's no damage to any cars or anyone injured.'

'What makes you say that?'

'Look at the picture of the white van and the Corsa.'

'Okay.'

'Look at the gap between them, it's small but still a gap.'

'Maybe the car bounced off the van when they collided.'

'This is why I don't think you can call it an accident. You see, the material at the front of most cars is polycarbonate, sometimes with a bit of carbon fibre thrown in for strength. It's designed to absorb the energy of an impact during a smash. As a result, bumpers, as they used to be called, crack, split and fall to bits in a collision. Hence, all the pieces of coloured plastic you see at the side of a road, even after a minor bump.'

'So, you think the front of the Corsa should be displaying some sort of damage if it hit the van?'

'Yep, definitely. If it bounced so far backwards, there wouldn't be much left of the front section of the car. Most of it would be lying in the road.'

'In which case, the van must have pulled out in front and the car stopped in time.'

'It's what we do, if we're coming out a side street and the target is on the main road. We pull across the front of their vehicle to make them brake, a 'hard-stop' we call it. It can get a bit hairy if the target driver is not paying attention, or the occupants are desperate to escape and decide to ram us. Most of the time the shock of a vehicle pulling directly in front of them is enough to make them stop.'

'Okay, we agree it doesn't look like an accident, more like a 'hard-stop'. Would the Met or Oxford Police use a van like this one?' Matt asked.

'No way. If we look too much like painters and decorators, the criminals might pull out guns and shoot us. If they realise we're the police, they'll think twice as they know it's not a good idea to fire at cops as we're likely to be armed as well.'

'I'm quite sure, this wasn't the police.'

'Do we know anything about the occupants of the Corsa, or the van?'

'Chris Anderson and a journalist called Louise Walker were in the Corsa, but they're still trying to trace the owner of the van.'

Emma's phone rang. 'Morning sir, yes I'm good,' she said, getting up and walking into the kitchen.

Matt carried on working. A few minutes later he put the car incident to one side. It looked to him just as Emma had said, a hard-stop. Questions about who the attackers might be and what they wanted could wait. What he wanted to know was what happened to Chris Anderson and Louise Walker. Did the men in the van kidnap them or did they escape? He believed the latter, given the presence of both vehicles and Chris's call to Kevin, but he needed confirmation.

He had tried calling Chris's mobile without result until one time it was answered, confusingly, by Kevin. Presumably, in their panic to flee after the altercation, Chris had left his phone in his car, the same car Kevin was driving back from the police compound; another dead end.

His email pinged, delivering another piece of the puzzle from Sikander. This time, a profile of Louise Walker. The office information guru wrote: 'Easy-peasy this one. Her newspaper publishes loads about their journalists, and she's active on social media. Even you could find this out, Matt. Then again, maybe not. See ya!'

He had to hand it to Siki, the attachments looked comprehensive: photographs, bio of early school life, her current job, and copies of articles written by her. After a degree in English from Glasgow University, she started working as a reporter at *The Herald* before moving to *The Scotsman*. Five years later, one of the nationals came calling, and she relocated to London.

He was reading one of Louise's articles when Emma burst in.

'That was Tony Quigley. Jacko and me are back on the job Monday! Yippee!'

She ran over and gave Matt a bear-hug. 'As much as I enjoyed a lie-in and shopping when the town is quiet,' Emma said, 'I do miss the excitement of work.'

'If you can call drug dealers taking pot-shots at you exciting.'

She broke away. 'You can talk, but you know it doesn't happen every day, not even every week.'

'Does a situation like the one you've just been involved in not give you a chance to reflect?'

She took a seat on the chair opposite. 'How do you mean, reflect?'

'Wouldn't you fancy doing something less dangerous?'

'Plenty of aspects of a cop's life are dangerous: anti-terrorist, undercover, people trafficking, to name a few.'

'Yeah, but plenty aren't.'

'Like what, traffic and schools liaison?'

'Don't be obtuse; you know what I mean.'

'I do. I've been with the drug unit for over eighteen months and the adrenaline kick you get when you find a dealer's stash or raid a drug den is exhilarating; better than any other job I've ever done.'

'That's not healthy.'

Matt's phone rang. 'We'll talk about this again, but don't get me wrong, I'm well pleased you're back.'

'Thanks.'

'It means I can work at home in peace.' After receiving a slap on the shoulder for his cheek, he picked up the phone. 'Hi. Matt Flynn.'

'Flynny, it's your favourite information and IT guru, bearing more gifts than a fat man with a white beard.'

'Hi, Siki, you're on a roll, mate.'

'You better believe it. The stuff I sent you about Louise Walker is good, yeah?'

'I haven't gone through it all yet, but what I saw looks up to your usual high standard. When I've read it all, I will feel I don't just know her, but I've been going out with her for the last six months.'

'Praise indeed, but this, my good fellow, tops it. Are you near a pen?'

'I am.'

'I hold in my sweaty hand, the address of the place where Chris Anderson made a call to Kevin on Wednesday night. You wan' it?'

Chapter 24

Two people walked into the Hotel Mercure in Praed Street, London. They immediately headed upstairs to room 127. The key to walking into a hotel, as their training had drummed into them, was to look and behave like a resident, even when challenged. If the hotel staff member was insistent on seeing a room card, Matt might pull out his HSA ID, or if the adrenaline rush had left him feeling arsey, stick his Glock in their face. If all else failed, or they didn't want to attract too much attention, he would claim to have made an error; wrong hotel, a common mistake in this part of London with dozens of them all within walking distance.

No such tactics were required today. They reached the room without being stopped. He looked up and down the corridor and then at Rosie, who nodded.

Matt rapped on the door.

'Who's there?' a female voice asked.

Matt was so used to saying, 'Room Service' when coming into places like this with the intention of grabbing someone or shooting them, he almost said it now.

'Louise, it's Matt Flynn and Rosie Fox. We spoke on the phone.'

The door opened on a chain. Louise Walker looked out with Chris Anderson standing behind her.

'Yep, it's them,' Chris said.

The chain unbolted and the door swung open.

'Hi Chris,' Rosie said on walking inside.

'Hey, great to see you both,' Chris said. 'We've been stuck here for the last couple of days without a clue where to go or what to do next.'

'Hi Louise,' Matt said.

'Good to meet you,' she said shaking his hand.

'A quick word about room security,' Matt said. 'If you need to do this sort of stuff again, door chains are next to useless. All someone needs to do is give the door a good kick and the screws holding it on will part company with the door frame. If you want to be secure, wedge something under the door like a rubber door stop, or jam the back of a chair under the door handle.'

'Will do,' Louise said, 'although I hope I never have occasion to use it.'

'Before any decisions are made, first things first,' Matt said. 'Do you have any coffee?'

'Yes,' Louise said, 'I went out yesterday and bought some. I like a caffeine fix too.'

Matt sighed but said nothing, one lecture was enough for the day. Walking out to shops so close to the mainline railway station from Oxford was asking to be spotted by a competent watching crew.

Since discovering the location of the runaway pair and realising they hadn't been kidnapped, but had escaped an attempted abduction, he'd given it a lot of thought. He wanted to know why anyone would attempt to do so and how to avoid a repeat performance in the future.

The picture he'd seen of Louise on her CV didn't do her justice. She was slim and curvy with shoulder-length brown hair and even without much make-up, would still be classified in the 'good-looking' category. However, the single beds spaced about a metre or so apart quickly dispelled any idea of two lovers running away from inquisitive parents.

Looking around, it was a typical budget hotel room with beds, wardrobe, cupboard storage space and a compact, tiled bathroom with power shower. Hotels like this were anonymous and plentiful, great for hiding in or keeping out of the public eye for a spell. Coupled with a false name, it was near-impossible to find anyone if they didn't want to be found. However, once a searcher knew the whereabouts of the person they were seeking, hotel rooms became death-traps with nowhere to run and with little in the way of weapons for a besieged individual to pick up and use.

With a hot coffee in his hand, Matt sat on the edge of one bed beside Rosie, Chris and Louise seated on the other. 'Tell us in as much detail as you can remember,' Matt asked, 'what happened when you came out the pub in Oxford. Louise, you make a start as, in my experience, reporters don't miss much.'

'A compliment; I've missed those,' she replied, glancing at Chris. 'There's not much to tell. We came out of the car park behind the pub and drove down the road, Chris driving and me on the phone to my boss. Seconds later, a van shot out of a side street and stopped right in front of us, blocking our path. I thought at first, 'bloody cheek of these white van drivers', God knows, there's enough of them in London. Then, two men got out and rushed towards our car. Chris shouted something like, 'It's them!' and I realised this was something other than a simple traffic accident.'

Matt nodded. How a bystander reacted to a life-threatening situation, a terrorist attack or a plane crash, often marked the difference between life and death. Many survivors repeated phrases such as, 'I couldn't believe this was happening' or 'I thought my eyes were deceiving me.' Soldiers and trained non-military personnel reacted on instinct, civilians waited until they could make some sense of the situation. Such a wait could cost them their lives.

'A guy opened my door and I hit him with my phone which seemed to do the trick as he fell on the ground. I then ran over to help Chris who was being dragged to their van in a neck-hold. I picked up Chris's laptop from the car and whacked the other guy over the head with it.'

'Well done you,' Rosie said, looking impressed.

'Describe the men who tried to grab you, Louise,' Matt said. 'Did they speak, do you remember anything they said?'

'Both guys wore everyday casual clothes, not scruffy like tradesmen. Both looked tall and stocky with short haircuts.'

'Yeah, like military guys, now I think about it,' Chris said.

'Did you hear them speak, hear the accents they used?'

'I only heard grunts,' Chris said.

'One of them said something,' Louise said. 'I thought at the time he sounded English, maybe London.'

'Rough or cultured?'

'Rough I would say.'

'They've sent a couple of military or ex-military heavies to lift a twenty-one-year student and his smaller female companion. It sounds like they need you bad.'

'I wouldn't like to be in their shoes when they report back to base with news of their failure,' Rosie said.

Rosie was right, those two wouldn't be making a repeat appearance any time soon. If Matt was in charge, he would now be sending someone better, but he didn't voice his concerns out loud.

'Chris, you owe us an explanation. I think you know more about this attempted abduction than you've told us so far.'

'I didn't realise when I first met you, honest I didn't. When I said I didn't believe the downing of the balloon was an accident, I assumed it had to be something to do with my dad's business.'

'Yeah, but now I think you know different.'

'Yes.'

'So, come on. Let's hear it.'

'I shouldn't be saying this as I could get drummed out of the organisation, but I'm a member of a secret computer hacking group.'

'INEXIS,' Matt said.

'Whaaat? How do you know? It's secret.'

'It's our job to find things out. Go on.'

'I'm interested in military stuff because of my dad, yeah?'

They nodded.

'To cut a long story short, I downloaded a load of documents from an American company called Dragon Technologies about their new helicopter, the Pulsar.' He went on to tell them about Dragon's dirty dealings and the guy who headed International Security at Dragon, Daniel Leppo.

'Let me see if I understand this,' Matt said. 'This American outfit, Dragon Technologies, make this fantastic new helicopter that everyone is going gaga about, but some people are baulking at the price.'

'Yep, it costs way more than an Apache and faults have been found in the AI software of the Arrow Battlefield System; it takes away pilot control and starts to work autonomously.'

Matt held up a hand. 'Let's not get too bogged down in technical detail here. We're interested in motives, not performance specs. Dragon employ incentives to entice military men and procurement managers into buying the product. Nothing new there in the defence business.'

'Yep,' Chris said.

'But, and it's a big 'but', they've moved way beyond a ticket to Wimbledon or a week in Ibiza, to call girls, drugs and blackmail.'

Chris nodded like a toy dog, his enthusiasm, getting the better of him. 'Not only that, but the killing of my family, the death of Latif Artha and now they're targeting me and Louise.'

'One at a time. Who's Latif Artha?'

'He was a weapons specialist at an outfit called QuinTec.'

'I've heard of them,' Rosie said. 'They test military kit on behalf of governments.'

'That's right. Artha published various documents about Pulsar, firstly saying it was overpriced and then again, when he'd discovered a fault in Pulsar's weapon system.'

'Several of the new developments incorporated into Pulsar,' Rosie said, 'must be high on a military wish-list. I can think of a few uses for a quieter helicopter and one invisible to radar.'

'Artha didn't dispute that it's a fine aircraft and, on paper, would give the military some significant advantages, if they can swallow the high cost. He moved his criticism away from cost when he found out that the weapons system, which is controlled by artificial intelligence, could malfunction under certain conditions. It can take control away from the pilot and start selecting targets on its own. Who knows what it will do then; kill civilians, attack markets, shoot at friendly troops?'

'That sounds dangerous,' Rosie said.

'You said something before about killing Artha,' Matt said. 'Did something happen to him?'

'He was driving along the M40 on a clear night when he veered off the road, down a steep embankment and crashed into an abandoned quarry. When they conducted the post-mortem, they found his bloodstream full of alcohol.'

'Classic drunk driver scenario; happens all the time.'

'This is what the verdict of the inquest into his death concluded. They failed to take into account Artha's religion. He was a strict Muslim; no way did he ever drink alcohol.'

Chapter 25

Matt and Rosie led Chris and Louise out of the Hotel Mercure in Paddington towards a waiting black cab. Once inside, Matt sat on the fold-down seat to allow him to monitor the traffic behind them. They were heading to a safe house in Islington, or Canonbury as the locals preferred to call this part of London.

'Safe houses' in any branch of the security services were no safer than any other house in the street. If HSA installed multiple security systems such as floodlighting, infra-red alarms and a couple of fierce dogs, it would soon give the game away. They were classified as 'safe' on account of their anonymity and having no connection with the people temporarily staying there.

If an intruder broke into Kevin Anderson's place in Oxford looking for the address of Chris's new location, they wouldn't find it. With the accommodation sorted, the most important thing now was to ensure they weren't being followed.

Chris tapped Matt's knee, breaking his concentration. 'What are we going to do when–?'

'Chris, not here,' Matt said, jerking a thumb behind him at the driver. 'We'll discuss it when we get there. Talk about politics, football, religion or anything you like, but nothing personal. Okay?'

'Sorry, I forgot.'

Monday morning traffic in London looked as it always did: buses, cabs, cars willing to pay the congestion charge and hordes of tourists pouring out of Paddington Station, lining the pavements at each set of traffic lights. Looks could be deceptive, though. The key to following a vehicle was to look the same as those around you.

Matt didn't look at the cars, instead he focused on the occupants, trying to spot a single guy, his face too intense or, a less common sight on the street, a car containing two or three male passengers. Of course, if they used two women, or a woman and a man, his job would become more difficult.

Matt didn't think they had been followed, nevertheless when they arrived at the street in Canonbury he instructed the cabbie to drop them thirty metres away from the safe house. If they were being tailed, it was a toss-up which option was safer.

Was it better for Chris and Louise to be exposed during the thirty-metre walk to the house and confuse any follower as to its location, or stop outside the house, allowing minimum exposure, but giving away the whereabouts of the safe house?

Matt chose the former, because if an abductor tried to attack them, he and Rosie were there to do something to stop them. If instead, they knew the location of the house the villains could wait until Matt and Rosie were no longer there before making their move.

'I don't think I've been to this part of London before,' Louise said as they walked, 'it looks so suburban and yet it doesn't feel like we travelled very far from the centre.'

'The Emirates Stadium isn't far if you like football, but I don't get the impression it would interest you too much.'

'My dad would love it, but his enthusiasm for the national game didn't rub off on me.'

Two doors away, Matt looked at Rosie who nodded. In situations like this they fell into a routine like an old married couple. She turned and monitored the rear while he scanned the gardens on either side of the street and the road ahead.

They walked up the path towards a brick-fronted house with a garage to one side. Matt turned the key, opened the door and headed into the hall to silence the alarm. Most houses in the street had alarms, locks on the windows and at least one deadbolt on both front and back doors. This house was similarly equipped.

'What do you think?' Matt said.

'It's better than the place I share in Shepherd's Bush,' Louise said.

'There should be food in the fridge–'

'Great!' Chris said with some enthusiasm. 'I'm starving.'

It elicited a strange look from Louise, but he didn't inquire.

'What I suggest we do is this,' Rosie said. 'You guys take a quick look round and decide on where you want to sleep. When you're done, come back into the kitchen. We can all have a drink and something to eat, if you're hungry, and then we'll sit down and talk about what happens next.'

Fifteen minutes later, they took seats around the large beech table in the kitchen. Chris was tucking into a thick ham sandwich, while the other three made do with a mug of coffee.

'First up, let's talk housekeeping,' Rosie said. 'By this, I mean clothes, food and some other bits and pieces. There's food in the house for seven days, eat the lot in three,' she said looking straight at Chris who stopped chewing, 'and you'll starve for the rest of the week. All right?'

Chris nodded.

'Neither of you are to go out of this house to do anything. If you run short of something, talk to one of us.'

'What about the back garden?' Louise asked.

'It's out of bounds. Do not open the back door under any circumstances. It's fitted with a special alarm and, if triggered, a couple of armed cop cars will turn up within five minutes.'

'A window then?'

'Yes, you can open a window, but remember to close it. Is everything to your liking so far?'

They both nodded.

'You'll both need changes of clothes and some nightwear. You should find the bathrooms stocked with toiletries, one with men's things the other for a woman. When we're finished here, Matt and I will set off and pick up some gear from your respective houses. I've written the alarm code and telephone numbers down here,' she said passing them a sheet of paper. 'I'll run through all the things you can do with the alarm later, like alarming only the upstairs rooms or sending an emergency signal to our switchboard if you need to. That's about it for housekeeping. Any questions?'

'How long will we be here?' Chris asked.

'Matt will cover that in a sec. Any other questions about housekeeping?'

'Will either of you be staying here with us?' Louise asked.

'We weren't intending to,' Rosie said, 'but we could make an exception if you like. One of us could stay here for your first night.'

'I would feel better if you would.'

She looked at Matt.

'I'll do it,' he said.

'Anything else? No? Matt, it's your turn.'

'Right, the answer to how long you'll be here will be determined by how long it takes us to neutralise the threat against you. From what we heard earlier, we're convinced the threat is posed by Dragon Technologies because you hacked into their computer systems. I don't think it's in retaliation for breeching their security, but they're trying to suppress the information you downloaded, frightened their dirty tactics will be exposed.'

'In which case, they'll need to suppress me,' Chris said.

'How do you mean?' Matt asked.

'Well, they can take my laptop with all the Dragon documents on it, but I saved them to the Cloud and also to a back-up drive. If they're savvy about this, they'll know the only way to stop the documents becoming public is to eliminate me.'

'Couldn't they just kidnap you,' Louise said, 'and ask you to delete the documents on the Cloud and then destroy your laptop? They don't need to kill you, surely?'

'I don't think they're as subtle as that,' Chris said.

'Hang on a sec,' Matt said. 'We don't know what they know or what they want. It could be the laptop or you as well; we just don't know. In many respects it doesn't change anything. Our aim here is to protect you, Louise, and the documents.'

'I understand the protection thing is for the next few days or weeks,' Louise said, 'but how do we, how do you, stop them trying to kidnap or kill us in the longer term?'

'Let me turn the question back to you,' Rosie said. 'What can you do to publicise their dirty activities?'

'I told you earlier how we tried to get the details published in my newspaper, but they got there first with a court injunction.'

'Yes.'

'I've been giving it some thought and I think there are still a couple of options we should consider.'

'Let's hear them.'

'We can either publish on a website like WikiLeaks and hope the story is picked up by newspapers around the world, or we can arrange for the subject to be raised in Parliament. I seem to remember something about not being able to prosecute MPs for anything they raise in the Commons chamber.'

'So, if we can get an MP to talk about this,' Chris said, 'Dragon couldn't do anything to stop them?'

'No, they can't. Also, when an MP raises those sorts of issues, newspapers are free to report it with impunity.'

'Fantastic! It sounds like a great solution. How do we do it?'

'I don't know any MPs,' Louise said. 'Maybe I could make contact with my own if I knew who he or she was. Do you guys know someone?'

Chris shook his head and for an instant looked deflated.

'I might know someone,' Matt said, 'I'll talk to him.'

'Fantastic!' Chris said, now full of life once again. 'I feel we're getting somewhere at last. Is there any more of that excellent ham?'

Chapter 26

Poor Matt. Not only was he having to spend the night babysitting their two charges, he needed to drive to Oxford yet again, this time to pick up some clothes for Chris. Rosie was doing the same for Louise, but the newspaper reporter only lived across town in Shepherd's Bush.

With Louise's flat only a short hop from Canonbury, Rosie decided not to go back to the office to collect her car. Instead, she walked to the underground station carrying an empty sports bag. After climbing on the train, she looked around the carriage for any suspicious characters. It was a hard thing to do as those who didn't have their faces buried in a newspaper, or weren't playing games on their phone or talking to a friend, looked the part.

She hadn't been to Shepherd's Bush often and didn't know the area well. After looking at the map on her phone, realised Louise lived only a few streets away from an underground station, pub, restaurants and within easy walking distance of Westfield Shopping Centre. Living in suburban Harlow, she missed the glitz and glamour many of those places offered and for a moment suffered a pang of jealousy.

She turned into Godolphin Road. Louise shared a two-bedroomed house with a fellow journalist who,

Louise assured her, would have left for work early in the morning. Just as well, as coming across a stranger who was dumping things from the wardrobe into a sports bag would give the poor girl a heart attack and elicit a call to the local cop shop. She climbed the stairs outside the building, stood for a moment and scanned up and down the road.

The girls rented the ground and upper floor of the building, commonly called a maisonette, while the basement had a separate entrance and was occupied by a different tenant. Access to the rear was through a tall metal gate, currently secured by a padlock.

If Dragon were serious in their search for Chris Anderson, and she and Matt had every reason to believe they were, they would be watching Louise's house, Chris's family home, and the house he shared with his uncle and aunt. If HSA were looking for someone, she and her colleagues would do the same.

She opened the door and walked into the house, making sure the lock snapped shut behind her. At thirty-six, Rosie was ten years older than Louise, but even then, the discarded clothes on the floor, unwashed dishes in the kitchen and the house looking in need of a good dust, took her by surprise. Two working girls lived here for sure, but it didn't mean they needed to live like slobs.

Ignoring the lounge and kitchen, she walked upstairs. Louise told her she would recognise her bedroom by how tidy it looked and by the presence of a guitar. Spotting the difference in the 'tidy' stakes was a difficult task, who was less messy being a better measure, but she couldn't help but notice the

Epiphone copy of John Lennon's classic acoustic guitar, the Gibson J-160E, in the corner. She didn't play, but when she was in her early twenties, she had gone out with a guy who played in a band. While she didn't like their music that much, she loved guitars and could happily while away an afternoon in a musical instrument shop.

Louise had given her a list of three outfits: jumpers, jeans, underwear and pyjamas, but nothing too dressy. They wouldn't be going anywhere. Before starting to load the bag, Rosie stood behind a curtain and looked out of the window. From a watcher's perspective, the first few minutes after someone entered a house was a good time to grab them. The person they had come to snatch would be too preoccupied in depositing baggage, taking off their coat and checking mail to notice anything strange going on outside.

A quick glance wasn't enough to detect movement inside an empty car or the difference between the slow cruise of a visitor looking for a parking space and a watcher giving the building the once-over. She stood for several minutes, her head still, but her eyes moving up and down the road in a systematic, gentle sweep.

A silver Toyota caught her attention. At certain times of the day, two men travelling in the same car looked unusual, and the ploy of the passenger holding an estate agent's property details in his hand didn't fool her. In these days of gender diversity and civil partnerships, two gay guys looking for a flat wouldn't be considered out of the ordinary. However, the clothes, stocky build and the furtive glances to the left and right by both men in the Toyota didn't ring true.

If they were looking for Louise's apartment, it was clear they didn't know the exact location as they ignored several empty parking places, but then again, it could also be a ruse. As they drove past, her guard would drop or, while she focussed on the Toyota, a guy in another car could be watching the house and trying to detect any movement inside. The cat and mouse tactics employed by watchers and counter-watchers could twist an ordinary mortal's brain into little knots, but she was used to it.

The curtain fell gently as if rippling in the breeze from an ill-fitting sash window. Rosie moved to the wardrobe. She filled the sports bag with clothes, not an easy task. Many of the items she was looking for couldn't be found on hangers, but were either lying in a heap on the floor, or weren't in the wardrobe at all, but thrown into a nearby chest of drawers. She zipped the bag and checked her weapon, making sure it was accessible and ready to fire.

Rosie moved to the window again and took a final look at the road. She couldn't see any sign of the Toyota or anything else that looked suspicious. She picked up the bag and headed downstairs. At the foot of the stairs, she walked towards the front door, listening for the sound of movement outside and trying to spot shadows on the other side of the opaque glass. Seeing and hearing nothing, she took a deep breath and opened the door.

Her caution was necessary. She didn't want to give the location of Louise's apartment away, the reporter would need to come back and live here at some point. She also didn't want to be surprised by an attacker hiding outside. In many ways, this could be an assailant's best approach, as breaking into Louise's apartment wouldn't give them any indication of her current location, but kidnapping and torturing Rosie would.

Standing on the step outside the front door, she looked around, as if trying to make sense of the weather, but searching for the silver Toyota and any supporting colleagues. She walked down the stone steps and headed in the direction of the underground station.

She set off at a brisk pace, keeping as far away from the road as possible. Godolphin Street was one-way, meaning the Toyota needed to drive around the block before making another pass, not easy with traffic, pedestrians and traffic lights. However, if the men in the car had driven past Louise's flat and parked further along the street, a couple of heavies might be waiting around the next corner, ready to confront her; she needed to be careful.

She felt better when she reached Uxbridge Road, a busy thoroughfare of afternoon shoppers, ambling tourists, delivery drivers and noisy day-time traffic. It wasn't a good place to attack or kidnap a victim with dozens of witnesses, multiple CCTV cameras and Shepherd's Bush police station further down the road. She walked with a renewed confidence in her stride, her adrenaline level, pegged one-to-one with the threat level, sinking slowly like thermometer mercury on a cloudy day. She glanced at the shops and businesses she passed: Caribbean restaurants, Halal supermarkets and the Christian Church of St Stephen and St Thomas.

Rosie reached the underground station without incident. On entering the concourse, she stood to one side, leaned against a wall and rummaged through her bag as if looking for money or her ticket. The ticket, she knew, was in her jacket pocket, but she used the time to scan all those walking towards the barriers and a small group of people loitering outside.

She zipped up her bag, slung it over her shoulder and, picking up the sports holdall, headed for the train. Rosie was good at this game, but the same could be said for the team following her.

Chapter 27

Matt arrived back at the safe house in Canonbury. The occupants, including Rosie, were sitting down for dinner.

'Smells good,' Matt said, walking into the hall, dumping the sports holdall with Chris's clothes inside on the floor and hanging up his jacket.

'Hi Matt, how was the journey to Oxford?' Rosie asked.

'No problem on the way down as I was moving against the traffic, but on the way back I got caught up in an accident on the M4. Took me over an hour to drive past.'

'What a shame. Have you eaten?' Louise asked.

'Nope, I'll go out in a minute and find something.'

'Don't bother. There's enough for us all.'

'You sure? I don't want to starve you guys for the rest of the week.'

'Don't you worry, it's not a problem. Grab a seat. The more you eat the less there'll be for Chris; I think he needs to lose a few pounds.'

'Hey,' Chris said. 'I'm a growing lad, I need plenty of fuel.'

'Never describe any food I make as 'fuel,' Chris Anderson,' Louise said, her face set in a scowl, 'or you'll feel the thick end of a spatula.'

'Ouch. That sounds painful.'

With everyone seated, Matt helped himself to a glass of water from the jug on the table, thirsty after so many hours in a car and drinking too much motorway coffee. He noticed a couple of bottles of wine in the wine rack and even though he didn't drink while on duty, he was surprised Louise or Chris didn't avail themselves to a glass or two.

Louise placed a large dish of spaghetti bolognese on the table and another bowl containing salad. 'You two serve yourselves first,' she said, 'you're our guests.'

Matt didn't need telling twice. After slaking his thirst with a couple of glasses of water, what he wanted now was something to eat.

'While you were out,' Rosie said when all their plates were filled, 'I looked over the documents Chris downloaded from his hack into Dragon's computers. It's dynamite stuff: names, places, amounts and, buried behind a password, photographs and videos of famous faces doing a load of things they shouldn't.'

'It sounds like blackmail is a key part of their game plan,' Matt said.

'They may have considered it as some form of insurance at the beginning, but when sales of Pulsar met some resistance, it looks like they moved into it big-time.'

'Yeah,' Chris said, his first pause from shovelling food non-stop. 'The US Military liked Pulsar well enough, but sales were slow as they were finding it hard to justify the high cost to their paymasters.'

'Don't forget, this information doesn't just reflect badly on Dragon as a company,' Matt said, 'it involves individuals in their organisation. If they're as tough as we think, they'll stop at nothing to prevent it becoming public knowledge. Otherwise, they'll find themselves being dragged up in front of a Congressional Committee and looking ahead to some lengthy jail time with their reputations in ribbons. Plus, working for an American company, they'll also have to face multi-million-dollar lawsuits for damages.'

'Whoa,' Chris said. 'The stakes are even higher than I thought.'

'If they can pay millions to sweet-talk their buyers,' Matt said, 'what's a couple of hundred grand to track you guys down and stop you publishing what you've got on the laptop?'

'Hell, you're dead right. Hey, you've just given me an idea.' The cutlery in Chris's hands stood motionless. 'Why don't I leave the laptop where they can find it? Then, they would think they've got all the information they need and call off the hunt.'

'Yeah, but you said everything's backed up.'

'In the Cloud and on a back-up drive at my Uncle Kevin's house, but they don't know that.'

Matt shook his head. 'You said it yourself, if they're smart enough, they'll know. If I worked for them, and Rosie will tell you I'm crap where computers are concerned, even I would guess as much.'

Matt went to bed about eleven after spending the evening playing cards with Louise and Chris. Rosie had gone home to Harlow a few hours before, back to an empty house as her husband was laid over in Orlando.

Matt headed upstairs after completing a check on the doors, windows and making sure the timer attached to the lamp worked and was set to the correct time. Despite a busy day with lots of driving, it still wouldn't make much difference to the quality of his sleep. A restless night was a habit he couldn't shake since his mother died, but for one night at least, Emma didn't have to suffer.

He started reading the printouts from the Dragon documents Rosie had been looking at earlier. Like her, he became astonished at the level of their lavishness in bestowing gifts and favours on the chosen few. Perhaps many other large corporations did the same, but he imagined few would risk documenting everything they did and taking photographs of their potential clients enjoying themselves. If they ever found out, these people wouldn't be their clients for much longer.

He turned off the light and tried to sleep. He soon fell into a deep slumber, better than at home. When he woke at two, something he did most nights, he didn't feel bright awake as usual but woozy. Not requiring a leak or something to drink, he settled down again, keen to get back to the best sleep he'd experienced for some time. Seconds later, the sound of breaking glass broke the calm of the still night.

He slid out of bed, pulled on his jeans and t-shirt and picked up the Glock. He slipped a spare ammo clip into his back pocket. Even though the gun held seventeen rounds, he couldn't be too careful. He also slipped into his pocket the small torch he always carried with him. It was small enough to slip into his trousers without discomfort, and it would prevent him falling down stairs or walking into something. If he did, it would end any chance of springing a surprise on his opponent or increase the likelihood of him catching a bullet while trying to pick himself up from the bottom of the stairs.

He opened the door of his bedroom and crept into the hallway. Nothing stirred from Chris or Louise's rooms; good, he didn't want either of them becoming targets. He headed downstairs, easier and quieter without his Timberland boots.

When he reached the bottom, he realised the intruder was inside the house as he could hear someone walking around the lounge. If Chris's laptop had been left there, they could now test the naivety or otherwise of the Dragon people. However, he knew he'd taken it up to bed with him.

Matt knelt at the bottom, leaning on the last step, and waited. The intruder came out of the lounge, his tread soft, but Matt still heard his step on the wooden door sill. The intruder turned towards the stairs while Matt held his position, waiting for the right moment. Now. He leapt up, and flashed the torch into the intruder's eyes. It blinded him, and at the same time, Matt smacked him hard in the head with the butt of his gun.

The intruder fell to the ground, but before he could check him, another gunman opened fire. Matt ducked back. The only thing separating him from instant death, the plywood which was used to box-in the struts of the banister, and the shooter aiming at the front door on the assumption that he came through it. A few seconds later, Matt crawled on the floor, reached around the stairs and using the body as a shield, pointed his gun down the hall towards the kitchen. He fired blind, straight down, through the open door.

He ducked back and waited. The intruder didn't return fire, but it meant nothing. The guy had most likely moved out of the way. He would be reconsidering his options after encountering someone with a gun. Matt would bet the presence of an armed opponent didn't feature in the intruder's original risk assessment.

Matt crawled closer to the prostrate intruder, searching for his gun. When he found it, he pocketed it. No way did he want this guy waking up and shooting him in the back. He lay behind the inert body and held up the man's arm. When it didn't elicit a burst of fire, he dashed into the shelter of the lounge doorway. With no access between the kitchen and the lounge, Matt couldn't sneak up on the other gunman and the gunman couldn't do the same to him.

He ducked down and leaning out of the door, he risked a rapid flash of the torch. When the gunman didn't respond, he knew with ninety-five per cent certainty he'd gone. The five per cent of doubt lay within the provenance of the most experienced and confident hitmen. The sort of man who could hold back from responding to Matt's volley, knowing the chance of a better and possibly fatal shot would come a short time later. He didn't believe these guys were in this class.

Matt crept towards the kitchen, his Glock ready to fire at the slightest movement. He reached the kitchen door and found his bullets had splintered part of the frame, and also discovered a splattering of blood. It didn't coat the cabinets or create a puddle on the floor to indicate a dying man, the body of whom he'd find in the garden among the rose bushes. It was just enough to tell him he'd wounded the intruder.

Torn material indicated a hasty exit through the broken window, but Matt wasn't taking any chances. He would deal with the other guy first and then make a thorough search of the garden outside.

He returned to the hallway. A sleepy Louise walked towards him, stepping over the body on the floor.

'What's going on, Matt?' Louise said rubbing her eyes, trying to wake up. 'What was all the noise? Whoa, did I just walk past a body on the floor? Who the hell is it; what's he doing there?'

Before he could shout a warning, the 'unconscious' man leapt to his feet. He grabbed Louise, wrapped his arm around her throat and held a knife at her ribs, which she could feel through her thin nightdress as, despite the dim light, he saw her flinch.

'Drop the gun tough guy, or she gets it.'

The voice sounded East London, rough, menacing, and Matt believed every word.

No matter how good a gunman's skills, a big guy couldn't shelter behind a slight woman. If Matt spotted a body part to aim at, shoot him he would. The problem was the lack of light. Streetlight from outside was shining through a frosted glass panel at the top of the main door behind the intruder, and some moonlight steaming in from the kitchen window behind him. It left the two of them in blurry silhouette.

'C'mon copper, I'm not gonna wait all fucking night.'

Matt couldn't see another option. He dropped his arm, bent down and slowly placed the gun on the ground.

'Kick it over to me.'

He lifted his foot to do so when a noise behind the couple made him look up. A dark shadow came flying through the air and something whacked the guy over the head.

Louise screamed and jumped forward, the knife tumbling to the floor. The villain collapsed behind her as if his legs were made of rubber.

She ran over and leapt into Matt's arms and hugged him tight, her body shaking with fear.

'Matt, I felt so scared.'

'No worries, girl, it's over now.'

The hall light came on. He could see now the bullet holes in the door, and the wall, the prostrate figure on the floor and Chris standing over him, holding something in his hand.

'Chris, what the hell did you hit him with?'

'The handle of a walking stick.'

'Where did you get that?'

'I found a couple of them in the umbrella stand at the door. I took one up to my room tonight for self-protection.'

Chapter 28

The clean-up team arrived at the safe house at eight in the morning. They proceeded to examine the downstairs part of the house, looking for forensic clues, while a couple of techies repaired the damage and beefed up security.

It was important to fix the broken window, of course, but vital to patch-up the bullet holes. It wouldn't do to bring a frightened family to a safe house only for them to find it full of the remnants of an earlier gun battle. Matt could have called the clean-up team the previous night as he didn't believe the aggressors, having lost one of their team and the other suffering from a bullet wound, would be back. He did, however, call out the Captivity Team to take away the prisoner.

He'd passed details of the shooting to the Met Serious Crimes unit who would check hospitals in an attempt to trace the wounded man. Matt didn't believe the guy Chris knocked out with the walking stick, would say much. If Dragon were prepared to kill Chris's family in a bid to get at him, they wouldn't baulk at killing a foot soldier who talked too much. Matt intended interviewing the prisoner himself, but first, he needed to spirit Chris and Louise away from there, as from their perspective, it wasn't a safe house anymore.

Before going to bed last night, he'd put a call through to the Director. Matt was loathe to wake him as the danger had passed, but Gill would give him a bollocking if he wasn't kept in the loop. After an incident like this and before blaming his own people, Gill would ask the question: were we the best-placed agency to carry out the job?

For Matt, the answer was emphatically 'yes' as HSA were pursuing Dragon, but the conversation raised an interesting point. Should the job of protecting two civilians fall within their remit? The police had plenty of expertise in this area with the Witness Protection Programme and the Royal Protection Group, but Matt believed he wouldn't get close to Dragon if they were the responsibility of someone else.

Having decided to move Chris and Louise, the next question he needed to answer was where? He'd talked to the Director about other safe houses they could use and a couple the Met could offer, when Matt came up with a better idea.

'We're packed,' Louise said walking downstairs. She looked almost back to her usual self after the shock-horror of only a few hours before; almost.

'Did you get much sleep?' he asked.

'Not much after the...the thing with the knife guy. I kept hearing his voice in my head.'

'I can't say what happened won't give you bad dreams as we all deal with things like this in our own way. I can put you in touch with some professional help, if it becomes a problem.'

'Thanks, I'll bear it in mind. Who are all those people?'

Matt explained that the forensics staff were looking for clues while the techies were repairing the house and making it safe for the next unfortunate incumbents.

'What happened to the bad guy? Is he dead?'

Matt smiled. 'No, he's not dead, but thanks to Chris, he'll have a big headache this morning. We've taken him away for questioning.'

'That's good news, isn't it, that you caught someone? You can find out who his associates are and, I don't know, use the information to close his organisation down.'

He placed an arm on her shoulder. 'I wish it was so easy. All the work we're doing here,' he said removing his arm, 'the research going on back at base and the questioning we'll do of the suspect, won't give us more than one or two bits of new information.'

'What? You can't be serious?'

'These guys are professionals, Louise. They don't leave clues and won't blab on their mates to us or anybody else.'

'Can't you force them?'

'What's this? Do I hear you advocating torture?'

'No, well…yes, maybe I am. It's important to find out what they know.'

'We'll try, but using torture can be counter-productive. Where's Chris?'

'In the bathroom. I swear he takes longer to get ready than my flatmate, and that's going some.'

'Give me your bag and I'll take it out to the car, see what's going out there. You stay here.'

He walked down the path, his eyes and ears alert as ever for any strange movement or sound, although he expected to hear it from antagonistic journalists, not malevolent criminals. The small group of reporters gathered outside must have been alerted by neighbours, as HSA and the Met hadn't issued any statements, and wouldn't when protecting witnesses was their main concern. They were being held behind a cordon by a no-nonsense member of the HSA clean-up team.

'Morning John.'

'Morning Matt. I understand you had a bit of bother last night.'

'You could say that.'

A tap on Matt's arm caused him to turn.

'Excuse me,' an eager face said, 'can I ask you what went on last–'

'No, you can't.'

Matt walked on, his eyes focussed on the car and not on the reporters who were looking at one another and shrugging. Matt wasn't a copper they recognised. He put the bag in the boot, closed the lid and headed back into the house.

On walking back into the house Matt spotted Chris.

'Wonders will never cease.'

'What?' he said, his face exhibiting the puzzled expression of a typical teenager faced with making a decision or answering a question before midday.

'Are you ready to go?'

'Ready as I'll ever be.'

He looked at Louise and Chris. 'On no account say anything to the reporters outside. If they make a move to take a picture, put your hand up and cover your face. All right?'

'Wait a second, Matt,' Louise said. 'One of the reporters out there might recognise me.'

'They might recognise me too,' Chris said. 'If they did, it wouldn't take long for them to tie me in with the balloon incident.'

'You're right, we need to do something. Have either of you got sunglasses or a hat?'

'You packed my bag,' Chris said, 'you know what I've got.'

Matt looked around, but a safe house only contained the items necessary for a short stay, although he felt grateful it extended to walking sticks in the umbrella stand.

'We could cover our heads with a jumper or a t-shirt,' Chris said, 'I've got a couple of them in my bag.'

'No, that will make the sharks out there ultra suspicious. Hang on, I've got an idea.'

Matt went into the kitchen and spoke to one of the forensics guys. A few minutes later he came out carrying two forensics over suits.

'Put these on, Louise, try to tuck as much hair into the hood as you can, see if we can confuse them. What else can we do to improve it?'

He thought for a moment. 'I know. Carry Chris's bag between you, as if it's heavy or contains something delicate. Human nature will come into play and I'll bet they'll focus on the bag and not on the faces of you guys. In fact, seeing the white suits might make them think it's something contagious and encourage them back off. What do you think?'

'Good idea,' Chris said nodding. 'It will be good to get something back on journalists for a change after all the rubbish they've written about me and my family. Sorry, no offence, Louise.'

'None taken. It sounds like a plan, Matt.'

'Good. Get ready and follow me out.'

Resembling two scientists from the Porton Down Research Laboratory carrying the last known example of Spanish Flu virus, they walked slowly to the car behind Matt, their backs to reporters and their faces almost obscured by white hoods. Matt didn't often buy a newspaper, there usually wasn't the time to read one, but he would do so in the morning. He'd love to find out what unusual ideas the reporters made of this.

They drove off without the usual thrusting of cameras at car windows or shouted questions, the standard accompaniment when anyone exited a house after a shooting had taken place. Matt felt sure he wouldn't be called into Gill's office in the morning, the Director's face like a man with a piece of gristle stuck down his throat, the morning edition of the *Daily Mirror* spread out in front of him.

They turned the corner at the end of the road. After a few minutes, when he was sure they weren't followed, he instructed Louise and Chris to remove their forensic suits.

'Thank goodness,' Louise said, 'it's getting hot in here.'

'Me too,' Chris said, 'although I like the idea of a disguise. We did a lot of dressing up at uni.'

'You don't mean what I think you mean?' Louise said, her expression one of mild shock.

'Don't be daft. I mean dressing up for themed parties like *Star Wars* and *Grimm's Fairy Tales*. Didn't you do it when you were there?'

'It wasn't popular during my time.'

'You were probably in the library.'

'Fat chance.'

After much rustling, Chris poked his head in the gap between the seats. 'Can I ask, where are we going?'

'How does Windsor sound?' Matt replied.

Chapter 29

Leaving a safe house unexpectedly was fraught with danger. The intruders knew that Chris and Louise had been staying there, and they risked losing touch if they didn't follow them to their new destination. One of the gang might have been standing in the throng of journalists outside the vacated house, or were in one of the cars driving behind them for long periods on the way to Windsor. As before, Matt made a judgement call as to the risk and decided not to engage in a drive-around before reaching Clifton Manor.

Sir Raymond Deacon wasn't at home when Matt and his two charges arrived at the house. Members of Parliament, including government ministers, were not required to be at the House of Commons until the session started at two o'clock in the afternoon. Government ministers, however, had the additional responsibility of a department to run. Matt knew he would be at his desk by eight this morning and wouldn't be back until after ten at night, or not at all if he stayed on to finish some important business. Then, he slept at the apartment he owned in Westminster.

The absence of the Home Office Minister didn't affect the new arrivals one bit, as David, Sir Raymond's personal assistant, ran the house when his boss wasn't there. Matt had informed Chris and Louise about Lisa's previous rape trauma, and when they dumped what little luggage they'd brought with them in their rooms, he took them both to meet her.

He knocked on the door and walked in. He received the now-traditional bear-hug from the young woman who had experienced so much.

'I didn't think I see you back here so soon,' she said, her breath coming in short gasps. 'You usually leave longer between visits.'

'I didn't think so either, Lisa, but circumstances have changed. How are you?'

'Oh, nothing much different, but I'm always pleased to see you.'

He held her away from him. 'Lisa, there are a couple of people here I'd like you to meet.'

Despite Lisa being briefed by David, Matt had no idea how she would react to having strange people in her house, and now in her room. Meeting people, other than doctors and psychologists, wasn't a high priority for her over these last few months.

Matt stood back to introduce the new arrivals. He didn't elaborate on the danger they were in. but simply told her they needed to stay somewhere safe for a few days.

Chris was tall, an inch or so above Matt and broad chested, and if possessing a meaner face than his round, boyish features, some could find him intimidating. Most people could read the signals that he was a jovial giant, but Lisa was out of practice, and recoiled when Chris stepped forward.

'Hi Lisa, I'm Chris. Great to meet you.'

Before Matt could say anything more, Louise jumped in.

'Hi Lisa, I'm Louise. Thanks very much for allowing us to stay. It's such a beautiful house you live in, you must love it here.'

'I suppose it is really,' Lisa said, her face red and her manner flustered, 'but I've lived here all my life. I hardly notice it now.'

Matt tugged Chris's sleeve, indicating he should back off.

'Perhaps,' Louise said, 'if you're not too busy, later on you could show us around?'

'Yes, I could, couldn't I? Do you like paintings?'

'Yes, I do.'

'Gory?'

'Oh yes,' she said smiling.

'Oh, you'll love many of the ones my grandpa collected. The more heads they chopped off and the more guts spilled the better he liked them.'

Matt slipped out of the room, Chris beside him.

'She's not used to visitors and knowing her background, not too keen on men. It's not you, so don't take it to heart,' he said nodding towards Lisa and Louise, nattering away like a couple of old classmates who hadn't seen one another for weeks.

'Happens all the time. I'm well used to it.'

'Look on the bright side, it's better than someone trying to kidnap you.'

'I couldn't agree more.'

'There should be enough to keep you occupied here. When you're fed up surfing the net, go down to the library. Raymond's always got stacks of newspapers and magazines as well as thousands of books. If you want anything at all, food, information, how to operate the television, just ask David. All right?'

He nodded.

'Same rules as the previous place,' Matt continued, 'although here I don't mind you walking around the grounds as they're fenced off, but no further. If something doesn't look right, come back to the house pronto and call me. Okay?'

'Yep.'

'If there's something you can't find here, ask David. Any questions?'

'I don't think so, I think we should be fine. It looks a great place. Thanks for bringing us here.'

'You can thank Raymond when you meet him. He might look like an old ogre of a government minister, but he's easy to talk to. He's a mine of information about loads of stuff.'

'Got it.'

'I'm heading off now, Chris. Call me if you have any problems. Same for Louise. Okay?'

'Yeah. See you later, Matt and thanks.'

He drove slowly down the long driveway at Clifton Manor. It wasn't because he was deep in thought or listening to something interesting on the radio. With such large pebbles under the tyres, if he drove too fast, they would attack the underside of his car with the alacrity of a band of gremlins. He stopped at the end and looked left and right along the long straight road bordering Clifton Manor.

Parked cars would stick out like drunks at a funeral. The surrounding area was flat and not blessed with many trees, meaning he could see far beyond Sir Raymond's property in both directions. The fact that he could see nothing to raise his suspicions didn't fill Matt with confidence as he drove back to London. He wasn't a pessimist by nature, only when it came to situations like this, with the role of hunter and the hunted now reversed.

His concentration was broken when his phone rang.

'Morning Matt,' Sir Raymond Deacon said. 'How are our new guests settling in?'

'Morning Raymond. They're settling in well. Lisa and Louise look as though they've hit it off. I suspected they would, but she's wary of Chris.'

'Tell him not to take any notice. The only men she could tolerate for a time were those in a white coat.'

'It's good for her to have some young people around.'

Raymond emitted his customary growl, reserved for errant civil servants. 'Are you trying to tell me something?'

'I wouldn't dare.'

'In the past, we've tried it with her cousins and friends, but you're right, it might work better now as a longer period has passed since Lisa's incident, and Louise will be staying there for a few days. Her cousins could only take a few hours of being shunned.'

'I hope it works, Lisa could use a break. How did you get on trying to identify an MP to raise the Dragon issue in the House?'

'Have you ever known me to fail? His name is Derek Spencer. He's MP for a constituency around Manchester and a man who calls a spade a spade. He takes a keen interest in defence matters and, in the past, criticised BAE Systems and Rolls Royce for selling equipment to rogue African states. He's an engineer and has experience of the defence industry when he worked for a couple of contractors to BAE Systems. He knows his stuff and won't be fobbed off with lame excuses.'

'Sounds like our man.'

'Even better, he's ambitious and wants a perch on the front bench. If you know anything about politics, you'll know he's been trying for months to make a name for himself. He aims to oust the useless incumbent, if I can be so blunt about a fellow colleague, Ed Greening, and nab the defence brief for himself.'

'It's not like you to give a firebrand MP a leg-up the political ladder. Are you going soft in your old age?'

He laughed. 'I've been called many things in my time, Matt, but never soft, and we'll have less of the 'old age' if you don't mind. In this particular case, I'm able to put any political reservations to one side with the best of them when the threat of a national scandal is so very near.'

'You're right, as always. If the MOD are close to buying Pulsar and later it's found that several MPs and military chiefs had their faces in the trough, who knows how many heads will roll?'

Sir Raymond sighed. 'That's only part of it. Firstly, yes, the Services are full of enthusiasm for this machine and are lobbying hard to lay their hands on it. Secondly, only today I learn that the deputy Prime Minister who said a few months back, and I quote, 'the UK Military will buy that over-priced, over-specified aircraft over my dead body,' unquote, is keen for them to acquire it. So, the stakes are very much higher than before. It does make me wonder though, who has got to him.'

Chapter 30

Matt walked into the interview room, Rosie by his side. They took seats behind a metal table. Facing them, the man Chris knocked out at the safe house. Rosie switched on the tape recorder. This session wasn't about gathering evidence but understanding motive. The police would use a more court-ready recording system when HSA handed this scumbag over to them.

'How's the head?' Matt asked, looking at the prominent lump.

'I've been better.'

'I bet you have.' In the daylight he didn't look as intimidating as he had with a knife poking into Louise's ribs. Aged around late thirties, he had short blond hair, a small scar down one cheek and intense blue eyes. In another setting like a pub or club, he might even be called rough but handsome.

'Listen mate,' Matt said. 'We've got you for illegal entry, possessing a firearm and threatening with a knife. If you understand anything about the court system, and I assume you're no stranger, you're looking at ten, maybe twelve years. If the police can tie your gun to other crimes, who knows, maybe more.'

The man facing them crossed his arms, a scowl creasing his face.

'Nothing to say? You might have guessed from the shoulder straps, me, my colleague and the guy standing behind you are armed. We're not regular police, we're Homeland Security. Which means when I hand you over to the police after we finish here, I could, if I'm feeling generous, leave out one or two things you did the other night. It's better than the cops can offer. They might say they'll speak to the CPS or the judge and ask them to go easy, but I'm talking about something concrete. Do you understand what I'm saying?'

'I think so.'

Using face recognition software and Sikander Khosa's consummate research skills, they now knew the prisoner sitting across from them was called Steve Ashley. They also had a copy of his criminal record. Notes left on the system by a helpful detective suggested he'd gone professional; moved from street robberies and post office heists to the ranks of a recognised criminal team, the Bermondsey Outfit led by Ivan Mander.

They were well known at the Met to be into drug smuggling and people trafficking and, in an attempt to diversify and develop other sources of revenue, a few years back, Mander set up a contract division. Not only did they hire out weapons, they could also supply a team of men, ready and willing to carry out shootings, set buildings on fire or kidnap a target.

In some ways, Mander had made a clever move. Parts of the drug and people trafficking business were becoming overcrowded with Romanian and Russian gangs fighting for territory. Both areas received much police attention, while the apparent random criminal act carried out by their contracting team was regarded by detectives as the most difficult type of case to investigate and solve.

Police detection methods were predicated on connections: the names of people known to the victim, the last person to see the victim alive, the recall of witnesses, the owner of fingerprint and DNA data collected at the crime scene. A contract criminal had no connection with the victim and unless they left some evidence behind or, in the case of the man in front of them, was caught, their involvement could be almost impossible to detect.

'Let's start with a name.'

'Easy; Steve Ashley. Can I go now?'

'Forget playing the smartarse, mate. Get serious for once. Why did you break into the house in Canonbury?'

'We made a mistake.'

'Who's we?'

'I don't know his name. I called him Rob, he called me Tom. I didn't know him; he didn't know me.'

'Doesn't matter, we'll find him soon enough. How did you make a mistake?'

'We meant to do the house across the street. A drug dealer lives there, see, and he owes this bloke a lot of money. The guns were just to put the frighteners on.'

Matt turned to Rosie who shook her head. It was the most the prisoner had spoken so far and the East

End accent Matt first heard at the safe house rang out loud and clear.

'Sorry mate, we need a better story than that. Only amateurs would make a mistake like getting the house number wrong, and while I don't think you and your pal are top-notch, you're no fools either.'

Ashley crossed his arms and looked shifty. Not because of any guilt he felt about what he'd done, more likely because the story he'd probably cooked up while waiting to be interviewed wasn't being bought.

'You're right, I must be getting it mixed up with another job. We was there to kidnap a bloke.'

'You're starting to make some sense, but I think you were there to kill him.'

'No way. We don't do jobs like that. Kidnap him we was told.'

'Why the guns if you only meant to kidnap him? The only people occupying the house, as far as you were aware, were a twenty-one-year-old boy and a young woman. It doesn't sound like a tough prospect for a couple of hard men like yourself and your mate.'

'In case we came across people like you.'

'I'm not buying it,' Rosie said. 'I think you went there to put a bullet into him, pure and simple. You tried killing him when you shot his family down in the hot-air balloon. Why stop there?'

'We didn't shoot down no hot-air balloon.'

'Who did, then?'

'I dunno. Americans, maybe?'

'So, you know about it?'

'Yeah, sort of.'

'Then you'll also know it's connected to what you and your buddy were being asked to do.'

'Maybe.'

'C'mon Steve,' Rosie said, 'you're not being straight with us. The balloon shooting was to kill the boy. When it didn't work, they sent you and your mate in to finish the job.'

'Hold up. We didn't go there to kill anybody, d'ya hear? You can't stick that fucking rap on me. The contract said lift him and then hand him over. Nothing else.'

'Who were you handing him over to?'

'A guy who would be waiting at the Clacket Lane services on the M25. Before you ask, I dunno anything about him.'

'Why did they ask you to lift him?'

'He stole stuff belonging to my customer is all I know.'

'What sort of stuff?'

'Documents. Important documents.'

On and on they posed the questions and with the consummate ease of a county batsman, the prisoner passed them back with little embellishment or enlightenment. A couple of times Matt asked directly for the name of their buyer, the name of his mate, and what they intended to do with Chris, but ignorance didn't hold him back; it was fear. The fear of incurring the wrath of his buyer outweighed any offer Matt could make at reducing his time inside.

He could understand his reluctance. Matt could lop-off four years from a twelve-year sentence, but this would still leave eight years of looking over his shoulder in case people paid by Dragon or friends of his former team mate tried to kill him.

Matt and Rosie walked upstairs to the office area. Several desks lay empty, hot desks used by field officers, and others for those who needed to interrogate the many systems HSA were allowed to access. Matt took a seat at the nearest empty desk with Rosie standing close, leaning on the partition.

'The interview didn't add much, did it?' Rosie said.

'No, but it cemented a few things. Without Ashley naming names, we know whoever hired him and his mate, they were after Chris, and we know they want the documents. The balloon shooting and the attack on the safe house were all about Chris. We suspected as much, but I think we've just had it confirmed.'

'It's a relief to finally see the pieces fitting together.'

'We also know that whoever is gunning for Chris is desperate to catch him. They employed a crack sniper to shoot down the balloon, and when they realised Chris wasn't on the flight, they brought in the two guys in Oxford. When they failed, they went to Ivan Mander and hired two more goons. Now they've failed, what comes next?'

'You don't think it's the same two guys who tried to kidnap them in Oxford?'

He shook his head. 'I don't think so, but I'll take this guy's photograph over to Windsor and ask Chris and Louise to have a look. I think the important issue is this. As far as I know, and tell me I'm wrong, Katić and Mander aren't connected. If the Oxford crew are a different gang, it further emphasises my point.

They're throwing everything at this; money, men, equipment, firepower. If one gang fails, another team steps up to the plate and tries to do their master's bidding. In which case, they won't stop until they get him.'

'You make it sound like no matter what we do, we can't protect Chris.'

'They can afford to make as many mistakes as they like, we only need to make one, and it's curtains.'

'He can't stay in a gilded castle forever. All the necessities of life taken care of and being surrounded by beautiful women. The poor guy will develop a complex.'

'Being ignored by beautiful women, more like, but we're short of options.'

'Don't be so negative, Matt. We've still got the MP to talk to, don't forget. When he tells Parliament what Dragon have been doing, it will hit every newspaper and television station in the country and be a huge embarrassment for the MOD. Dragon's shares will plummet and so will their sales. They'll have more to worry about than some university student from Oxford. That should put an end it.'

'Yes, but you know what they say happens when you antagonise a dragon?'

'Don't start getting all literary on me now. What do you think we should do with him downstairs?'

'Keep him for another day, make him think he's with us long-term and see if he becomes more cooperative. If not, we should hand him over to the Met Serious Crime Unit.'

'What if he does tell us something useful? Are you willing to forget a few of the events of that night, such as his attempt to kill you, take Louise hostage, or the fact you found a gun on him?'

'No way.'

'You're a hard man to please Matt Flynn.'

'I do my best.'

Chapter 31

Matt and Chris walked into MP Derek Spencer's office in the Houses of Parliament. They were accompanied by a tall, good-looking girl with the strong, muscled legs of a two-hundred-metre sprinter. Her presence changed Chris's demeanour from the worried and neurotic expression he'd worn since setting off from Windsor, to that of a lusty schoolboy ogling a vivacious young teacher.

If the Amazonian stature of Geraldine, Derek Spencer's research student, was a surprise find in the musty corridors of Parliament, the sight of Derek Spencer MP was even more so. He expected to see a careworn old buffer with a pasty complexion, receding hair line and a taste in clothes not improved since boarding school days. Matt was surprised to find a fit, mid-thirties man with a thin, noble face, trimmed and gelled black hair, wearing a stylish blue suit, blue shirt and matching tie.

'Pleased to meet you both,' Spencer said standing up from behind his cluttered desk and shaking their hands. 'The conversation I had yesterday with Sir Raymond really piqued my interest, hence when he suggested we got together, I happily agreed to do so. Before we start, let me make something clear to ensure there are no misunderstandings about what I can or can't do. I'm a backbench MP with an interest in defence matters, not the Minister of State for Defence. I don't have the ear of the Prime Minister or make government policy. My only power is in trying to influence those who do.'

'Sir Raymond told us as much,' Matt said.

'Good. Nevertheless, while I don't enjoy a direct line to the Prime Minister or Defence Secretary, I have enough clout in this place from my membership of and chairing a couple of key Defence Select Committees. I'm therefore confident that if you can confirm what Sir Raymond outlined, I'll have no trouble repeating the allegations on the floor of the House. Does this sound like a way forward?'

'Sounds great,' Chris said, a smile creeping across his face for the first time today.

'Excellent. Let's get started. Perhaps if you can begin your story, Chris. When and how you first got involved with Dragon, then bring me up to date with their attempts to silence you.'

Chris came to the meeting prepared. Over the next twenty minutes, he explained how he'd downloaded the documents from Dragon, what they revealed, the efforts the company were making to take them back. Also, why he and an agent from HSA were in the Houses of Parliament today talking to an MP.

'Good Lord, you tell quite a story, but excuse me if I remain sceptical until I see some proof. In my defence, my father is a lawyer and some of his manner has clearly rubbed off. I must say, looking at you now, Chris, I do recognise you. Your picture was in all the newspapers at the time of the tragic balloon crash.

You have my condolences, it must have been a terrible time for you.'

'It was, back then when I was under the impression it was an accident. Now, it's started all over again with Dragon trying to kidnap or kill me.'

'I understand. You said you have some documents to show me. Did you bring them with you?'

'The documents are saved on the net. If I can use your laptop, I'll show you.'

Spencer closed a couple of documents he didn't want them to see and turned the laptop towards Chris.

'Be my guest,' he said.

'So, how did you and HSA become involved with Chris, Matt?'

'It's a long story and I won't bore you with too many details. We were tracking the movements of a Serbian hitman who we believed was in this country to do a job. This turned out to be the downing of the Anderson family balloon.'

'I'm finding it hard to get my head around,' Spencer said, a look of shock on his face. 'So, right from the word 'go', Dragon have been trying to eliminate anyone involved in bringing their nefarious activities to light?'

'Yep, that's how it looks.'

'The documents are ready,' Chris said.

'It didn't take long.'

'I just needed to sign in to my Cloud account.'

Chris shifted the laptop to Spencer's side of the desk. For the next half hour, he talked him through a variety of downloaded reports and emails, while Matt took a look through a pile of today's newspapers lying on the desk.

When the two men finished, Chris moved his chair back to its previous position and waited for Spencer's reaction.

'This is devastating stuff,' he said after a few moments. 'If these emails are genuine, and there is no reason to doubt their authenticity, Dragon are responsible for wholesale bribery, corruption, the murder of your family, Chris, and that of Latif Artha.'

He pushed his chair back, walked to the window and stared through the dirty glass. He removed a handkerchief from his pocket and blew his nose. A minute or so later, he turned to face them.

'I'm not sure if either of you are aware, but Latif was a great friend of mine. I attended his funeral, that was when I was under the impression he had died in a car accident. Although, at the time, I was sceptical when the police said he was found with high levels of alcohol in his system, as he didn't drink. I assumed the bottle of scotch he always brought for me had smashed in the crash and somehow confused them. I had no idea his death was in any way deliberate. No idea.'

'I'm sorry for you to hear about his death in such a blunt way,' Matt said.

'No, no. I suppose it's better I hear this from a member of the security services than reading some salacious rumours in the tabloids. It's just come as a shock, that's all. Let's get back to business.'

The MP retook his seat behind the desk. 'The stakes are high because Dragon are desperate to sign a deal with the UK and NATO. With this vote of approval, it's expected the US Military will weigh in with a much larger order, some say three times bigger than the first. If we in the UK don't sign and open this can of worms, it could cause the US to cancel or at least reconsider. If this happens, I suspect Dragon Technologies will collapse.'

'As bad as that?' Matt asked.

'From what I hear in the committee rooms, they have sunk so much money into the development of the hybrid engine that makes Pulsar fly so quietly, they've been touting banks and shareholders ever since, looking for additional funding. The Defence Minister knows all this and it should give him reason enough to at least pause, as it throws doubt on the future availability of spares and upgrades, but the man is gung-ho for it.'

'Perhaps Dragon got to him as well,' Chris said.

'I wouldn't like to go around accusing a government minister of any wrongdoing without proof, although I do appreciate, details could well be contained in these files. However, if a financial crisis does engulf Dragon as a business entity, it won't be the last we'll see and hear of Pulsar. Other defence contractors are eager to get their hands on the helicopter's advanced technology so will be keen to pick over the pieces.'

'Vultures picking over the bones,' Matt said.

'Quite.'

'So, do you think you can help us?' Chris asked.

Spencer stood and paced the room, his face twisted in contemplation. 'Noises coming out of the PM's office are saying I've been too critical of defence spending in general, and Pulsar in particular. Some in the Tory press are calling me 'anti-defence' and in others, anti-British, the pillocks. This dossier of yours, Chris, changes everything. No way can I sweep the information it contains under the carpet, no matter what newspapers choose to call me.'

'So, you'll help us?'

'Have any of the documents been published?'

'I tried in one national newspaper,' Chris said, 'but Dragon found out and issued an injunction.'

Spencer snorted. 'The nationals run scared at the slightest whiff of scandal, but I know others who'd bite our hands off for even a sniff of this. Even if they fail to be receptive, there are dozens of internet sites I could name who wouldn't bat an eyelid about publishing. However, I think the best course of action would be for me to take this straight to the floor of the House.'

'Is there a downside?' Matt asked. 'The documents were obtained following an illegal hack of Dragon's computer systems.'

'I know, and while newspapers can be gagged by court orders, Members of Parliament are protected by Parliamentary Privilege. This means I can say whatever I like on the floor of the House and I can't be prosecuted if it offends, is libellous, scandalous or defamatory.'

'Excellent.'

'The people it'll most annoy will be the Defence Secretary and his team as they are the main cheerleaders for Pulsar, plus any MPs and cabinet members who are or have been in receipt of Dragon's lavish hospitality. The Deputy Prime Minister recently voiced his support for the project and this makes me even more suspicious.'

His smile faded as a thought crossed his mind like a black cloud on a summer's day. 'The Prime Minister will be furious and blame me of trying to destroy our relationship with the US, rebuilt in the light of the Syria debacle. The press, of course, will enjoy a field day. If they don't accuse me with being a heretic and start a campaign to have me burned at the stake, I will be very surprised.'

The conversation had moved from the optimistic hue of earlier to the damn-near insurmountable. This was all reflected in Spencer's face, now looking like a man who was walking out to the gallows to be hanged.

'The whips will try to censure me, as will the deputy leader,' he said in a quiet voice, almost to himself. 'They might threaten to withdraw the whip, but would they go as far?'

Matt looked at Chris who shook his head.

'The odds seem stacked against you,' Matt said after a tense minute or two. 'We'd both like to thank you for listening. If you can let us have the names of the people you know in the media who might be receptive to an approach.'

'Hold on there, you two, don't lose heart, just give me a minute to think this through.' He walked to the window again and gazed at view.

Chris looked over and Matt shrugged. Spencer was either trying to think of a way of dropping them gently, or seeing if he could make it work without it kiboshing his career.

'It may look at the moment like overwhelming odds,' Spencer said, 'but this place can amaze you at times. Start the ball rolling with something like this and people you don't expect will leap out of the shadows and join your side. For this and the memory of Latif, I will help you; don't worry about it. After all, I didn't come into Parliament to ignore important issues or turn my back on corruption.'

'Excellent news,' Chris said. 'What happens now?'

'Until this information is in the public domain, I don't think we should meet here; there's too many people coming and going. Let me think. Yes, let's get together in a day or two at a flat I use nearby where I have a small office and can print some of this stuff out. In the meantime, there are a couple of people I need to speak with, to make sure when I get on to my feet, I'm not a lone voice.'

Matt shook his head. 'It doesn't work for us, Mr Spencer,' he said. 'People are out there looking for Chris as we speak. The longer we delay, the greater chance that they'll find him.'

'You're right, you're right, I'm not thinking straight, I do apologise. Okay, let's make a date for tomorrow night at my flat. I'll need to move a bit quicker, that's all. Let me give you the address.' He scribbled it down on a piece of House of Commons notepaper and handed it to over. 'How does around eight o'clock sound?'

Chapter 32

Rosie left the office at six-thirty and headed for the tube station. On days when she intended to go somewhere else, she would come in by car. On others, when she didn't need it, and to vary her movements, she took the train.

The civil unrest which plagued Northern Ireland in the 1970s and 80s taught the security services one major lesson, routine and habit could get you killed. Dozens of part- and full-time policemen and military personnel were killed during the so-called Troubles. This, because they drove to work at the same time every morning, took the same route they did the day before, and came back home at the same time every night. It presented a gift to terrorists intent on killing any member of the security forces irrespective of their sex, race or religion.

Targets for an HSA operation might include terrorist groups, criminal gangs or large organisations acting illegally. Dragon Technologies could now be added to that list. These groups were often well-funded with access to plenty of manpower and all manner of equipment and documents including cars, guns and false identification papers. Most were capable of targeting agents who were investigating them. Every day, Rosie examined the underside of her car for explosive devices, checked the street where she walked for spotters and followers and, on returning home, scanned the neighbourhood for strange cars or people.

Neither she nor Matt knew who had compromised the safe house. While Matt redeemed himself by stopping the two gunmen from killing Chris and Louise, she had to suffer the office banter and the wrath of the Director alone. Gill praised Matt for the professional way he had stopped an impending bloodbath, but spat venom, principally at her. By a process of elimination, it was easier to tail her back from Shepherd's Bush, than following Matt all the way back from Oxford.

The Director could be a hard man to cross. With the memory of an elephant, he could recall the finest detail of operations undertaken twenty years before, and therefore an indiscretion like this one would not easily be forgotten. On the plus side, he didn't hold grudges and balanced successes to failings. Like Napoleon, he liked his agents to be lucky. By this he didn't mean an ethereal attribute neither visible nor measurable, but the sort of luck someone created through their actions, helping them to succeed more times than thcy failed.

Surfacing from the underground at Liverpool Street Station, she headed towards the train platforms. Services to Harlow were a bit erratic at this time of the evening, some trains with a gap of only a few minutes between them and others, a gap of twenty-five minutes. One was about to leave in two minutes' time. She stepped aboard with seconds to spare. She took a seat, loosened her coat and pulled out her ringing phone.

'Hi Matt, how are you doing?'

'I'm good. Where are you?'

'On a train.'

'I wanted to give you an update, but I'll do most of the talking so you don't have to say much.'

'Fine.'

'I've just been to see Derek Spencer with Chris. We're now heading back to Windsor.'

'How did the meeting go? Did he believe Chris's story?'

'He believed him all right, but he can foresee plenty of problems ahead, like making him unpopular with the Prime Minister, and his party threatening to withdraw the whip.'

'Sounds painful.'

'It's quite a serious step, so I'm told. It could mean Spencer is no longer considered part of the Conservative Party. At the next election, his party would field an official candidate in opposition to him.'

'It does sound serious. Is it likely?'

'He thinks he'll be able to drum up enough support from other MPs and newspapers which will create a big enough stink to prevent the Government from taking any action against him.'

'Looking good. When's the big reveal set to happen?'

'We're meeting Spencer tomorrow night at his flat and by then he expects to have a better idea how it's all going to play out.'

'Excellent work, Matt. I think I can see an end in sight.'

'If this comes off, I can too. After receiving so much flak, Dragon will be forced to back off from targeting Chris and Louise, and give us space to pursue the people behind the deaths of Chris's family and Latif Artha.'

'Let's hope it does. Are you in the office tomorrow?'

'I need to be in London around eight in the evening to meet Derek. I might drop by some time in the afternoon.'

'Call me a sceptic but I'll believe it when I see it. Bye Matt.'

Ten minutes later, the train arrived at Harlow Town station. She got off and walked towards the multi-storey car park. She stepped aside to allow the throng of people travelling the same way to pass, and rummaged through her bag for her car keys. In fact, her car keys were in her jacket pocket. She did it to find out if the tall guy in the black coat, a man she caught looking at her on the train, was heading her way. He was. She shut her bag and walked towards her car at a brisker pace than before. When she reached the second floor, she ducked into a corner and waited.

At this hour of the evening, the door to any floor in the car park didn't stay shut for more than ten seconds. By the time it had opened and closed another three times, the tall man came through. He walked down the aisle of cars, but stopped. He looked around, as if trying to remember where he'd parked his car, or perhaps searching for her.

She waited, conscious of the myriad of CCTV cameras dotted all over the car park. At this moment, the camera controller would be calling his boss to tell him about the strange woman lurking in the corner on floor two. The tall man set off as if he'd spotted his car, but his bird-like mannerism of looking left and right at regular intervals was pushing her suspicions-meter into the red zone.

The ramp to lower floors was on the side where her car was parked. After allowing the guy time to reach his car, she headed for her own, safe in the knowledge she would be out of the car park before him.

Outside, she joined Edinburgh Way and turned at the first roundabout towards town. No one followed her out, but now, barrelling along a busy urban road, it became harder to tell. Stopping at the roundabout beside Harlow LeisureZone, she spotted the face of the man from the car park in a car lying two cars behind.

She didn't panic, but waited until a couple of cars that were in the process of negotiating the roundabout on her right-hand side came closer. She zipped out in front of them, eliciting loud blasts from several horns, and proceeded to keep her foot on the gas all along the next section of carriageway.

This time, the roundabout wasn't busy, just as well as she had no intention of stopping. The remaining part of her journey home was along single carriageway roads. They provided excellent cover during the day, busy with shoppers, delivery vans and school buses, and would put any number of vehicles between her and her follower, but not at this time of the evening. Realising if she continued on her course, he would soon catch her up, she took a sharp left into the car park at the Tesco Superstore. She slotted her Seat into the first space she came across among the hundreds of anonymous cars belonging to late evening shoppers and waited with the engine running.

She didn't fear being approached by her pursuer or being cornered in a dead-end, of which Harlow had many. She was armed and wouldn't give up without a fight. No, her one dread was revealing the address of her home and putting Andrew and her neighbours in danger. It didn't cross her mind that her behaviour was somehow irrational or paranoid. In all their training, they were taught to trust their instincts. If a situation didn't feel right, they didn't waste time debating the issue. Such a delay could be the difference between being killed and walking away unscathed.

She waited ten minutes before getting out of the car. She stood on the door sill and panned the car park, looking around for her pursuer's blue Vauxhall. His car had looked new and clean, most likely a hire. It would stand out against all the silver saloons cruising the vast car park, looking for a space, as many were streaked in mud and grit from recent heavy rains. She waited another five minutes before heading out.

She turned into Church Langley and headed towards her house. Cruising past her driveway at low speed, she looked for cars she didn't recognise and any strangers hanging around. Seeing nothing that looked out of place, she turned back, drove into her driveway and locked the car in the garage.

When she walked into the house, she would pour herself a glass of white wine from the fridge, take it upstairs and stand behind the curtain like a pervert spying on a good-looking neighbour across the road. She would not relax this evening until she was convinced no one had followed her.

Chapter 33

Derek Spencer picked up another document from the heap and started to read. A few minutes later, he placed it on a second, smaller pile, replete with red pen marks. He used them to highlight a word or phrase, and with notes in the margin to improve clarification and to remind him of a key point. It was methodical and tiring work but the Member of Parliament would take all night if he needed to.

Many MPs and cabinet ministers didn't bother with this sort of slog and instead, left it to an unpaid interns or budding students of politics. When they walked into the Commons chamber, they weren't weighed-down with a large and untidy pile of papers. All they brought with them was a one-page summary with some key points highlighted, presenting a more succinct version for the benefit of the television cameras.

However, with such explosive material, it was important for him to be master of his brief. The floor of the House of Commons could be a bear-pit of a place, and if not armed, loaded and cocked, his opponents would find a chink in his defences. Then, they would exploit it to the point of derision.

He moved the papers from his lap to the floor, walked into the kitchen and switched on the coffee machine. He had known the flat's owner, David Fisher, since school, when David was the star of the rugby team and reputed to have bedded most of the female sixth form. David's job as export manager for a household goods company took him all over the world, and he liked to leave his Pimlico flat occupied while he was away. In truth, he also enjoyed having an MP as a house guest. It gave him something to boast about to his colleagues at work, making them believe he had the inside track.

While waiting for the coffee to brew, his mind returned to the Dragon documents left by Chris Anderson and Matt Flynn over an hour before. It wasn't unusual for defence companies to pull out all the stops at the launch of a new product, as military equipment was expensive and many were wedded to their existing set-up. If their over-enthusiastic trough-feeding had stopped at the odd holiday and a few coke-fuelled parties, it would not have bothered anyone, save a few crusading newspapers and some aspiring politicians.

The political heat it would create could be smoothed over by the Prime Minister's silver-tongued spin-doctor, following the resignation of one or two fall-guys, but Dragon didn't stop there. What could not be overlooked, apologised, or never excused was the murder of Chris Anderson's family and Derek's good friend, Latif Artha.

He'd first met Latif when attending a demonstration of the weapon system fitted to the new Lockheed Martin F35. Soon after, they became best friends and not so long after that, lovers. He didn't grieve in public when Latif died in a car wreck, as even though his party leader publicly supported gays, he didn't promote or confide in any colleagues who were.

He knew now from copies of emails sent between Jack Dawson, head of Corporate Security at Dragon in Houston and Daniel Leppo, his second-in-command, that Latif didn't die as a result of a lapse of concentration or an animal running across his path. A hit-and-run driver forced him off the road and into a quarry. It wasn't an accident as claimed by the police, but a deliberate act to silence a vocal opponent of Dragon's flagship product.

His emotions had started to waver when talking to Matt and Chris earlier this evening, but he reminded himself of the support promised in the House tomorrow. It would include several MPs from his own party and many more in the Opposition, keen to be involved in the Government's embarrassment and perhaps be responsible for the sacking of a minister or two.

He returned to his seat with his cup of coffee and his main weakness at the moment, a Tunnock's Caramel Wafer, a taste first developed on a trip to Scotland to visit the Faslane nuclear submarine base. He picked up an A4 pad and began to draft the speech he intended to deliver tomorrow during a defence debate. He had received word from the Speaker of the House that if he indicated he wanted to speak, he would be allowed to do so.

He wrote: 'Honourable members, I'm afraid the discussion we have listened to in this house about the new Pulsar Helicopter, fine aircraft that it is, should no longer be about its cost or efficacy at selecting targets and eliminating enemies. It needs to be about the murderous dealings of its manufacturer, Dragon Technologies.' Loud heckling would come from the Tory benches, mainly those, he suspected, in receipt of the Dragon largesse, but he would plough on regardless. 'I now have in my possession documents which clearly show how Dragon has bribed Ministry of Defence officials, cabinet ministers and MPs. If that wasn't enough, they have tried to silence anyone who voiced dissent or with the temerity to stand against them. This includes,' and here he would raise his voice, 'the murder of Chris Anderson's family in a so-called balloon accident, and a weapons specialist at QuinTec, Latif Artha, in a so-called car accident.'

He would pause there as the House would be in uproar, even if only quarter full. His choice of words now would be crucial as they would be shouted over a wall of noise and a sea of angry faces, so only one or two words would be audible.

After completing and editing the speech, he would draft a summary statement which would be memorised and handed out to the press. He hoped to reveal much of its content in subsequent sound bites during television interviews, so he could present a consistent story, leading to more clarity in the morning editions.

The click of the outside door opening could be heard over the Nora Jones CD playing quietly in the background. He looked at the clock, too early for David to return from the opera. In fact, lousy evening or not, David would never pass up the chance to stay the night at his girlfriend's place, the randy sod.

The lounge door opened, but the chiselled face of his charming friend didn't appear. Instead, two men he had never seen before walked in. Both looked stocky with short hair, dressed in black, and not resembling the Polish cleaner or the handyman David employed to do odd jobs.

'Who the hell are you? What are you doing in my house? I'm going to call—'

Before he could finish, a punch smacked him on the side of the head. It knocked him out of the chair and on to the floor. He lay there for several seconds, his brain fuzzy and his vision seeing double.

'They're not here,' one of them said.

'Search the other rooms,' said the guy standing close to him.

Firm hands gripped Spencer's cardigan and hauled him to his feet. The face before him was black, clean-shaven, but with a pock-marked face. His breath smelled of cigarettes. He held a handful of Spencer's shirt collar and squeezed it tighter, knocking the air out of his windpipe and making him gasp.

'Where are they?'

He was choking and could barely speak. 'Where are...who?'

The blow to the side of his face felt as heavy as a rowing oar. 'Don't fuck with me buddy. The people who were here earlier; where are they?'

The pain in his head throbbed like a disco strobe light, making it hard to concentrate. His eyes couldn't focus, his vision like looking through a child's kaleidoscope.

'They're gone.'

'Where?'

'I don't know. I didn't ask them, and they didn't say.'

'What did you talk to them about?'

'Something...something I'm doing for them in Parliament.'

A slap this time.

'What sort of stuff?'

The American noticed the papers lying on the floor. He let him go, picked up a sheaf and flicked through them. 'What the fuck's this?'

He wanted to say, 'can't you read' but he didn't want to be punched again.

'Is this what you talked to them about?'

He said nothing, trying not to incriminate Matt and Chris. The man grabbed his collar again and tightened it until he felt like he was going to black out.

'Yes,' he gasped.

He heard the other guy enter the room. 'The rooms are clear; no sign of the targets.'

'Shit! Did you check the closets and the bathroom?'

'What do you take me for, a fuckwit? Of course I did.'

'Damn it. He told us they'd be here.'

'What do we do now?'

'Take a look at this,' he said handing over the papers in his hand to the other guy.

'This is it,' his companion said after a few moments. 'This is the stuff the client said he's looking for.'

'Yeah, he figured the targets he was meeting would give this bozo something,' the guy holding Spencer said, 'but it's way more than he thought.'

He let Spencer go and the MP slumped into the chair, his energy and fight all but done. The two men talked in animated voices, but he couldn't hear a word over the incessant ringing in his ears, the result of the head punches and slaps.

Minutes later, his questioner reached into his pocket and pulled out a gun and fitted a silencer. Before Spencer could raise himself up and make an attempt to escape, the gunman turned and pointed the weapon at his head.

Chapter 34

He extracted his Homeland Security Agency ID and presented it to the young copper standing at the door of Derek Spencer's flat in Pimlico. The copper gave Matt and Rosie a good look over before indicating they could go through. They climbed the stairs, walked into the open apartment and approached the middle-aged man hunkered down beside the pathologist.

Matt learned of Derek's death following a phone call from a member of HSA's administrative staff. David Fisher, the apartment's owner and Derek's flatmate, discovered the body of the MP early this morning. Fisher had been staying at the house of a girlfriend the previous night and only returned home for a change of clothes. Despite possessing a sound alibi, Fisher would be questioned by the relentless police investigation and considered a suspect until proved otherwise.

Matt's first reaction had been one of rage, selfish perhaps at losing their last genuine hope of removing the threat to Chris and Louise. When the anger subsided, he felt sad that their involvement had caused his death. He didn't know Derek well, but from his dealings with him and Sir Raymond Deacon, he no longer regarded all politicians as career-centred money grabbers, as popularised in the press. He knew many of them to be genuinely interested in bettering the lives of their constituents. This involved working unsociable hours and tackling difficult jobs to bring many improvements to constituents' circumstances, often without their contribution being recognised.

'Detective Inspector Blackstone?' Matt Flynn asked.

'Who wants to know?' a large bulk said without turning around.

'Matt Flynn and Rosie Fox, HSA.'

The man turned and looked them up and down. A well-worn, jowly face, its centrepiece a rosette nose reflecting a regular pub habit, or a man who couldn't stand the cold. The top of his head was as threadbare as an old sofa with thin strands of grey hair doing their best to hide a flaky scalp. He got to his feet in what looked like a painful movement, his knees cracking as he did so. He stretched as if recently waking up.

'Why the hell are you HSA folks taking an interest in my case?'

'It's not every day a Member of Parliament is murdered,' Matt said.

Blackstone scratched his head, flakes of dandruff falling on to his jacket collar. 'Thank Christ for that or I'd been getting my balls chewed off every hour for not catching the people responsible. Excuse my French,' he said nodding at Rosie.

'I'm used to worse,' she said.

'Apart from the late Derek Spencer being an MP,' he said through narrowed eye slits, 'why are you guys here?'

'We've been tracking a Serbian gunman who arrived in the UK a couple of weeks ago. It's led us here.' It was an old line, but vague enough not to give anything away.

'How's your gunman connected to this?' the DI asked, nodding at the body of Derek Spencer. 'Is he the guy I should be looking for?'

Matt shook his head. 'It wasn't him. He's at this moment in the custody of Interpol.'

'And here was me thinking you nice people from HSA were going to give me something for a change.'

'Sorry, Detective Inspector, not today.'

'How does your gunman connect to our victim?' Blackstone said.

'We're not sure yet. Derek was doing some research for us.'

'So, you know the victim?'

'I wouldn't say we know him, but we've met him.'

Blackstone's eyes narrowed. 'When did you last see him?'

'A few days back, we had a meeting with him at his office in the House of Commons.'

Matt's lie skated over thin ice. He and Chris had been at Spencer's house the previous night and their prints would still be on the glasses in the kitchen. That is, if Spencer hadn't had the time to wash them up before being killed. As one of the last people to see the MP alive, Matt could easily be spending the next six hours in a stuffy interview room if he admitted as much.

Blackstone nodded. A simple check with Spencer's secretary would confirm the House of Commons meeting. Matt hoped Spencer didn't also put yesterday evening's get together in the diary.

'When was Mr Spencer killed?' Matt asked, keen to move onto the front foot.

'Forensics estimate the time of death any time between the hours of nine and midnight last night.'

'How did he die?'

'Shot in the head.'

'One or two bullets?'

'Two.'

'Any witnesses.'

'Not a dickey. Now it's up to the forensics boys, and I'm keeping them here until they find something. I can't tell you much more.'

'Thank you, Detective Inspector. Do you mind if we take a look around?'

He looked at both of them with a suspicious stare, the jaundiced eye of a seasoned veteran. 'Be my guest, but don't touch anything.'

'Sure thing.'

'Hang on. You got a card? I may need to speak to you at some point.'

Matt handed Blackstone his contact details. He followed the DI and took a closer look at the body of Derek Spencer. It was currently being photographed by the police photographer as the pathologist gave his afternoon's work a preliminary examination.

Spencer died from a double-tap, Special Forces parlance for two shots to the head. The first shot to kill the victim, the second to ensure he was dead. Was this a sign of Dragon upping the ante by employing Special Forces personnel after two of Ivan Mander's villains attacked the safe house and failed? When added to Rosie's scare the previous night, it suggested as much.

The room looked tidy with no signs of a struggle, the only indication of anything untoward happening were the bloodstains on the wood block floor and the inert figure of Derek Spencer MP. Matt knew from talking to Derek last night that after they left, he intended reading the documents given to him by Chris. Looking around, he couldn't see any trace of the documents now.

Knowing how forensic investigations worked, if a SOCO team came across the papers, and why wouldn't they, lying in a heap on the floor or in the out-tray of Derek's printer in the corner, they would have bagged them. He couldn't see any bags and it was unlikely they would have taken them out to the van yet. Instead, they would have joined the small number of bin bags sitting in the hall.

It would be interesting to read Blackstone's report about the murder and find out what he believed Derek Spencer was doing in his chair before he was shot. The absence of paperwork and anything else, including a television or radio, suggested he was drinking a cup of coffee while staring at the wall. He didn't think an experienced DI like Blackstone would dare write something so stupid and suffer the resultant ridicule.

He left Rosie in the lounge and walked into the kitchen. With the majority of the police activity taking place in the lounge, the forensic team hadn't reached the kitchen as yet. Sitting on the worktop in the company of a couple of dirty plates and mugs, were three glasses: the whisky drunk by Spencer before he and Chris arrived, the beer given to Chris, and the water to Matt. Picking up his water glass, he gave it a quick wipe with a paper handkerchief. He reached for Chris's beer glass and did the same. Just when he was replacing it on the worktop, a voice behind him said, 'What the hell are you doing in here?'

Matt turned to see a white-suited SOCO standing there. It was a long, narrow kitchen and it was possible with Matt's back turned he'd obscured the SOCO's view of his illegal tampering of the evidence. The handkerchief disappeared into his pocket.

'Matt Flynn, Homeland Security,' he said turning. 'Detective Inspector Blackstone said it was all right for me and my colleague to take a look around the crime scene.'

'Ah, right. If Blackstone says it's okay, who am I to argue? You work for HSA eh? I always fancied moving there. What's it like?'

He was aged mid-thirties but with boyish enthusiasm etched on his rotund face, his mind no-doubt filled with images of guns, explosions and handsome agents karate-chopping the enemy. He'd probably been taken in by what the Director called the 'Bourne Effect,' in reference to the Robert Ludlum books and Matt Damon movies about a rogue secret agent. To say so in an interview would be enough for the interviewer to terminate the discussion and refuse the candidate further consideration. They didn't want anyone joining the organisation glorifying the role they performed.

'I'm not sure the forensics side would be much different from what you do with the police. A dead body is a dead body.'

'Yeah, but we also have to deal with all the mundane stuff as well, the wife skewered with a carving knife by her husband after his coffee was served cold, or the builder falling off a ladder into a cement mixer. You guys cut out all the boring crap and only work on the shootings and high-profile cases, the interesting stuff that gets splashed all over the newspapers.'

'It's not always so interesting, I assure you.'

'Shit, I'm being called, I better get back. Hey, it's been good talking to you, it might encourage me to stick in that application.' He made to walk away. 'One last thing,' he said, a sly smirk on his face, 'don't let me catch you touching anything.'

Chapter 35

Detective Inspector Emma Davis stood on the windswept headland. Her binoculars were pointing out towards the Irish Sea in front of her, but she couldn't see a thing. This wasn't quite true, she could see the moon and a couple of stars peeking through the thick clouds, the white-topped waves of the water, whipped up by a stiff breeze. What didn't appear in her vision were ship lights, in particular, the lights of the *Tudor Rose*, a thirty-five-foot single keel yacht making its way across the Atlantic from the Caribbean.

The Metropolitan Police hadn't all of a sudden taken an interest in trans-Atlantic shipping, but for many months Emma's team had been following the career of London drug dealer Simon Wood. Starting small about five years back, they believed he was behind a complex web of small-time dealers and now running an organisation turning over six figures a week. Word on the street suggested he was making a bid for the big-time by importing an industrial quantity of his new drug of choice, cocaine, but Emma's team had no idea where, when or how.

A breakthrough came when intel from the French authorities informed them of a yacht spotted off the coast of Guyana, engaging in a rendezvous with a freighter from Turkey. The yacht was now heading towards the UK. This was one of many pieces of intel arriving into the offices of the drug unit every day. If not for the diligence of Detective Constable Lorna Mayhew, no one would be aware that Simon Wood owned the yacht in question, the *Tudor Rose*.

Emma walked back to the car feeling cold and miserable. She knew Jacko would have the engine on and the heater running full blast. He couldn't stand the cold.

'Christ, it's bitter out there,' she said climbing inside.

'Tell me about it. I used to come down here when I was a kid; scarred me for life.'

'You used to come here? Where are we near, Portreath?'

'Not exactly this place: south Cornwall.'

'How do you mean it scarred you for life? Did you do a Keith Richards and fall out of a tree or something?'

'I was speaking metaphorically, if you must know. As a kid, I had to endure walks along the cliffs with a bloody gale blowing and being forced to go into the water and freeze my balls off.'

'I'd imagine a week or two in the fresh air and the clean living of the countryside would be a godsend to a boy from a council estate in East London.'

'Don't get me wrong. I liked coming here but I hated staying with my grandmother. She was eighty something with spindly hands and a powdered, white face making her look like a vampire.' He shivered. 'The vision still gives me nightmares.'

'Is there any coffee left in the flask?'

'Plenty. I haven't touched it as I'm drinking this,' he said, holding up a can of Coke.

'Rots your teeth and makes you fat.'

'Coffee gives you high blood pressure or summat, so touché to you.'

She poured a cup and looked out of the window. There wasn't much activity out on the ocean, and the same could be said for the assembled police presence lined up on the grass. It consisted of numerous marked and unmarked police cars and vans belonging to Devon and Cornwall's finest, all assembled at great expense to give Mr Wood and his accomplices a warm welcome home.

The longer this went on, the deeper a feeling of dread pervaded her mood, like a sea mist shrouding the cove in the cliffs below. Did Wood somehow feed them false information and leave them at the wrong cove, proving yet again they could never catch him with dirt on his hands?

Due to lack of availability, the locals couldn't provide a helicopter to track the yacht's progress. Instead, a radio bod was monitoring transmissions between the yacht and their accomplices who were located somewhere along the coast. In any case, she thought, consoling herself, a helicopter would alert the yacht to the police presence and might force them to change course and dock at some other cove. If the yacht headed back out to sea, the Royal Navy patrol ship, Sir Ivanhoe, taking part in NATO manoeuvres in the Irish Sea, would be alerted. Then, the Jack Tars on board could claim all the credit without doing any of the work.

'Christ,' Jacko said, 'how long does it take?'

'How long does what take?'

'To sail into Cornwall from the Caribbean.'

'I dunno. The ETA was 2:30. What time's it now?' She looked at her watch, '3:15. They're only three quarters of an hour late. Maybe they're finding the sea a bit rough and not making good progress.'

'Or maybe it's a change of plan, and they're heading round the coast to Dorset.'

'It's not like you to be so pessimistic.'

'Yeah, but I've got better things to do with my time than to sit here in this bloody car. No offence Emma, but I'd rather be clubbing or sleeping.'

'So would I, but—'

The radio sparked into life. Emma grabbed it and hit the 'Receive' button.

'All cars. All cars. Transmission received from *Tudor Rose*. They are docking at Mullion Cove, repeat Mullion Cove. Invoking Plan B. Alpha One and Alpha Two in lead, proceed to Mullion Cove ...'

'Action at last,' Jacko said as he eased the car away from the grassy slope back to the tarmac road. They set off in pursuit of the other police vehicles.

The drive to Mullion Cove took less than forty minutes. The convoy had made rapid progress on empty roads devoid of tourist caravans, delivery vans, milk tankers, there to hinder such activity during daylight hours.

The radio operator didn't tell the whole story in her transmission and was forced to correct it later.

Yes, they were to drive to Mullion Cove, but their drug smugglers didn't fancy docking in a busy tourist spot and waking up those nearby in tents and caravans. Instead, they selected a secluded cove about two hundred metres further up the coast, a place where a vehicle could drive on to the beach. According to a police spotter, he could see a 4x4 parked there, no doubt to await the arrival of the yacht.

By the time they arrived there, the yacht had already docked. The curved shape of the shoreline gave the large police party, now on foot, an adequate level of cover as they made their approach along the beach towards the illicit late-night activity. Superintendent Walden, the lead copper from Devon and Cornwall Police, decided to wait until the merchandise was being unloaded before giving the 'Go' order. He also deployed two shooters in the rocks and dunes to stop anyone trying to a make a run for it.

The cold and fatigue Emma felt faded away as they hurried towards the yacht, support vehicles as yet unseen coming up behind them. The large group of officers refrained from shouting or rattling their batons. In any case, any noise they did make was drowned out by the crashing of the waves. The first cops arrived almost within touching distance of the Range Rover before being spotted. It was fisticuffs at close quarters, but the weight of numbers and drawn batons soon overwhelmed the two men from the Range Rover, waiting there to receive the contraband.

A guy on the docked yacht appeared on deck with a gun and started firing, one bullet hitting the windscreen of the car, spidering the glass. They all ducked down until they heard another shot being fired from the police lines. When someone shouted the all-clear, she looked out from her position behind the car and saw the man with the gun lying on the deck clutching his shoulder.

'Hands in the air, all those aboard the *Tudor Rose!*' Superintendent Walden bellowed. 'You are outnumbered and we are armed!'

One by one the crew from the yacht came up from below deck and stood facing them with their hands in the air. Emma and Jacko, only observers for this Devon and Cornwall operation, watched as officers climbed on board and handcuffed them. A medic attended to the injured man.

Standing close to the car while all the activity was taking place on the yacht gave Emma a chance to have a look at the cargo already unloaded. She counted five bags weighing three or four kilos each stacked in the boot. It was impossible to be certain without opening one and having it tested, but she would bet her pension the white powder inside couldn't be used to sweeten her coffee.

'Looks like there's a fantastic haul aboard the boat, if this is what they unloaded in only a few minutes,' Jacko beside her said.

'Oh, I think so,' she said smiling. She felt pleased to be involved in capturing such a large consignment of dope. Not only would it stop many lives being ruined, but it avoided her and Jacko looking like prats. This was a sizeable group of cynical coppers, all ready to take the piss, if the crew aboard turned out to be no more than a large family on a round-the-world voyage.

'Shall we move in a bit closer and find out if our man is one of the crew?'

'Make my night if he is.'

They walked towards the yacht, the crew sitting on the deck, their hands behind their backs. With the lighting gear not yet rigged, it was difficult to distinguish faces. It was also hard for them to get nearer with all the big coppers standing around looking relaxed and enjoying a smoke, now the only danger they faced was tax on their overtime.

'Inspector Davis, Sergeant Harris, where are you?' Superintendent Walden shouted.

'Over here,' Jacko replied.

'Come up here, if you please.'

They pushed their way through idling coppers and others with their jackets off, links in a human chain unloading the bags of cargo from the yacht. They walked over the gangway where the Superintendent shook their hands with unexpected vigour. 'This is a huge find we've got here, Inspector Davis, the largest in this part of the country for many years. I offer my thanks to you and your colleagues for bringing it to our attention.'

'Thank you, Superintendent,' she said. I hope you receive the promotion you're hankering for, she thought. 'Do you mind if we take a look at the crew?'

'I'm not sure your man's aboard. I didn't recognise him among those we handcuffed.'

'I'd like to make sure.'

'Be my guest. They won't bite, they're all handcuffed.'

'Thank you.'

She walked towards the bow, the crew sitting on the deck under the watchful eye of a young copper. She looked along the faces, weather-beaten and bearded, but if they intended this to be some form of disguise, she could see through it.

'Hello Simon,' she said to a scruffy man wearing jeans and an Antigua-inscribed t-shirt.

'Hello Emma.'

'Detective Inspector Davis to you, Wood.'

'Oops, sorry. A couple of weeks aboard a boat with these miscreants and my manners go out of the window, or porthole I should say.'

'You'll have a long time to work on your behaviour where you're going. Courts take a dim view of big-scale importing like this.'

'Don't I know it? Lean closer.'

She did as he asked, believing him to be above the usual druggie tactics of biting or spitting. Perhaps he wanted to broker a deal by implicating his shipmates.

'Before I get back to London,' he said, 'slip me your bank details and I'll drop a million into your account.'

She straightened up. 'Bribery to add to the drug shipment charges? I would advise you to stop digging a deeper hole than you're in.'

'It's not a crime if you accept my kind offer, is it?'

'You're wasting your breath, Wood.' She walked away.

'C'mon detective, you know it makes sense. Set you up for life it would.'

She met Jacko on the deck. 'Let's go, Jacko, and get some sleep, someone back there is polluting the air.'

'You should take a look at the stack of dope down below,' he said, 'must be another thirty or forty bags.'

'Quite a haul, then?'

'Amazing.'

They crossed the gangway to the shore, getting strange looks from the assembled coppers, no doubt because they didn't get invited up on deck by their boss.

'Inspector Davis!'

Walking past the side of the yacht and glancing across, she saw Wood leaning out of the handcuffed group, looking at her.

'Say you'll reconsider.'

'Get lost Wood. There's nothing you could offer me that I want. You're going down, end of. Get used to it.'

'You fucking bitch, you don't know who you're messing with. Nobody, repeat, nobody says 'no' to me, you hear? Even if they put me inside, don't you worry, your days are numbered. You're dead, Davis.'

Chapter 36

Matt walked into HSA's London offices and headed for a spare desk. For once, he felt pleased to be there. At home, Emma was doing his head in, buoycd one minute with the capture of Simon Wood, depressed the next at something else gone awry.

The work she did could be stressful, even in days when they didn't draw a weapon and shoot a drug dealer. He never wanted her to move to the unit in the first place as he knew a guy who worked there for about five years and quit after a colleague was killed. His nerves were shattered, and he couldn't hold down another job. The last Matt heard, he was surviving on benefits, his wife and kids living elsewhere with another man.

Rosie appeared at his shoulder.

'Morning Matt. I take it you're here for our ten o'clock with Gill?'

'Yeah, for once I'd rather be here getting a bollocking from Gill than sitting at home receiving an ear-bashing from Emma. It's a strange world, eh?'

'I don't dare ask. You may or may not receive a bollocking, but whatever he hears from us will have a bearing on how his meeting will go with the PM later this morning.'

'No pressure then.'

'It's not looking good if the statement the PM made last night is anything to go by. He looked angry on the ten o'clock news.'

'Did he say anything about the murder investigation? Have they got any leads?'

'I saw DI Blackstone on Sky News this morning. He said they believed the killing had all the hallmarks of a professional job. Looking at HOLMES this morning, I don't see much follow-up going on with forensics.'

HOLMES2, the Home Office Large Major Enquiry System, was used by all UK police forces during large and complex investigations. A dedicated operator assigned to the team keyed into the system all data, reports, sightings, witness accounts and anything else generated by the investigation team. Detectives are then able to find out what others in the team are doing, search for connections to a lead, and combining their skill and experience with the acquired knowledge of the system, identify new lines of enquiry.

'Which means the SOCOs didn't pick up much,' Matt said. 'Damn. It would be good to get a lead or two. Any mention of the glasses in the kitchen?'

'As you would expect, they were sent for analysis with everything else. Will they assume Derek Spencer liked to mix his drinks? I mean, the evidence suggests he started off with beer and a whisky chaser, followed a glass of water and finished up with coffee. Or will they think he entertained guests?'

'I think you'd enjoy it if I got banged up as a suspect.'

'How can you say such a thing?'

'When we were at Spencer's flat, I didn't spot any cameras in his building or the street outside. If Blackstone thinks we're a lead worth pursuing, he'll hit a brick wall.'

'You hope.'

'I'm not quaking in my boots, if that's what you think. I didn't kill him and neither did Chris, but you know as well as me the big sausage machine of a police murder investigation has to keep turning. If they pull us in for questioning, it could be hours or even days before we're cleared.'

'At least.'

'I suppose if the worst came to the worst, the Director would bale me out.'

She shook her head. 'He won't interfere in a major police investigation.'

'Not even if it involves one of his agents?'

She nodded. 'He says it would destroy the trust we've built with them. I must say I agree.'

'Talking of Gill, here he comes.'

'Fox, Flynn, in my office now,' the Director boomed as he strode past.

Matt, with some reluctance, got out of his chair and followed Rosie. On entering Gill's office, he closed the door. The seating in the outer office worked on a hot-desk policy. Matt and other agents who didn't come into the building often, would take any free desk while someone like Sikander Khosa, their key researcher who came in every day, tended to sit in the same place.

Gill's office, on the other hand, radiated the confidence and opulence of a company chairman, with a large desk, bookcase, settee and expansive views over central London. However, the boss didn't mind working beside the troops, something he did during the renovation and redecoration of his office. In doing so, he clearly missed the opportunity to vent some pent-up frustration as he was a dedicated door slammer.

'I spoke on the phone to the Prime Minister, and to that little prick he calls a deputy this morning, and they are not happy bunnies. The PM is accusing us of being responsible for the death of one of his MPs and said in no uncertain terms, if I can't control rogue elements in this organisation, he will.'

Matt wanted to say something but knew it was better to wait until Gill instructed him to speak. Templeton McGill, a decorated, former Major in the Royal Marines and once an agent and later a senior strategist with MI6, didn't like being interrupted when angry. He knew more about world politics and the way governments worked than anyone else in their organisation, so anything Matt or Rosie could say at this moment wouldn't add to it.

'I don't believe there are any rogue elements in this organisation. Do you, Matt?'

'No, I don't.'

'Can you look at the behaviour of both of you and tell me it is beyond reproach?'

'First up,' Matt said, 'I don't understand how Dragon knew we were meeting Derek Spencer. I checked to ensure we weren't followed.'

'Parliament is like the common room of a private school, everyone latching on to the latest rumour or tittle-tattle and passing it on to anyone who'll listen. All to prove that they have their fingers on the pulse. Those in the pay of Dragon would be on the phone to them as soon as word got out.'

Matt groaned. 'I should have seen this coming. Spencer told us he was planning to talk to some MPs, trying to drum up support for his speech.'

'Poor guy, he was obviously unaware, as we all are, of Dragon's considerable reach.'

'The second thing bothering me,' Matt said, 'is how did they put together a hit team at short notice?'

'What, you're suggesting we send them a bouquet of flowers for doing such an excellent job?'

In another situation he would have laughed but the Director's stony face didn't encourage it.

'No, but it makes me think the team were already in place. Spencer's been a thorn in Dragon's side for months and perhaps a few days back, they decided it was time to silence him. When they found out we'd be there as well, they probably brought their plans forward, as not only would they catch Chris, they could also frame him for Spencer's murder.'

Rosie glanced over at Matt. She didn't need to say anything or change the expression on her face, but he knew the question on her lips: *Where the hell did this little gem spring from?*

'Damn, I think you're right,' Gill said. 'I should have said it to the PM and stopped the sneering comments of his deputy dead in their tracks. In my experience, it doesn't take long to brief an attack team, but finding and bringing together the right men can take days even in a large outfit like a battalion.'

The Director steepled his fingers, his deep thinking pose. 'Right,' he said, a few moments later, 'we can put the blame game out of the way. I'm seeing the Prime Minister after this meeting and instead of going in there with my tail between my legs, I can present him with a valid explanation. Good, it should keep Number 10 quiet for a few days at least. Now, how do we stop Dragon?'

'If the Met can't find Spencer's killers, we're out of leads.'

'Rosie?'

'I agree with Matt. Derek Spencer was in some ways a last resort, although he did say he knew the names of several newspapers that would be happy to publish Chris's material, but their names died with him.'

'Maybe his secretary will know,' Matt said.

'It's one approach,' Gill said, 'but don't forget, all along Dragon have been one step ahead of us and if we implicate her, they might kill her too.'

'What's on your mind?' Matt said.

'Are you sure of your ground? You're convinced Dragon brought down the Anderson hot-air balloon, killed Latif Artha and now, Derek Spencer?'

'As sure as I'll ever be without concrete evidence. It's the only thing connecting all the victims.'

'I agree,' Rosie said. 'Why else would they remove the documents Spencer was reading when he was killed, unless they knew their content? They were printouts of the material Chris downloaded from Dragon's computers, no use to anyone but them.'

'As ever, the voice of reason, Rosie,' Gill said, smiling for the first time. 'It convinces me.' He leaned forward and looked intently at each of them in turn, a vulture trying to decide which one to eat first.

'We've reached this point by reacting to what Dragon and their confederates have done. Am I right?'

They both nodded.

'It is in no way a criticism of your performance, not only have you prevented any harm coming to Chris and Louise, but you've also captured one of their abduction team. Now, I think it's time to take the fight to them.'

Matt smiled. He'd hoped the Director would say something like this. 'What do you propose?'

'At the moment, we don't know much about who in the Dragon business is orchestrating this. I'm sure you'll agree with me, we'll get nowhere by kicking in the door to their offices with all guns blazing.'

'You're right,' Rosie said.

'This is a deficiency we must now address. The number and extent of their attacks suggests to me whoever is behind this is not in the US, but here in the UK.'

'We believe the head of International Security was sent here by the US company to recover the stolen documents.'

'Quite. We now need to become familiar with their organisation in this country, find out who the main players are, who they associate with, how they're being financed, and who's pulling the strings.'

Through the glass wall panel, Matt saw Sikander talking to someone and laughing. Matt suspected he wouldn't be so jolly when this lot landed on his desk.

'Once we've done this,' Gill continued, 'we'll make a move on the main players. Given they've shown no reservation about using lethal force, I don't think the Prime Minister can complain if we respond in kind.'

Chapter 37

Rosie left the car park at Harlow Town railway station and drove towards home. The Director had been like a bull in a china shop at the start of their meeting earlier today, and would have continued if he believed they were in any way responsible for Derek Spencer's death. Initially, she suspected it to be the fault of Matt for not being aware that a Dragon team were tailing him.

The more she thought about what Matt had said to Gill in the meeting, the more she reckoned he was right. No way could Dragon rustle up a couple of hitmen in the time between Matt and Chris meeting Spencer at the House of Commons and the following night when they killed him.

Chris was staying at a secret location few people in HSA knew anything about. The obvious way for a Dragon team to find out where their target was holed up would be to put a tail on Matt by waiting outside HSA's offices in London until he emerged. However, Matt didn't go there often enough to establish a regular pattern, and in this age of openness and freedom of information, the address of HSA didn't appear in the public domain.

She knew logic like this didn't hold much water in the hallowed halls of Westminster. It was a place more interested in apportioning blame, and trying to shape how a story would look in subsequent news bulletins and newspapers, before moving on to the next big thing. To them it would probably sound like a hollowed-out excuse and Gill would take some flak, further demeaning HSA's credibility with its paymasters.

It hadn't been a good couple of months for the organisation. They'd been involved in a public spat with SIS - Secret Intelligence Service - after an HSA team led by Joseph Teller killed a top Syrian terrorist when they raided a house looking for someone else. SIS were trying to groom the terrorist as a potential informer and claimed HSA's actions set the programme back eight months.

In addition, even if the PM was not in receipt of Dragon's generosity, a number of his close coterie were. If word got out that HSA were investigating Dragon, Gill was sure those same cabinet ministers would be whispering in the PM's ear, calling for a review of HSA's operating mandate and the sacking of its Director. They needed a success story soon, but if the boss was depending on his saviour being the exposure of Dragon, he might have a long time to wait.

She turned into the Tesco superstore, the same place she had driven the day she thought she was being followed, and found a place to park. Before opening the car door, her phone rang.

'Hi Matt,' she said after she glanced at the phone screen.

'Hi Rosie, it's just a quick call. Where are you?'

'I'm at Tesco in Harlow. The cupboard's bare and I need to stock up.'

'You told me before, you didn't like shopping there.'

'I've thought about changing but it's so convenient, I can nip in on my way home from the station.'

'Do I hear words like routine and habit?'

'You're right, maybe I do need to go somewhere else, even just for operational reasons.'

'The only reason I mention it is I think Dragon have upped the ante. They didn't hesitate to shoot Derek Spencer and the other night, someone followed you. They know we're involved and I think they're targeting us. If they are, I don't think they would think twice about killing us. You, me, everyone connected with this case needs to be on their guard 24/7.'

'I feel the same. I will Matt, count on it.'

'See you tomorrow at eight, all right?'

'Any idea where we're going?'

'Yes, but I don't want say on the phone.'

'Fair enough. See you tomorrow.'

She pocketed her phone, got out the car and headed towards the supermarket entrance. From the trolley stack, she pulled one out and walked inside. What Rosie put in her trolley varied from week-to-week, depending on her work schedule and Andrew's flying commitments as he could be away from home for three or four days at a time. Her diary was clear of overnight engagements for much of the following week as they'd exhausted all their options at exposing

Dragon and now needed to change tack and take the fight to them.

Andrew was scheduled to be away for most of the following week as he was flying to the US on Monday. On long flights like this, the flight crew were allowed a three-day layover to rid themselves of jet lag and to relax, and he wouldn't be back home until late Friday. He was a slim guy, but she didn't know how he did it. His job involved sitting all day in the cockpit of an aircraft, and he liked eating stews, curries and pastries. There wouldn't be any of that stuff in her trolley tonight. Among the salad, hummus and low-fat milk designed to keep the skin on her face from exploding into little red spots, she dropped in a few of her favourites: Chicken Kiev, strawberries and creamed rice.

Her phone rang: Andrew.

'Hi babe, can't talk long, only just landed.' His breathing sounded hard as if walking. Andrew's employers ran a low-cost business and were cheapskates when it came to landing gates. They would baulk at the charges for a gate close to the terminal building and as a result, passengers and crew often had to walk a fair distance or take a bus. This is what he told her, but for all she knew, maybe he wasn't walking but shagging Cindy, a cabin crew supervisor he seemed to be spending a lot of time with in the toilet.

'There's a meeting scheduled with the Customer Services Director this evening about the way we handled a bunch of drunken girls we just took over to Alicante for a hen weekend. We could be garlanded with praise and held up as an example to other crews, or get kicked in the balls for dumping a drunken rabble on the Spanish Police. It could go either way but whatever happens, I'll be late.'

'A meal for one it is.'

'Where are you?'

'Tesco.'

'Can you get me–'

'Hold it buster, you're not here next week. Remember, you're off to the States.'

'Ah, you're right, as always. What would I do without you, eh?'

'I wonder.'

'No need to elaborate. Look, I've got to go. I'll see you in the morning. Bye.'

She dropped the phone into her jacket and not for the first time, wondered why she carried on with this relationship. She'd always imagined that living together would be a shared experience, but she continued doing all the things she did when she was single, Andrew making only an occasional contribution. Her job could be stressful and some nights all she wanted was to sit down and talk to someone, chat about her day and let the fear, loneliness and the anxieties spill out. Instead, she found solace in a glass of wine, the section of the supermarket that somehow her trolley had brought her to.

No need to buy beer as she didn't drink the stuff and ditto with spirits, however, she did like wine. In this, she and Andrew were compatible. They both liked red, although he favoured the thick and heavy types, such as Malbec or Barolo, while she preferred lighter wines like Merlot and Beaujolais. A compromise would be reached and something like Shiraz would be selected pleasing neither, but today she could suit herself. Into the trolley she popped two bottles: a bottle of Tempranillo and a bottle of Sangiovese, a taste developed on a trip to Italy during her gap year before university.

With a week on her own, she toyed with the idea of having some friends over to the house for a meal. Despite possessing a confident intercom voice, reassuring nervous passengers about forthcoming turbulence or pointing out scenic sights on their route, at heart Andrew was immature.

In social situations such as a dinner party or office party, he used alcohol to instil confidence but the boorish boarding house bully appeared when he'd imbibed too much. As a consequence, he had fallen out with many of her friends and some, like Matt and Emma, would only accept her invite if Andrew was away. She decided against it, not out of loyalty to her partner, as she would support him in many things except insulting or arguing with her friends. Instead, she did it to keep her diary clear in case something concerning Dragon required her immediate attention.

She pushed her trolley out to the car park, feeling pleased with a food bill thirty pounds lighter than normal. This time, it wasn't burdened with a twelve-pack of beer and a selection of pork pies and Scotch eggs. She'd parked at the back of the car park as she fancied stretching her legs after a day of meetings and sitting on a train, but regretted it now as she weaved past open car doors and untethered children.

Unlocking the car, she opened the boot. She lifted each bag and transferred them without trouble, but on coming to the last, the side split as she was about to put it inside, tipping some tubs of yogurt on the boot floor. Reaching inside, she carefully lifted the split bag and placed it inside another bag. She picked up all the loose items and placed them in the now-reinforced container.

She stood and stretched the tightness in her back, when she heard a noise behind her. Turning, a fist came towards her. It was like walking into a brick wall and her knees buckled. She didn't hit the floor or her head on the sill of the boot, as her legs appeared to be floating upwards. It was a strange sensation in her confused state, but made utter sense when the boot lid closed and darkness descended all around her with a thud.

She waited several minutes until her fuzzy head cleared. It did, but the ache from the punch remained and would take longer to fade. She knew all the dodges for escaping from inside the boot of a car as they'd practiced it enough in training. Only then with the lid closed, did she discover she suffered from claustrophobia. Their instructor, an ex-army veteran called Dave Bull, showed her that by controlling her breathing and thinking positive thoughts how to control the panic, but if left unchecked it was capable of overwhelming her.

In her mind she began to go over the escape options. No way did she want to offer the kidnapper or kidnappers the initiative. She could pull the boot release lever, standard in the US but not in Europe, although her Seat hatchback was fitted with one; kick out a brake light and stick her hand through the gap, or undo the retaining clips to the rear seats and climb into the passenger cabin, Glock in hand.

Any of those things she would do if she could move, but she couldn't flex a muscle. The kidnappers had taken her gun and tied her hands and feet in plastic bindings and jammed her between the bags of shopping and the bodywork of the car. They couldn't have incapacitated her better if they'd tried.

Chapter 38

Matt left the house at seven, leaving Emma in bed dozing. Only the Saturday commuters of Ingatestone showing any signs of life. He joined the A12, quiet for a change, and headed towards Harlow on his way to pick up Rosie. With Joseph and Sikandar, they were all heading out to a secret hideaway where they would plan the strategy for an attack against Dragon.

They often did this when a dangerous part of a project lay ahead. They would move out to an offsite location where they could scream, shout and talk over good and bad suggestions without fear of being overheard or segments of the mission being compromised. To some of the more hot-headed in the security services, they believed that planning took the spontaneity out of a situation like this.

There were times when they didn't have a choice but to act on instinct. When they were given the opportunity like now, planning ensured they arrived on the scene with the right equipment, everyone with a clear understanding of their roles and all aiming at the same objective. Mistakes could cost lives and often led to a later inquiry. Such exposure could have a negative impact on the organisation, especially if elements of their operational methods were leaked to the press and seen by their enemies.

He decided not to use the cottage in Surrey or the warehouse in Sussex where they tested new vehicles and equipment, but the spacious home of Sir Raymond Deacon. Matt wanted to include Chris in their discussions to glean as much information as he could about Dragon. If they needed to hack into Dragon's UK computers, Chris and Sikandar would be there to do it.

He arrived in Church Langley forty minutes later and drove into Rosie's road. He parked the car in her driveway behind Andrew's Range Rover, her Seat nowhere to be seen. She often put her car in the garage. It wasn't to protect the paintwork, even though Matt had told her that red cars faded in sunlight. It was to stop enemies attaching a tracker device or worse, a mercury tilt bomb to the underside of the car, a regrettable risk in their profession.

He knocked on the door but received no reply and couldn't detect a noise inside to indicate the presence of anyone awake. He felt a little annoyed to think Rosie had overslept just when they were about to decide on a crucial part of the investigation, but it soon subsided. It was a selfish response, as she could be nursing a dose of flu or had suffered a bad night due to howling dogs or, more appropriate to his area, the screeching of foxes. Besides, it was a Saturday morning, a day off for most people. He needed to cut her a bit of slack.

He knocked again, and this time it elicited a response from the occupants inside. A shuffling noise behind the door grew louder and at last he heard the sound of deadbolts unlocking. The door opened and to his surprise, Andrew stood there.

'Morning Andrew,' Matt said.

It didn't look much like morning to Rosie's partner. He was still in his pyjamas, a blue dressing gown covering, his hair tousled as if he'd just come away from a frantic pillow fight. The shadow of a beard was making its way into the world with more effectiveness than its owner.

'Matt, hi,' he said as he tried to stifle a yawn. 'Excuse me, I'm knackered. What time is it?'

Matt looked at his watch. 'Seven-fifty.'

'Thank goodness, I thought it was the afternoon. Christ it's cold out here, you better come in.'

Matt walked inside and closed the door. Andrew padded towards the kitchen and Matt followed.

'Coffee?' Andrew asked, reaching for the water reservoir of the coffee machine.

'Yeah, thanks. White no sugar.' Matt took a seat around the kitchen table.

'I might be half-asleep but I do remember how you like your coffee.'

'Were you out last night?'

'Got back from Stansted about one in the morning,' he said, spooning coffee into the filter and switching on the machine. 'We were doing a round trip to Alicante, normally a breeze, but on the way out, we had a load of drunks on board and spent time liaising with the local police in Spain after many of them were arrested.'

'Male or female?'

'Female; a hen party. They were all drunk as skunks and started throwing their clothes around the aircraft.'

Matt laughed.

'It sounds funny and would make a good YouTube video to see some bloke hit on the head with a pair of knickers. However, we had a lot of families and elderly people on the flight and many of them were not amused.'

'I can imagine.'

'One white no sugar,' Andrew said placing a mug in front of him.

'Cheers.'

'What brings you here on a Saturday morning?' Andrew asked, taking a seat opposite Matt. 'Assuming, of course, it is Saturday morning.'

'If you're having trouble remembering the day of the week after being in Spain, you'll be lost next week when you head to the States.'

'Ha. It's easier over there as we get three days in Orlando before flying back. A bit of R&R by the pool and my head soon gets back into gear.'

'I'll bet, and Rosie tries to tell me you work too hard.'

'I do, don't you worry about it. There's been no sign of Rosie this morning. I take it this isn't an unannounced visit. She is expecting you?'

He nodded. 'Yeah.'

'She might still be in bed,' he said, pushing the chair back and standing. 'I'll go and make sure she knows you're here.'

He noticed Matt's puzzled face.

'She often sleeps in the spare room if I'm due in late or making an early start, so I haven't seen her this morning.'

Andrew climbed the stairs, his heavy footsteps a warning to Rosie that he was on his way. A minute or so later he walked back down.

'She's not there; the bed's not been used.'

'What?' Matt said, getting up from his chair, his face slowly draining of colour. 'Did you check the bathroom? Other rooms?'

He nodded. 'I checked every room upstairs. The bed in the spare room is made up and unused, and when I opened the front door to you, the deadlock hadn't been undone. So, she isn't out running. I don't think she slept here last night.'

Matt walked to the window overlooking the back garden to make sure she wasn't out there drinking a cup of coffee or doing a spot of gardening. Andrew checked the lounge, other downstairs rooms and the integral door to the garage. When they both drew a blank, he pulled out his phone and called her number. It diverted straight to voicemail, as if switched off. This was a big no-no in HSA; phones had to be charged, on and carried at all times.

He looked at Andrew, his half-asleep face now alert and anxious.

'When did you last speak to her?'

'I phoned her from the airport, last night. She was in Tesco doing the weekly shop.'

'What did she say?'

'I can't remember. I did most of the talking, telling her I would be late home but the usual stuff.'

'Did you call her after she'd been at Tesco?'

'No, why would I?'

'To tell her you were on the way home.'

'No, I didn't get away until after midnight. She would've been in bed by then.'

Matt thought for a moment. He reached over and opened the fridge and pulled open a cupboard where he remembered they stored tins and dry foods.

'Does it look as if the shelves have recently been restocked?'

'A big shop like the one she does at the end of the week,' Andrew said, 'would put bags of pasta and tins of tomatoes in the cupboard and fill the fridge for sure.' He shook his head. 'No, they haven't been.'

Matt closed both doors. 'Andrew, I need to go but don't leave the house today. Okay?'

'Yes, but why?'

'Within the hour, some forensic guys will come here.'

'Forensics? What do you think has happened to her?'

'I know as much as you do, but in our business we have to assume the worst and believe she's been kidnapped.'

This was the civilian version. Fearing the worst in their business was finding an agent with a bullet in their head inside a burned-out car.

'Kidnapped? Why? Who by?'

'I don't know any more than you do at this stage, but I need go. I'll talk to you later.'

Matt walked out to his car and on the way pulled out his phone. He called in and asked for the security office. 'This is Matt Flynn, code number 675786.'

'Morning, Matt. What's the issue?'

'Rosie Fox. I'm declaring a Code 7.'

'Roger 675786. Rosie Fox is Code 7.'

Code 7 in HSA speak was a shorthand way of saying an agent had disappeared, believed killed or kidnapped. All available agents would now be recalled to London and all leave cancelled. The entire resources of HSA would be deployed in finding Rosie Fox, dead or alive.

Matt climbed into his car and headed towards London. Driving out of Church Langley he decided on a detour and turned into Rosie's local Tesco supermarket. Saturday morning, the car park contained plenty of cars, but not many shoppers as it was early and the supermarket didn't close until midnight. The absence of old ladies attempting to park in small spaces and children running loose while their mother collected the shopping bags from the boot, made it easy for him to drive up and down the lanes trying to spot Rosie's red Seat Ibiza.

He felt frustrated at not finding the car but buoyed by confirming one fact; she'd been taken away in her own car. They knew plenty about the vehicle, as HSA owned it. Not only could they put its details on ANPR and have patrolling cops out looking for it, it was also fitted with a tracking device.

His phone rang. Matt pulled into a parking space.

'Hi Gill.'

'Morning, Matt. It's terrible news about Rosie.'

'It is, but I'm not writing her off yet, not until I see some solid evidence.'

'I'm not either, Matt and I'll section anyone who does. This will be treated as a kidnapping by HSA until we know otherwise. Where are you now?'

'Tesco car park in Harlow, her last known whereabouts and the place most likely the kidnap took place; assuming she didn't go anywhere else after shopping other than straight home.'

'Can you see her car there?'

'No, it's not there. If they put Rosie in her car and didn't transfer her to another vehicle or dump it, we'll soon find it. I'll send some analysts down here to review CCTV and see if we can confirm if this is the kidnap site.'

'Good. Are you heading into the office?'

'Yes. The planning meeting scheduled with Rosie and the team to decide our attack on Dragon is on hold for the moment.'

'I called a meeting of the board and I want you in attendance. See you later.'

Matt smiled to himself, not a happy smile but the grimace of the troubled. 'The Board' was a euphemism for a group consisting of government minsters, an Assistant Chief Constable from the Met, the Deputy Director of MI5 and the Head of Border Force. With the resources those individuals could command, if Rosie could be found, this was their best chance.

Chapter 39

Matt came out of the Director's office, his head reeling. MI5, Border Force and the Metropolitan Police currently offered HSA high levels of cooperation whenever required. To hear their bosses say their organisations would do whatever they could to help find Rosie, went way beyond his expectations. The problem for Matt was when they asked him for details of how they could assist, he didn't have much to tell them.

He gathered six agents and four researchers inside the conference room and shut the door. HSA agents could also access the euphemistically named 'the padded cell', a secure conference room lined with a material that prevented the intrusion of phone and wi-fi signals. This wasn't to stop those inside making calls or checking Facebook while they were supposed to be paying attention to the speaker, but to stop those with the capability of listening in to their discussions. Matt didn't believe this case required that level of security and the normal conference room would suffice.

Matt walked to the front of the room and stood beside the electronic whiteboard. He tapped a few keys on the connected laptop and Rosie's picture came up on the screen behind him.

'I'm sure you all realise by now why we're here. Rosie Fox has been kidnapped. At the meeting of the board this morning, they decided to give us any cooperation we need from all areas of the security services. Let's make a start and review what we know.'

He backed away from the laptop and looked around at the assembled team.

'I went to Rosie's house this morning to pick her up and take her to our planning meeting, but she wasn't there. It was clear from an undisturbed bed, the lack of food in the cupboards, and the empty garage, that she didn't come home last night after a shopping trip to Tesco. Her partner, Andrew Milner, couldn't offer an explanation for her disappearance. I don't think he is in any way involved in her kidnap, but I sent a forensic team over there just in case.'

'What does he do?' Joseph asked.

'He's a pilot at Stansted Airport.'

'Does his work schedule explain why he didn't realise she wasn't at home last night, and we only found out this morning?'

'He came back late after a problem in Spain. If Rosie's not sleeping in the main bedroom, he assumes she's gone to the spare room, so she doesn't get disturbed when he comes in. Last night he felt too knackered to check.'

'Sounds plausible,' Joseph said, 'but what if he's hiding something. Maybe a domestic gone wrong, or she's away with a boyfriend?'

'I work with Rosie a lot and I think something would slip if she had a boyfriend. Plus, I saw Andrew this morning, just out of bed. I don't think he was putting on an act. I may be blinded by Dragon's aggressive tactics these last few weeks not to see a simpler answer, but I don't think so. If you guys think I'm wrong, feel free to put me right.'

'No, you're all right, mate,' Joseph said.

'I think you're on the right track, Matt,' Jess Harvey, a fellow agent recently drafted into the Dragon team, said.

'Okay,' Matt said, 'let's move on. I called Rosie last night as she turned into the Tesco car park in Harlow and Andrew called her about five minutes after me. Both calls were between seven-thirty and seven forty-five in the evening. I drove around the car park this morning looking for her car, but couldn't see it. She could only be kidnapped when she returned to her car after shopping or on the journey back to her house.'

'If it was me trying to grab someone,' Jess said, 'I would choose the Tesco car park over a street anytime.'

'Me too,' Joseph said. 'Even though there are CCTV cameras, it's easy enough to do it without revealing faces or the vehicle.'

'They did that all right when they took Rosie in her own car.'

'We don't know much more at this stage,' Matt said. 'I'm looking for ideas how we can progress this. We have people updating ANPR, locating the car tracker and checking Tesco's CCTV. Siki, how are they getting on?'

'Someone's looking at Tesco's CCTV pictures in Harlow as we speak,' Sikandar Khosa, their chief researcher said. 'The ANPR information has been loaded, but I just found out, the tracker's been disabled.'

'Damn, I thought it would have given us a head start, if only to a burned-out wreck,' Matt said.

'That's probably how they've disabled it, set the car on fire or drove into something like a quarry.'

'What about town centre cameras, Siki?' Jess said.

'In Harlow?'

'Yeah. If we can locate the car on CCTV, it might tell us the direction they're going and maybe give us a picture of the occupants.'

'I'm on it,' Khosa said, writing it down.

'I don't think anyone in this room is in any doubt,' Matt said, 'that Dragon are behind this. The way I'm thinking now, I could go over their offices and put a gun to the MD's head. If he doesn't tell us where Rosie is, I'd happily stick a bullet in him.'

'We'd all like to do the same,' Jess said, 'but it won't help us find Rosie if he knows.'

'Finding Rosie and doing what we were planning to do this morning, taking the fight to Dragon, have just become intermeshed. This seems like as good a time as any to discuss how we do it.'

'We go back to the plan you outlined a few days ago, Matt,' Sikander said. 'We get Chris Anderson to hack into Dragon's UK systems, find out who the main players are, what they do, how they're funded and where we can find them.'

'I'm not sure this sort of stuff will be documented,' Jess said.

'Sure, it will,' Joseph said. 'I can see them emailing the US asking for approval to carry out some things and requesting more money, that is, providing we're not dealing with a loose cannon over here. The UK people will need to make contact with their US counterparts on a regular basis, asking for guidance and giving them updates. It might be in code but Siki and Amos should be able to unravel it.'

'We could retaliate by kidnapping one of their people,' Kamal, the youngest member of the team said.

'It has its merits,' Matt said. 'The upside being we could trade their guy for Rosie, but it could lead us into a situation we don't want to be in. What if they send us one of Rosie's ears or fingers through the post? Do we do the same to their guy?'

'For sure, but if we get the right guy, we might be able to put a stop to the activities of their dirty organisation.'

'I don't like it, Kamal, if feels more like revenge than a fair trade.'

'It doesn't matter if you like it or not,' Joseph said. 'We're looking for the best option to bring Rosie back. Her safe return isn't only your concern, Matt, we all want her back.'

'Do you think I don't know it?' Matt said, slamming his fists down on the desk in front of him, 'but I feel responsible as we've been working on the Dragon case together.'

'Boys, boys, calm down,' Jess said. 'We need to focus on the task in hand. Rosie is a friend to us all, we all have a stake in this.'

'Agreed.'

'You're right Jess,' Matt said, 'arguing will get us nowhere and it won't bring Rosie back. We all need to get back to work and do something. Jess, follow up on the ANPR checks and Tesco cameras. Amos, you take town cameras. Joseph, talk to Border Force and make sure she isn't being taken out of the country.'

'And you?' Joseph asked. 'What will you be doing?'

'C'mon Siki,' Matt said, 'we're going to Windsor. We need to speak to Chris Anderson.'

Chapter 40

Rosie's kidnap was at the forefront of Matt's mind as he approached Windsor. He realised that he and Sikandar could also become targets, not to mention endangering the people they were going to see. So, Matt took a circuitous route to Clifton Manor. Sikander Khosa didn't notice as he had never been to the house before and spent the journey looking at his phone.

'Thank God we got here in one piece,' Sikander said when the tyres of the car began crunching over the gravel driveway, the manor house in the distance. 'I never thought I'd make it. Do you always drive so fast?'

'How would you know? You were too busy playing games the whole journey.'

'I had to do something to try and ease my anxiety.'

They got out of the car and approached the house. Matt knocked on the door and when it opened, was surprised to see Lisa standing there.

'Matt how wonderful to see you,' she said enveloping him in a big hug.

Matt was so stunned at seeing Lisa downstairs he didn't notice the puzzled look on Sikandar's face or spot Louise standing behind her.

When they parted, he approached Louise and gave her a hug. 'Hi, Louise, how are you?'

'I think it would have been so much worse without Lisa here. We've had so much fun, haven't we girl?'

'Yes, we have.' She took Matt's arm. 'C'mon Matt, and I'll tell you all about it.'

Matt extracted his arm. 'Sorry Lisa, not now, maybe later.' He nodded at his car companion. 'This is Sikandar Khosa, a researcher from our office. We've need to do some work with Chris. Is he around?'

'He's in his room,' Louise said. 'I'll take you up there if you like.'

'Fine,' Lisa said. 'I know Matt likes his coffee, I'll go and make some.'

Matt walked upstairs, Louise beside him. 'Where are you hiding the old Lisa? The difference is amazing.'

'We've talked for hours on end and I found out we've got the same taste in music and the same luck with boyfriends. It's all gone on from there.'

'Whatever you did, you've worked wonders. Raymond must be thrilled as she rarely ventured downstairs these past few months, never mind open the front door on her own.'

'He's not an easy man to read, but he did take me aside to thank me.'

Matt smiled. 'Careful, Louise. If he likes you, he might offer you an estate in Scotland or persuade one of his pals in the cabinet to make you a dame.'

'He can keep the title. I'll take a slice of Scotland any day of the week.'

They reached a closed oak door, so solid he doubted their combined efforts could force it open if locked.

'Chris is in there,' Louise said, pointing with her thumb. 'I would knock if I were you, he hates being interrupted, but maybe that's just us. If you don't need me, I'll go and help Lisa.'

'Thanks.'

Matt knocked, opened the door and walked in. It was around midday so it wasn't a surprise to see Chris up and about. The shock was seeing him dressed and with his hair brushed. Perhaps living in a manor house was rubbing off.

'Don't you people believe in privacy?' He turned to see the intruders. 'Oh, sorry Matt, I didn't realise it was you.'

He was sitting at the desk, his laptop open in front of him.

'Hi, Chris,' Matt said. 'Are you well?'

'Me? I'm bored rigid to tell you the truth. Since Louise and Lisa became best-buddies, they bugger off together for most of the day and the only people I get to talk to are my mates on social media.'

'I trust you keep your location secret?' Sikandar asked.

'Credit me with a bit of sense.'

'Chris,' Matt said, 'this is Sikandar Khosa, a researcher from our office.'

'Hi,' Chris said.

'Hi Chris. Good to meet you.'

'We're here to ask you for a little favour,' Matt said.

'If it helps me get out of here and back to my old life, name it.'

'We'd like you to hack into Dragon's UK computers.'

'What? No way. Think of the grief this has caused me already. I can't believe you're asking me to do this.'

'Chris, calm down. Their UK business is more or less a sales office, all the serious stuff is back in Houston. We just need you to look up some emails and documents.'

'What if they find out?'

Matt gave him a quizzical look. 'You're winding me up.'

'What?'

'You're an experienced hacker, Chris, this is what you do. If you can't cover your tracks, no one can.'

'What I mean to say is, after all the trouble I've caused, I'm going to stop hacking and live life like a normal person.'

'I think that's a great idea but could you do it just one last time?'

'They found out last time and if I was them, I would've installed more sophisticated software to prevent it happening again.'

'Fair enough, but I suspect the UK operation isn't as IT savvy as the one in the US. In any case, what do you care? If they do find out you're behind it, they can only come after you once.' He almost said, 'kill you once' but realised just in time. He didn't want to freak the guy out.

'I dunno.'

'C'mon Chris, we're depending on you here, we need this.' Matt held back the 'Rosie card' as the less people who knew about her kidnap the better. They needed Chris's cooperation, he would play it if he had to.

Chris looked first at Matt then at Sikandar.

'It's important, yeah?'

'In this one instance it is. I wouldn't be asking you otherwise.'

'Okay, I'll do it, but only this once, right? After this, I'm finished with this game. I'm going to delete my software tools and unsubscribe from all the hacking forums I use.'

'I wouldn't delete the software, Chris,' Sikandar said. 'Take it off your laptop by all means, as it will reduce the temptation to use it, but archive it to a separate hard drive or memory stick would be my advice.'

'Yeah, good idea. I'll do that instead.'

Chris turned to his laptop and did what hackers did best. Within five minutes, they were in. Matt and Siki watched as Chris explained what the program was doing as it probed the open ports on Dragon's UK servers, but Matt still couldn't describe the process to anyone else.

'Right, we're in. Where do you want to look first?'

'We need the names of the main people.'

'You'll find that sort of stuff on their website, there's no need to hack into their systems.'

'Yeah, but I'm not interested in job titles, I want to know what they do, where they're located, how they're paid, all sorts of things.'

A few minutes later after looking at soulless organisation charts and company appointment announcements, they switched their attention to personnel records. There, they found, among others, the name and personal details of the Chief Executive, Walter Ingham; Head of Sales, Gary Dennis, and Head of International Security, temporarily seconded from Houston, Daniel Leppo.

'Leppo is the guy I told you about before,' Chris said. 'He's the guy sending the threatening emails about Latif Artha and me.'

'I remember. He's at the head of my calling card list. See what else we can find about him.'

The door opened and in came Lisa bearing a tray. 'What are you boys up to?'

'Top secret, for our eyes only.'

'Boys and their toys. The coffee's there on the dresser. Don't let it go cold.'

'Cheers Lisa,' Matt called to the closing door.

'Take a look at the financials,' Matt said. 'Leppo's over here to do a job, he needs big funding to employ all the muscle he's been using.'

'For sure,' Chris said. 'I imagine the guys in Oxford and Derek Spencer's killers don't come cheap.'

Chris tapped away at the pc while Matt and Sikandar helped themselves to coffee.

'He's good,' Sikandar said. 'I did a bit of hacking when I was younger, but I couldn't do what he does.'

'I can't see you being younger. You probably looked the same when you were ten.'

'Maybe, but with a bit less of this,' he said patting his considerable stomach.

'A question no one's asked,' Matt said in hushed tones, 'is why Dragon kidnapped Rosie in the first place? What are they getting out of it?'

'Maybe they want to do a trade with the documents, reveal the whereabouts of this place, or use her as leverage to force us to pull back?'

'It's one of the three, for sure. Which one would you put your money on?'

'The first one.'

'At least neither of us believes they've nabbed her for revenge and killed her straight away. Which suggests to me, Rosie is still alive. If we play our cards right, we can bring her back.'

'Hey guys, come and take a look at this and pass me a Coke if Lisa brought one up.'

It took Matt a few moments to understand what was being displayed on the laptop screen. When he did, he realised Leppo had been dipping into a five-million-pound slush fund, billed as 'Consultancy Services' in the accounts. By drilling down, they discovered numerous large withdrawals to companies and people they didn't recognise, but the dates were roughly consistent with every violent incident, and each one was authorised by Leppo.

By digging some more, Chris not only found irrefutable proof of a concerted, well-funded attempt by Dragon to get their documents back, he also discovered a list of the properties the company owned or rented. Now they had something substantial to get their teeth into.

Ten minutes later, they left Chris's room armed with print-outs of the key information and a plan of action forming in Matt's mind. At the top of the stairs, with the sounds of hysterical laughter emanating from the kitchen, his phone rang.

'Hello, Matt, where are you?' Gill asked.

'Clifton Manor. Chris Anderson's been digging into Dragon's UK computers and uncovered some good stuff. We'll use it to start the hunt for Rosie.'

'Excellent; you're going to need it.'

'Why?'

'We've had a message from the kidnappers. 'Stop your investigation into our activities now, or the woman dies,' is all it says.'

Chapter 41

Matt and Joseph got out of the car. They were in rural Surrey, close to the village of Sutton Abinger. Perhaps this place was too under-populated and spread out to call it a village, more a hamlet. Whatever the term, it looked a fine place to live, with a quintessentially English pub and many magnificent houses, their gardens trim with big 4x4s in the driveways.

'Man, this is so out in the sticks,' Joseph said.

'You don't like it?'

'No way. Where would I get my latte and newspaper in the morning? I'd need to go all the way to somewhere like Guildford to meet any women. Give me Islington any day of the week.'

'You can take the boy out London...but I guess you need to be at a certain stage of life to live here.'

'Yeah, retired and rich, I think they call it.'

They'd decided not to use surveillance to stake out six properties owned by Dragon, identified from Chris's hack of Dragon's UK computers. It would take too long, time they didn't believe they had. Instead, they would use a direct approach, visit each property and spin a lost motorist story or something similar if they encountered anyone. If the property looked likely or lay empty, they would attempt to gain entry and confirm what it contained. If this wasn't possible as they had spotted people and cars, suggesting some other activity, they would mark it out for further action.

Matt and Joseph walked down a tree-lined lane, past silent houses, many of which didn't seem to be occupied, the inhabitants perhaps lying low believing the two men to be evangelists or council officials conducting a survey. Maybe the occupants weren't retired at all, but working in Guildford or London to pay the mortgage on such large and expensive properties.

Soon the scattered houses disappeared and the countryside closed in.

'Are we walking to Guildford?' Joseph said.

'It feels like it but their place should be just ahead.'

Fifty metres further on a sign, 'Dragon Technologies UK Training Centre,' came into view.

'At last,' Joseph said. 'A man can only take so much fresh air in one day.'

'Missing the smog of London already?'

Not far from the property, they found a track leading into the woods. Matt didn't need to say anything to Joseph about not talking; the city boy kept any comments about the boggy ground, the smell of decaying leaves and the lack of sunshine to himself.

A building appeared through the trees. The bottom half was painted white with what looked like modern double-glazed sash windows, the upper part hung with red tiles. In common with the other Dragon-owned buildings they'd seen so far, it looked well-cared for and the grounds well-tended, suggesting Dragon were a rich company and didn't mind spending money on the upkeep of their properties. The place looked large enough to hide a kidnap victim without too much problem.

They walked on, and after first making sure no dog walkers or ramblers were around, they left the track and moved in for a closer look. The grounds of the training centre were surrounded by a five-foot fence, not an obstacle to deter the persistent, more a statement to the casual passer-by to keep away. Out of sight from any watchers inside the building, Matt crouched down and pulled out an eyepiece. Joseph did the same.

'Only one car,' Matt said. 'Suggests a caretaker.'

'Yeah, if they were running a training course you would expect more. Mind you, one car might mean a couple of guards for Rosie.'

A few minutes later, Matt dropped the eyepiece back into his pocket. 'Let's move over there,' he said, pointing to the opposite side of the clearing. 'We'll get a better view of the front windows and keep watching until we see some movement.'

'Fine by me.'

Matt stood and stretched. His phone vibrated. In normal operations, phones were only to be used in an emergency or if needing to impart crucial information. When it came to more dangerous situations such as breaking into one of the properties, they would be set to 'Do Not Disturb' as the vibration even from a silenced phone could alert a guard to their presence.

'Jess.'

'Matt, I think we've found the place.'

'Describe it to me.'

'A house on a quiet country road, looks like a bolthole for one of the bosses or a place for visiting executives. Two big 4x4s outside and now and again a guard comes out for smoke. He's packing.'

'It sounds like you've struck gold. Are the weapons heavy duty?'

'No, a handgun in the waistband.'

'It's a better bet than here. Give me the address. We'll come over and join you.'

Matt and Joseph headed back to the car, a greater sense of urgency in their steps than before. Matt was aware, and he hoped Joseph was too, any eagerness to rescue Rosie needed to be tempered with cold professionalism. Only a fool would rush in and try to release the kidnapped agent unprepared. Fools didn't last long in this business.

It didn't take long to drive to Ockham, and Jess's directions were good. They soon found the house being watched, lying as it was on the southern fringes of the village. They drove past and parked in a lay-by a quarter of a mile further on. They walked towards the house, but this time with no bridleway to ease their passage they had to make do with tramping through bracken and skirting the more serious outcrops of brambles.

Bushy pine trees obscured their view of the house, not the fortuitous effects of nature, but a deliberate attempt by the present owner or the last, to shield the house from neighbours or prying eyes. The planter had to be paranoid as few people lived nearby and

Matt doubted many walked past on what looked like a quiet B-road that led deeper into the surrounding countryside.

A few minutes later they found Jess and Kamal, hiding behind a large bush with good visibility of the property.

'Don't shoot,' Matt said in a low voice, 'we're the good guys.'

'Hi Matt, Joseph,' Jess said. 'Come and take a look.'

She moved to the side to give them some space. Jess was the newest member of the team and at twenty-five, among the youngest. She was pretty with short black hair, even white teeth and an easy smile, but not a woman to cross. In her previous role as a fraud detective, she'd decked one of her colleagues when he refused to carry out her order, and could shoot more accurately than anyone else in the team.

Following Jess's outstretched hand, they could see the house between two tall pine trees. The trees didn't provide the effective screening the original gardener intended as due to high winds or tree disease, the branches at eye level looked spindly and dry and several had fallen on the ground.

Through the gap and using his eyepiece it looked to be a much-extended cottage with a long, pitched roof. The shape of the roof suggested not many rooms upstairs, but with the large floor space the house occupied, he would expect the downstairs area to be spacious. Obtaining more detailed information about the layout inside would be vital before entering the property. He would task Sikander with finding a Land Registry entry or estate agent details.

'The two 4x4s you see have been there since we arrived,' Jess said. 'We were here about half an hour when a guy came out for a smoke. When he turned to go back inside, I saw the gun in his waistband.'

'I can't think of an innocent explanation for having armed men in a rural house, can you?' Matt said.

'Not even for an armaments company like Dragon.'

'What do you think, Joseph?'

'I'm with you guys, this looks like the place.'

'Kamal?'

'Same. The cars, the heavies, the gun. It all fits.'

'Have you seen any other movement?' Matt asked.

'If you look long enough at the windows, you can see people moving around inside. We think there's three of them.'

'We need to confirm the exact numbers before any attempt to storm the place.'

'I agree.'

'What are you thinking?' Joseph asked.

'If we all agree–'

'Hang on there,' Kamal said. 'The guns and the men do look bad, but what if it's only their base for launching the attacks they've made on Chris Anderson?'

Matt thought for a second. 'You might be right. They could be using the house to plan missions and to come back here to sleep and regroup.' He paused, thinking. 'Either way, we hit it. If we don't find Rosie, we'll be knocking out part of their capability for kidnapping or killing someone else. Plus, we might nab someone who can tell us where Rosie is being held.'

Matt looked at Kamal who nodded. 'Fair enough.'

'Good,' Matt said, 'we're all agreed. We attack it, but not in daylight and not with only four of us.'

'Glad to hear it,' Kamal said.

'Jess, you and Kamal stick around here a bit longer and confirm their strength. When you do, bugger off and get something to eat. Joseph and me will head back to the office. I'll get Sikander to research the house and rustle up a few more bodies. We'll meet back here at 23.00 with flak jackets and full ammo magazines. Then, we'll hit them with everything we've got.'

Chapter 42

Matt drove towards the rendezvous point in Ockham a few minutes after eleven. In the time between first seeing the house and now, he'd returned to the office in London and briefed the Director. Then, he picked up some spare flak jackets, had something to eat and rested before completing an MFA, Monthly Firearms Assessment, known to all as the 'monthly.'

Every month all agents were required to pass an assessment of their competence with a range of firearms. The instructors didn't set the same test every time, and not the twelve shots at the target's body so beloved of television crime dramas. They didn't need to assess an agent's prowess with a weapon, blasting a dummy full of holes, but to measure an agent's accuracy and control under stress. It was an important consideration in their game as HSA had never been set up as a 'shoot to kill' operation, but an agency capable of deploying lethal force if the situation demanded it. With more accurate shooting, the perpetrator didn't need to die in every instance.

The incident Matt faced two weeks ago, Louise Walker being held by an intruder at the safe house, would have turned out differently in daylight or with the hall light switched on. Agents concentrated on finding parts of the intruder's body not covered by the hostage, easy to do with a slim girl like Louise and a large man like the intruder. HSA agents practiced shooting various sections of the body with their weapon in different positions. They tried to mirror unfavourable situations, such as when the agent's gun was at their side, as if agreeing to an assailant's request to put the weapon down.

Passing the 'monthly' was a mandatory requirement for all agents, while office-based staff, the likes of Sikander and Amos, undertook a quarterly test. In every UK police force, armed officers were suspended from active duty and subjected to an internal inquiry if they opened fire. In HSA, no one would suffer any sanctions for firing their weapon if the situation demanded it, but they would lose their operational licence if they didn't pass their 'monthly.'

Matt also called Emma. He hadn't seen much of her these past few days. He was so wrapped up in the Pulsar case, and she had been working late, planning raids across London and the south east to bring down Simon Wood's drug operation.

Matt parked the car, removed the guns, thunder flashes and flak jackets from the boot and set off towards the rendezvous point. He looked at the sky, the moon and stars obscured by thick clouds. Any type of weather was fine for a raid like this, even stair-rod rain offered some advantages, but he hated a full moon. It made hiding difficult and sneaking up behind an opponent near-impossible. Also, despite the intervening years, his head was still filled with his grandmother's stories of elves and leprechauns dancing around tree stumps, trying to think up mischief as the full moon shone.

Dark nights like this did present him with a problem: it made the job of finding the rendezvous point way more difficult. If not for the lights burning in the target house, he would have walked past. He dipped into the woods and a few minutes later came across a small and well-armed huddle. He expected to be the last one to arrive. He was right.

'Hi,' he said quietly as he hunkered down. He looked around at the five faces, giving each a nod. He felt confidence at seeing the resolute expressions, despite the cold and damp place they found themselves in, the leaves and grass dripping with earlier rain.

'Any changes?' Matt asked.

'Nope,' Jess replied. 'The lights came on, they shut the curtains. The same guy appears at the back door for a smoke at regular intervals.'

'How regular?'

'It's about every forty minutes.' She looked at Kamal who nodded.

'A man who likes his nicotine. How many of the opposition are inside?'

'A total of three, definitely three.'

'Good. When did our smoker enjoy his last fix?'

'Fifteen minutes ago.'

'Okay. It gives us about twenty minutes to get ourselves together, over to the house and in position.' He pulled from his jacket a floor plan of the house and illuminated it with an astronomer's torch, the red light didn't ruin night-time vision as a conventional torch would do. They all crowded round to look.

'Lee, you'll cover the front of the house and Steph, you the back. The rest of us will wait at the back door for the smoker to appear. Joseph, you take him out as quietly as you can and when he's out of the way, we'll chuck flash grenades into the house. When you hear our grenades go off, Lee, throw yours in through the front windows. We'll move inside, grab the guards and tie them up. If Rosic's in the house, our reaction will be determined by how badly injured she is. If she's dead, I wouldn't want to be one of the guards.'

He switched off the torch.

'Lee, you and Steph will round up any strays who make it outside, and deal with any unexpected arrivals. Any questions?'

He looked around at the faces. He couldn't see them well, but felt their grim determination.

'C'mon guys, let's go and release Rosie.'

The smoker didn't come out at the forty-minute mark, but they didn't mind waiting. When he didn't appear after fifty minutes, Matt decided to give him until sixty before changing the plan. An assault with three gunmen inside would be a lot more difficult than two, but no way did he want to come away from this place empty handed. A minute before decision time, they heard loud voices. The door unlocked and a large body emerged.

He stood, legs apart, looking relaxed and pulled out a pack of cigarettes. He selected one and sparked up. He clearly enjoyed the first puff as his cigarette hand dropped down to his waist and he tilted his head back and blew smoke rings into the night sky. Joseph struck. A ligature appeared around the smoker's neck and as his hands came up to try and pull it off, Joseph pulled him backwards, off-balance. Matt rushed forward, a stun gun in his hand and after jabbing the prongs into the guy's neck, pulled the trigger. The guy collapsed, incapacitated in a similar way to being hit by a police Taser. Joseph tied his hands and legs and Matt applied a gag.

They dragged the body to one side, then opened the door of the house. One by one, the agents threw in thunder flashes. They were percussion weapons, not fragmentation, designed to emit a loud bang to disorientate those inside, not kill them with flying shrapnel.

Matt, with two agents behind him, entered the house, carbines drawn. Behind them, Kamal was stationed to stop anyone feeling outside or sneaking up behind them. Joseph peeled off to check the rooms while Matt and Jess moved dead-ahead into the lounge. He found a man sitting inside, but he didn't look fit to pass water, never mind pick up a gun and shoot them. Matt pushed him to the floor and secured his hands behind his back.

'Where's the other guy?' he hissed into his ear.

Matt received a garbled response and Matt left him where he fell. He looked over at Jess. 'I'm getting no bloody sense out of him. Search the room, look for hiding places, then we'll check the others.'

'Will do.'

Matt walked into the hall and entered the first door he came across, a small television room. Joseph was standing there, his gun held in two hands aiming at something. Pushing the door further, he now saw the third guard in the house, a well-built character with a military-style haircut. He was backed into a corner, holding Rosie, a gun pointing at the side of her head.

At first glance she didn't look hurt. He could see no blood on her face or bruises on her arms and her clothes looked intact. The only problem he could see, the frightened look on her face. No bloody wonder, their presence in the house increased her chances of being killed by several factors.

'Put the gun down, pal,' Matt said. 'There's six of us and one of you.'

'Don't try to smoke me, mate. Eric's outside, he's waiting for the right moment to drop the lot of you.'

'The guy who went out for a fag?' Matt said shaking his head. 'We've met him. He won't be offering you any help.'

'You come near me and she gets it.'

'Last chance. Put the gun on the deck or you're gonna die.'

A look of panic crossed the gunman's face, an expression Matt didn't like. The overhead light gave Matt a good view of the man's left shoulder. Matt fired. It wasn't the arm holding the weapon but in reaction, the gunman let loose a round. It almost sheered the tip of Rosie's nose, but with luck it missed and struck the wall instead.

His grip of Rosie relaxed and, like a good trooper, she ducked down exposing the upper parts of her assailant's body. The guy lifted his weapon. Before he could bring it level and let off a shot, Matt fired again. It hit him in the middle of his temple and the guy dropped to the ground like a lifeless theatre puppet.

Rosie ran over and hugged Matt hard, banging her fists on his back. He could feel her body shake. 'You bastard, Flynn. I could have been killed.'

'No, the usual greeting is, thanks for rescuing me, you guys did a brilliant job.'

'You know what I mean, coming in here all tooled up. He could have panicked and shot me.'

She stood there for half a minute before kissing him on the cheek. 'Thank you,' she said and let him go.

Matt turned to Joseph beside him. 'Why didn't you drop him? You had a better angle.'

'I waited for you. After completing your monthly today, I knew you would be more accurate than me. I was right.'

Chapter 43

'Miss Fox, Doctor Harrison will see you now.' Rosie threw the magazine on the table, rose from her seat and followed the well-dressed receptionist into Doctor Harrison's office. Rosie thought the outer area was plush, but the office of the occupational psychologist was equipped with deep pile carpets, an enormous desk and what looked like original artwork on the walls. It was difficult to reconcile this with the sparse offices she and the other HSA agents occupied only two floors below.

'Ah Miss Fox,' Doctor Harrison said, from behind the desk consisting of not much else but a large sheet of thick green-tinted glass and four chrome legs. It was a good thing the doctor wasn't a woman and wearing a skirt, as this trendy piece of furniture didn't include a modesty board.

He walked over and shook her hand. 'Good to see you again, Rosie. How are you today?'

'Getting better by the day, I would say.'

'Good to hear it. Please take a seat.'

He directed her to the soft seats by the window. This was their third meeting and, for Rosie, the most important. A good report here, and she could return to active service. Something not right or a specific problem identified, could send her out to grass for several weeks, and something more severe could see her kicked out of HSA.

'When we last spoke you said you were having trouble sleeping. How are you sleeping now?'

'Much better.'

'What are you doing different?'

'I'm thinking less about the kidnap incident, not easy to do while at home or kicking my heels in the office all day. I also tried your suggestion about taking a bath in the evening.'

'Good. As I explained to you before, sleep is nature's way of restoring some semblance of order to your thoughts. In deep sleep, your brain acts like a sophisticated filing system, sorting negative thoughts into one place and putting positive thoughts, like the successful projects you've worked on, into another. It helps you to attain a sense of perspective.'

'I think I'm getting there.'

'Are you taking any medication?'

'We discussed this last time. Even before the kidnapping incident, I didn't take pills unless I really needed to. In the last few days, I've been offered sleeping tablets, feel-good powders and all manner of herbal concoctions from well-meaning friends and relations, but I rejected them all. I'll deal with this without the aid of any crutches.'

'I know we discussed it last time, and then, as now, you've made your position perfectly clear. I only asked to find out if anything had changed.'

'No need. It hasn't and it won't.'

Rosie took a deep breath. She knew not to rile the pedantic doctor as he could put a red line through her assessment. She mistrusted every mind doctor she had ever come across, from the behavioural psychologists at the Met, the clinical psychologist her doctor recommended, to Doctor Harrison with his wall full of impressive certificates.

She knew Harrison had an important job to do. While working for the Met, the hurdle to reach was being mentally stable and physically fit. In HSA, the barrier was higher. Mental stability would allow Rosie to walk the streets of London with a gun on her hip. Harrison had to decide if she could also handle a range of stressful situations with repercussions all the way to the Prime Minister's office.

'Have you experienced any flashbacks about the kidnap incident?'

'Less and less. Now and again I have dreams about it. Although elements of the kidnap are included, it's often in strange places and with a different outcome.'

'Ah,' the doctor said and went on to explain about fragmentation and rationalisation, her brain inserting previous successful kidnap scenarios into the one she'd experienced. 'This is your brain's way of saying what you've been through is an aberration, look at all the times it went right. You're looking back at something that didn't go right and trying to find ways to correct it.'

'Yeah, that's what I thought.'

'Good. You are no longer thinking about the kidnap incident in negative terms, for example, woe is me, look what happened to me. Instead, you are thinking that if this thing occurred again, this is what I would do about it. Good. It's a major step forward from our first meeting. You've moved all the way along the spectrum from negative to positive thinking.'

'Really?'

'Don't you remember? All you could talk about then was the incident. How dark it was in the boot of the car, how horrible the men were to you and so on.'

'Yeah, I suppose I did dwell on it for a bit.' She could have mentioned the severe claustrophobia she experienced, but based on previous dealings with the good doctor, he was an expert on the subject. He could go on for hours, including quoting from articles he'd published in various medical journals.

The interview continued for another twenty minutes. There came a point when Rosie was about to tell him to shove his questions, she didn't want to answer any more, when he started gathering his papers into a neat pile.

'I think we've covered everything,' he said. 'What do you think?'

'I agree.'

'Do you have anything you'd like to ask me, or is there anything bothering you which you'd like us to discuss?'

'No,' she sighed. 'You've answered every question I can think of.' Exhaustively she could have added, but didn't.

'Good, I'm glad to hear it. You will be pleased to know, I'm recommending to the Director that you can return to active service.'

She was stunned and didn't realise at first what he had said. When her brain finally processed it correctly, she said, 'Thank you doctor,' and rose from her seat.

'There is one condition.'

'What is it?'

'You pass a Firearms Assessment.'

'What? I passed one ten days ago.'

'I know, but I'd like you to take it again.'

She sighed. 'Okay.'

Rosie walked downstairs in buoyant mood and stepped into the open office with a renewed bounce in her step. The feeling of belonging returned once again, no longer like someone with one foot on the pavement outside and clutching her P45.

She passed the desk of Siki, his mouth busy munching a Picnic and in his hand, a can of Coke.

'Hey, Rosie,' Siki said, wiping the back of his hand across his mouth to clear the last vestiges of chocolate. 'How d'ya get on?'

'I'm back,' she said smiling.

'High five, girl.'

She responded in kind.

'I knew they wouldn't kick you out. You're too good and important to this place.'

'Thank you for your kind words, Siki, you are too. Where's Matt?'

'Oh, he's around. I don't know exactly where, but he is in today.'

'No problem, I'll catch him later.'

She headed to her desk, sat in the chair and surveyed her little domain, a place she believed she might never see again. She didn't share Siki's confidence about her return to active duty being a slam-dunk, but she also couldn't believe they'd sling her out on her ear. Instead, she would be pushed upstairs to Admin or consigned to a less conspicuous role not involving guns. At worst, back to the Met as a desk analyst in a front-line unit like Anti Terrorism.

Moving the mouse, she woke up her computer and began looking through the many emails received since the previous night, her last visit to the office. In the time taken to walk down two floors from Doctor Harrison's office, the doctor had sent one to the Firearms Unit. Sitting in her inbox was the date and time of her next Firearms Assessment.

Mention of a Firearms Assessment alarmed her more than it should, as without warning and several times a day, her hands started to shake. Not the tremors associated with a frightening film or following vigorous exercise, but physical shudders like those experienced by severe Parkinson's disease sufferers. It made drinking a cup of coffee or eating a bowl of cereal a distressing experience, and if it happened while holding a gun, she couldn't hit the side of a barn, never mind the barn door.

'Hi Rosie, why the glum face? I hear you passed. It's great to have you back.'

She turned to see Matt staring at her, an unreadable expression on his face.

'Oh, hi Matt. Thanks. Sorry, I was looking at some emails and got sort of engrossed.'

Matt pulled over a seat and sat facing her. 'How did you do?'

'I'm fine by all accounts.'

'Not suffering from depression, flashbacks, bad dreams or any of that crap?'

'Christ no. You sound like our jolly psychologist, Doctor po-faced Harrison.'

'He is a bit of a misery guts, right enough. How do you want to play it? Do you need a few more days to rest or are you itching to get back into active service?'

'Sod all this resting. Since the kidnap I've done nothing but read reports and shove papers around. I'm ready to get back into it.'

'Are you sure? It's only been a few days since you were convinced Daniel Leppo and his pals were about to top you. If you need to take time to sort yourself out, no problem. Jess and Joseph have been briefed on the next stage of the plan and–'

'I'm fine Matt, really. I don't need any more time off. The Doc says I'm good to go providing I pass an unscheduled monthly.'

'Okay, enough of my fussing. Here's what we're planning.'

Chapter 44

Matt screwed up his Bounty bar wrapper. He was about to let it fall on the floor, when loud tutting from the driver stopped him. He put it in the compartment beneath the radio instead.

'I think I preferred it when you were still in captivity.'

'You have a cruel tongue,' Rosie said. 'If I was, who would keep your scruffy self on the straight and narrow?'

'Maybe I don't want to be kept on the straight and narrow. Maybe I like being untidy.'

Since the kidnapping, Rosie had passed a medical, Firearms Assessment and a psychological evaluation, all concluding that she didn't suffer from any after-effects of her enforced incarceration or Post Traumatic Stress Disorder. In Matt's opinion, she did suffer from 'nuisanceitis,' pestering him non-stop to return to operational work, but he believed the cause to be nothing more serious than boredom. To ease her back into active duty, he'd allowed her to accompany him on this mission on the strict understanding that she would only be his driver. Any rough stuff would be down to him.

At one time they suspected Daniel Leppo was behind the kidnap, now they knew for sure. He didn't go as far as swapping business cards with Rosie, but she recognised him from his picture on the Dragon website. When he came to the house where she was being held, he spoke to her guards as if they were hired hands. He made it clear what he wanted them to do and warned them he would put a bullet into any guy who hurt their captive. If his statement was designed to make Rosie feel better, the next bit didn't. If anybody was going to do it, Daniel Leppo said, he would.

'Matt, don't you think-'

'Hold on a sec. There he is. Remember, follow me in the car.'

'I might be fresh out of the psychologist's chair but I haven't lost my marbles. I'll be there.'

They watched as a sharply-dressed man appeared at the rear entrance to Dragon's UK sales office in Hertfordshire. Matt exited the car and walked over to Walter Ingham's Mercedes D Class. On getting closer he ducked down. When Ingham unlocked the central locking and reached for the door handle, Matt opened the passenger door and slid into the thick seat. Ingham was stepping into the car when he spotted the stranger sitting there and froze.

'What the hell–' was all he could manage before he noticed the gun aimed at his balls.

'Get in, Ingham, or lose your manhood forever.'

'What do you want?' he said, defiance in his voice despite doing what Matt asked. 'Is it the car? Do you wanna steal it?'

'I've got a car, but I wouldn't mind a big Merc like this. No, I'm not here for the car, just drive.'

Away from the sanctity of the Dragon building, Matt instructed him to drive along the main road. 'Where are we going?' Ingham asked, after he had negotiated the traffic lights at the crossroads.

Matt poked him in the ribs with the gun. 'Shut the fuck up. You'll go where I tell you and don't try speeding or flashing your lights to alert police; I'm one of them.'

'I was born in Brooklyn, buddy. I know bullshit when I hear it.'

Matt sighed. 'I'm an agent with HSA. Think of it as a combination of the NSA and FBI with a British accent. In short, it means I'm armed and authorised to shoot you if you don't cooperate.'

'You can't do this! This is the UK, I've lived here for–'

Matt jabbed the butt of his gun hard into Ingham's thigh.

'Ahh!' He screeched.

'You're testing my patience, Ingham. Now, shut the fuck up and drive.'

Ingham did what he was told as Matt directed him to a safe house in north London. It was one where he knew he could park the car at the back of the house and get Ingham inside without raising the antenna of over-zealous neighbours.

Matt pushed him into a chair in the kitchen, pulled his arms behind his back and secured them with plastic ties. He didn't do it as he feared retaliation or escape, but he hoped the feeling of helplessness would have a debilitating effect on the subject.

'Hey what are you doing? I'm an American citizen–'

Matt slapped him across the face.

'Only speak when I ask you a question.'

'I'll sue your ass when I get out of here.'

He received another slap. 'You're not listening, Ingham. Don't speak unless I ask a question.'

Matt picked up another kitchen chair and placed it opposite his prisoner and sat down. Ingham looked the epitome of a successful businessman: tanned after-shave-soaked skin, expensive shirt and suit. If the company boss wasn't such an out-of-condition, overweight slob, a punch from one his fists would deliver a knock-out blow to most men. Not that his fists were big, but one hand was embellished with many large gold rings and having the weight of a thick gold bracelet, and on the other a chunky Breitling diving watch.

The expression on his face, irritation mixed with anxiety, made him look like a man used to getting his own way. He wasn't adjusting well to his new-found position in the second-string.

'You are Walter Ingham, Chief Executive of Dragon Technologies UK, yes?'

'Yep.'

'Are you a director of the US company?'

'I'm on the board.'

'Good. So, you know about Pulsar?'

'It's our star product.'

'You'll also know about the dirty tricks your people have been pulling, including blackmail and murder, to ensure every country you target buys it.'

'Now wait a minute, fella. I'm a businessman, not a criminal. I don't know anything about murder. You can't–'

'Your role here in the UK is what? To sell Dragon's products to the likes of the UK Military and NATO?'

'I came here to establish Dragon's presence in Europe. We've never been a big player in this arena, now we've got our chance with this fantastic new product.'

'And you do this how?'

'The same way any other business sells their products. Show them how Pulsar performs better than the opposition and when they're hooked, give them the support plan and financing package they want.'

Rosie had followed him to the safe house, ostensibly to run Matt back to the office, and was sitting in the next room. Matt called her in. If Ingham had been involved in her kidnapping, he had to be a good actor as he showed no hint of recognition, but then Rosie didn't either.

'Who's this?' Matt asked the prisoner.

'What's this, some kinda test? Never met her before in my life. Hey, you're not gonna try to blackmail me with a prostitute–'

Matt punched him on the side of the face.

'She's not a prostitute, you fucking shithead,' Matt said as he grabbed a handful of coiffured hair and pulled hard. 'Make another comment like that and I'll break something.'

'Aghh,' the captive screeched.

'Stop playing the idiot, Ingham. You, or people working in your organisation, kidnapped my colleague here and threatened to kill her.'

'I swear, I had nothing to do with any kidnapping. Where are you getting these wild accusations from?'

Matt let go of his hair and eyeballed him. 'I'll make it simple for you. People working for Dragon are trying to recover documents stolen from their computers.'

'Hell yeah, I know about that. Everybody in the company does. Jack, that's Jack Dawson, Head of Corporate Security, has been put in charge of getting them back. The schmuck who stole it got away with sensitive commercial data and we want it back, sure we do.'

'What's Dawson done to retrieve the data?'

'I don't know, I'm not part of the loop.'

'Even if the trail led to the UK?'

'Even if. See, you need to understand, fella, we're an armaments company. We're paranoid about leaks to the press so most information is kept in silos; a need to know basis. I don't need to know what he's doing to get the data back, so they don't tell me.'

Ingham was growing more confident by the minute, thinking he could bluff his way out. Matt wasn't finished with him yet.

'Who's Daniel Leppo?'

'He works for Jack Dawson. He's Jack's man on the ground over here.'

'Do you know Leppo?'

He shook his head. 'He doesn't come into our offices much, and what he does with his day is down to Jack.'

'Horse shit, Ingham. We know Leppo's on your payroll!'

'What?' he said looking at Matt in shock. 'How the hell would you know that?' His eyes narrowed, 'Who have you been talking to?'

'He is, isn't he?'

His head fell. He'd been found out. 'Yes.'

'You know him better than you're admitting.'

'I don't, I swear to you I don't.'

Matt pulled out his gun, squeezed the side of Ingham's cheeks with his hand and with the other, shoved the barrel into his open mouth.

'I've had enough of your lying, Ingham. You've got five seconds before I pull the trigger.'

'Agh...'

'Matt, don't,' Rosie said.

'5, 4...'

'Okay, okay,' he spluttered.

Matt withdrew the weapon but stayed close to the shaking, perspiring figure.

'Yeah,' Ingham said, 'I know him and I know he's a nasty son-of-a-bitch, but it don't mean I condone his methods.'

Matt lifted the gun to his face again and nudged it against his cheek.

'It's the truth, I swear it is. He does his own thing as directed by Jack. I just pay the bills.'

'Where does Leppo hang out?'

'He's got a house in Hemel Hempstead and access to a warehouse we own in Hitchen.'

He turned to Rosie, watching with professional detachment. 'What do you think?' he said, in a voice quiet enough so the captive wouldn't hear. 'Do you believe him?'

'I think he's telling the truth. Leppo is the one we should be after.'

'I think so too,' Matt said, 'but I don't think Ingham's hands are squeaky clean either.'

'Me too. I think he's dirty.'

'He knows what Leppo's been doing and did nothing to stop him. Too busy counting the bonuses he receives for making Pulsar sales.'

'Leppo's over here to recover the documents,' Rosie said, 'but someone has to be orchestrating the incriminating videos and blackmail. It might be Ingham. What do you want to do with him?'

He pulled out his phone.

'Who are you calling?'

'The Captivity Team. Dragon Technologies will need to operate without their Managing Director for a while. We can't have this guy going back to work and warning Leppo that we're coming after him, can we?'

Chapter 45

The HSA agents arrived in Hemel Hempstead shortly after eleven. Ten minutes later, they drove past Daniel Leppo's rented house. He lived close to Hemel Hempstead Football Club. Somehow, Matt couldn't see Dragon's Head of International Security using his spare time to stand on the terraces drinking mugs of Bovril and waving his team scarf. It was a detached place, not near any neighbours but central for main road links.

Due to Leppo's uncompromising behaviour, Matt decided they would return the compliment. Included in the team were Matt and Rosie, Joseph and Jess and a unit of five 'heavies', consisting of a door opener and several heavily-clad room searchers who arrived in a prison-style van. They parked close to the house, but out of sight and switched off all engines and lights.

Matt got out of the car and stretched; it had been a long week. He walked to the boot of the car and extracted a flak jacket and put it on. He handed one to Rosie who did the same. Matt made sure his gun was loaded and ready to fire before scanning the area around the house. He checked its position relative to neighbours, the layout of the garden and garage, the wind, and the weather. He also made sure no dog walkers were loitering, preparing to take pictures on their phones before inviting friends and neighbours to join them. In the house where Rosie was being held, they'd used subterfuge to deny the kidnappers time to kill their hostage, but for this one they would deploy classic police tactics: hit them hard and fast.

With the door banger in position they waited. *Bang-bang-bang* and the front door of the house fell open. One of the heavies on the team, a big man, over six-four and built like a prop forward, stepped inside and shouted, 'Police! Hands in the air! Let me see your hands!'

The assault team piled in and moved through the house like a well-oiled machine, pushing doors open and sweeping them with the barrel of their guns. They didn't meet anyone until the kitchen. Matt, walking behind two of the assault team, could see a broad-shouldered guy sitting at the kitchen table. He fitted the description Rosie gave of Leppo's right-hand man, King, a man who had threatened to rape her.

He obviously didn't hear the noisy police entrance, perhaps due to the thick walls of the house and the radio on the worktop playing loud rock music. The guy wore an FBI-style shoulder holster and, on spotting the intruders, reached for his gun.

'Leave it!' the lead officer shouted.

The hand continued to travel along the leather strapping and made contact with the weapon. He gripped the handle and, almost in slow motion, the grey metal body emerged.

The lead officer's gun responded with two short bursts. The gunman's previously white t-shirt now exhibited two large blood-red marks, their circumferences gradually expanding. He toppled from the chair and fell to the floor.

Matt ducked out of the room and nodded to Rosie standing beside him, but her face displayed no emotion at the killing of her tormentor. He set off in search of Leppo, the man's image etched in Matt's brain. He and Rosie checked the main ground floor rooms as the assault team had done minutes before, but found nothing. Believing he might be hiding, Matt opened what he thought could be a store cupboard and discovered stairs leading down. He nodded to Rosie to follow him.

'Shouldn't we wait until the assault team are finished upstairs and send them down?'

'Why let them have all the fun?'

Matt descended the stairs, Rosie close behind him. She closed the cellar door to block the light at their back, not wishing to make themselves easy targets, with the added benefit of shutting out the noise of the heavy-booted team upstairs. Her actions didn't give the HSA agents a problem, as the stairs and the cellar below were illuminated, perhaps with safety lighting or because someone was already down there.

The cellar looked large and spacious without all the clutter of a family home; no outgrown bikes, unused mattresses or scrap books. Instead, it displayed the neat, orderly sparseness of a rental. At one end, a tidy pile of packing cases, their contents clearly labelled, while at the other, the armed figure of Daniel Leppo, hunched over the blood-stained form of Chris Anderson, tied to a chair, his head slumped. An iPhone, attached to a mobile speaker was playing Beethoven's 1812 Overture in the background.

'Drop the gun, Leppo!' Matt called. 'We're armed!'

Leppo didn't turn on hearing his shout or look around to find out who uttered it. Instead, he ducked behind the inert figure of Chris and pointed his weapon at them. 'Get back or I'll shoot!'

He had taken a good position behind the chair as, despite a stocky and muscular appearance, the chair and Chris's slumped body hid his profile effectively.

'The game's up, Leppo. King isn't coming down to help you. Let Chris go.'

'You must be crazy. I hold all the cards punk, not you.' He turned the gun and placed it against Chris's head. 'I don't like people pointing guns at me. Put your guns down or the kid gets it.'

'You're making a big mistake,' Matt said. 'You don't have the stolen documents, and he can't give you them if you shoot him.'

'Ha, you think I'm stupid? I know where his laptop is; he just told me. My boys are on the way right now to pick it up.'

Matt felt a wave of panic. If Leppo had managed to kidnap Chris, he had to be aware of the Windsor house. The vision of Lisa and Louise being confronted by a couple of armed men didn't bear thinking about. He needed to stop this charade now and warn them.

'Getting hold of the laptop won't be the end of this.'

'You bet it will.'

'No. The documents are also saved to a separate hard drive and to the Cloud. They can be accessed from any computer.'

'You're bluffing.'

'Maybe I am, maybe I'm not. Let's face it, Leppo, you've messed up this like you did with all your other botched attempts to silence him. You could have asked him yourself if you hadn't been so bloody heavy-handed. I imagine Jack Dawson's patience is wearing thin with you.'

Matt couldn't see his face, a combination of the dull light in the cellar and the blocking effect of the chair, but the tone of Leppo's voice suggested some element of doubt creeping in.

'I'm not going to tell you people again. Put your fucking guns down!'

Without a clear shot, they couldn't move from this stalemate position, so Matt decided to do something to break it. He bent over and placed his gun on the floor and Rosie did the same. The HSA agents were spaced a metre or so apart. If Leppo approached to pick up their guns, they would go for their spares in the rear holster. Leppo might be quick, but before he realised what was happening, one or both of them would nail him. Leppo didn't budge, suggesting he suspected such a move.

'Now, back away!'

Matt took one step back to the right and so did Rosie to the left, increasing the space between them.

Matt expected him to come out from his hiding place, but Leppo surprised him by dragging the chair to one side. He did it at a slow, methodical pace, making sure he didn't expose any part of his body. The two figures dissolved slowly as they moved into a darkened section of the cellar, untouched by the light bulb's illumination. Seconds later, they disappeared completely.

'Don't move you two! Stay where you are!' Leppo's disembodied voice shouted. 'You can't see me but I can still see you.'

A door creaked and Matt could tell from increased levels of light and the sharp drop in temperature that it led outside. He waited, not knowing where Leppo was and if his gun was trained on his or Rosie's head. Seconds later, he heard a car engine start. He sprinted into the darkened area and fell headlong on to the dusty cellar floor. He'd tripped over an object left there for that very purpose.

Matt got up and limped to the door. Rosie, cautious at seeing the fate of her colleague, walked closely behind him. Their caution wasn't for nothing as Leppo had left several other obstacles in their way, including a chair and a packing case. Matt pushed them to one side and headed outside. An armed officer lay bleeding against the wall, blood trickling down a face wound, but Daniel Leppo, Chris Anderson, and the car Matt had heard, were nowhere to be seen.

Chapter 46

'Quieten down, everybody. C'mon you lot, let's have some hush.' Superintendent Tony Quigley looked around at the expectant faces in the packed room, his jowly face locked in a serious expression. 'That's better,' he said, 'I can hear myself think now.'

It didn't look like a big audience in comparison to many of the drug raids that Emma Davis had taken part in, but it was one of the noisiest. Everyone was buoyed by the news of Simon Wood's arrest and his first appearance in court. The judge didn't hesitate in rejecting Wood's well-paid lawyer's plea detailing his client's poor health and terminally ill mother, both fabrications in Emma's view, and he refused an application for bail. The judge went as far as saying if the jury found Wood guilty, sick or not, he would have no choice but to hand out a long custodial sentence.

'This is the second raid of Operation Redoubt, our plan to shut down Simon Wood's drug business for good. The target tonight is a large spice lab which we believe is being operated by Roderick Lamar. Most of you will know him as the nephew of Simon Wood.'

Excited murmurs leapt around the room with the alacrity of fire in a dry forest. It was hard getting anyone interested in Wood six months ago, now with the man in custody and having closed one of his cocaine warehouses last week, they couldn't get enough. Superintendent Quigley had trouble keeping a lid on the enthusiasm.

'Quiet now,' the Super said. 'This Lamar character we believe is Wood's right-hand man. There's talk of Lamar minding the shop while Wood's inside. Most people think he's read the runes and expects his boss to be away for the foreseeable; maybe he fancies his chances at taking over the whole operation. Our job is to go there and close his main source of income and, in addition, nab the geezer with his paws on the merchandise. Not only will we take a shed-load of spice off the shelves, it'll put another big dent in Simon Wood's illegal operations.'

This time the Super didn't try to stop them as feet were stamped and hands banged on the sides of their chairs. Soon they ran out of steam, not because of any dimmed enthusiasm for the cause, but everyone was keen to find out the role they would perform in this evening's raid.

Spice wasn't a single drug, but a wide range of laboratory-made chemicals designed to mimic the effects of the main psychoactive compound contained in marijuana, called THC, tetrahydrocannabinol. A highly addictive substance, spice was capable of turning lively teenagers into zombies, as the residents of many towns and cities in the UK could testify. In prisons, the drug was a serious problem, its addictive nature encouraging repeated use to prevent the onset of an angst-inducing 'downer.' To drug barons it was manna from heaven as it provided them with a steady flow of eager customers who would dig themselves deeper and deeper into debt. Spice was now at the heart of the drug/debt culture in most prisons and the main reason for increasing inmate violence.

They left the briefing room twenty minutes later and piled into vehicles; four detectives in two cars and half a dozen uniformed officers in a van, with another for the prisoners. Jacko didn't say much as they headed east towards an address in Essex. It was a large county and the laboratory was located in the extreme south, near Grays, many miles away from Emma's house in Ingatestone to the north of the county.

'Did Arsenal not do well last night, or something?'

He looked over, a strange expression on his face at this poor woman who knew bugger-all about the beautiful game.

'They didn't bloody play, did they,' came the grumpy reply.

'How am I supposed to know? What's bugging you tonight? Sally give you the old heave-ho again?'

'She wouldn't dare.'

'What then?'

He didn't respond.

'C'mon Jacko,' she teased, 'what's up? Tell Aunty Emma, why doncha?'

'Emma, I've got a hangover, leave it out, will ya?'

She got the message, turned up the radio and stared out of the window. East London passed by in a murky blaze of street lights and neon signs, accompanied by the *whisk-whisk* of the windscreen wipers. She'd been to places like this before during raids and seen them from the window of the train when commuting into London. Matt grew up in the East End, his parents Irish rural stock eager to escape the grinding poverty of a subsidence farming community. She couldn't imagine living in some of these places; damp, rat-infested tenements, neighbours speaking a language she couldn't understand, strange smells clogging her nostrils at all hours of the day. Plus, the vacant look of the dispossessed standing on street corners.

Her job brought her in contact with many such people. Enterprising men from Pakistan and the Middle East, unable to find work due to a lack of practical skills or a mastery of English, turned to selling the principal exports of their home country, marijuana, opium and heroin. They soon realised they had a great advantage over the local London dealers, as they could speak the language of their suppliers. Through this, fortunes were made and it ensured a regular supply for the aimless people whose only escape from lack of money, despair and failure was inside their heads.

In this business, Simon Wood was something of an anomaly. He was privately educated and with a degree from a leading UK university. He didn't have a reputation as a violent man, a requisite for those trying to establish a long-term foothold. He did have a knack of surrounding himself with a group of trusted lieutenants who would do whatever he needed. Lieutenants like the man they hoped to meet tonight, Roderick Lamar.

Emma and Jacko reached the rendezvous point before everyone else, a rutted farm track surrounded by woods and fields. Despite trying to keep the small convoy together as they barrelled along the A13, the vans fell behind. They'd lost the second squad car about twenty minutes before when the officers inside stopped for a piss, but they arrived a few minutes later and the two vans, a quarter of an hour after that.

Based on intel, the spice laboratory was located in the building she could see in the moonlight about two hundred metres in the distance. The size and shape suggested an old hay barn, but not one derelict and falling to bits. This one looked solid and fit for purpose, either converted by a cash-strapped farmer or more likely by drug dealers, diverting cash from Spice sales to create a sophisticated rural laboratory.

With the team all in one place, Emma called them together. The faces of the detectives could be seen, but the armed response team were near-invisible with all-black clothing, black helmets and visors.

'Is everyone clear about what we're here to do?'

The detectives nodded, the ARU clanked their equipment.

'The place we're interested in is the large warehouse over there,' she said pointing at the faint outline in the darkness. 'Can you all see it?'

'Just about.'

'We hammer the door down and once inside, grab anyone we find. Handcuff everyone, no excuses or exceptions. Clear?'

'Yep,' several voices said.

'I know you're all wearing bulky and awkward gear,' she said feeling a touch under-dressed in a simple flak-jacket, 'but try not to damage the laboratory equipment. We'll need it for evidence. Right. That's it. Any questions?'

She looked around, but didn't hear anything. 'Let's go,' she said.

They walked up the track, muddy in places and rutted by the big tyres of large farm machinery. The men in the ARU didn't seem to mind as they all wore boots, but the more lightly-shod detectives kept to the edge where the grass verge offered more solid ground.

The windows of the warehouse were blacked out, but little chinks of light escaping suggested someone might be at home. While the door banger got himself prepared, Emma walked to the corner of the warehouse and looked around. In what appeared to be a tarmacked car park, big enough to house eight or maybe ten cars, she could see four. Here was proof that this journey into deepest Essex was not wasted.

The laboratory door jumped open under the force of the door banger, a scratched hunk of metal with 'Terminator 2' written on the side.

The assault crew piled in, Emma, Jacko and the other detectives following behind the black Kevlar-clad figures. Emma smiled when she saw the contents of the warehouse, everything bathed in bright overhead lights. On three long metal benches she could see metal pots, filters, glass jars, bottles of chemicals and, scattered around on all surfaces, a dusting of green leaves.

Spice production was usually done in two stages, a lab first made the chemical and turned it into a white powder. Second, wholesalers would dilute the powder with something like acetone and spray it on to leaves such as tea. The contents of this warehouse looked to Emma like a second-stage lab, and she would bet the pile of boxes in the corner would be filled with leaves ready to be coated, or packets of the finished product. She made her way inside to take a look when the lights conked out.

'Bloody hell! Torches out everybody!' Emma called, 'and for Christ's sake no shooting unless you make a positive identification of a target.'

She didn't see anything that looked like an office on the way in, and she assumed the electricity control box would be at the other end of the room. She made her way there by torchlight, careful not to bump into any of the lab equipment or the Kevlar-clad assault team.

In an untidy room at the back, looking more like a storeroom than an office, she spotted the electricity box, high up on the wall. She reached for a chair to give her a leg up when she heard the sound of car engines firing up. She searched around for a door and hoped the boys out there in the lab area were doing the same.

At last, she made it outside, the cold air hitting her with the force of a slap after the clammy heat of the lab. She looked left and right but couldn't see any cars. Emma ran around the corner of the warehouse, her gun at the ready; nothing. Walking further down the track, she could see through a row of trees, the tell-tale red brake lights of a number of cars moving away in the distance. She ran across the car park and let out an animalistic screech to the trees when she realised there was another road, tarmacked and leading the opposite way from the track the police team had used.

She threw her arms up to the heavens; what an almighty balls-up. When first sighting the cars in the car park, she should have guessed the drug gang had an escape route and if so, detailed a member of the armed response team to guard it. She pulled out her radio and called it in, but without a decent description or registration plate, a passing patrol car had little to go on. She didn't feel hopeful.

She walked back inside the warehouse, the lights restored and the lab lit up in its former glory. Sarah Leggett, one of the detectives in her team, was sifting through the pile of boxes in the corner. Emma could see they contained nothing but air. Seeing them and the departing cars one word popped into her head: setup.

She walked towards the young detective. 'Did someone switch off the lights or did we have a power outage?' Emma asked.

'With modern consumer units like the one they have here, it's impossible to tell, but my money's on a pre-arranged plan. As soon as they heard us banging the door, they legged it out the back. The last one out kills the lights to slow us up, and they disappear down the road. Easy-peasy.'

'Someone should have been watching the vehicles.'

'It's easy with hindsight. Don't beat yourself up about it, boss.'

She looked around the room for Jacko but couldn't see him and guessed he would be outside having a smoke. She walked past lab equipment, much of it being pawed over by restless coppers, all dressed up and with no sign of a party. Stepping outside, she didn't see him standing amongst the small knot of coppers, helmets on the floor and flak-jackets lying open to the cool night air.

'Anyone seen Sergeant Harris?' she asked.

'Not for a while,' one replied. 'Not since the lights went out.'

'Me neither,' said another.

She walked around the outer perimeter of the building, feeling apprehensive at finding Jacko injured. She wondered if he'd sprinted out at the first sound of engines firing, and the villains had run him over or left him beaten up on the grass.

She started to walk over the drug gang's escape route when her phone rang.

'Emma, my good lady, how are you? Are you looking for me?'

She didn't know many Jamaican men and none knew her mobile number.

'Who is this?'

'Roderick Lamar.'

'How did you get my number?'

'That's for a discussion at some later point.'

'What do you want? Are you phoning to gloat about your amazing escape?'

'What do I want? Wrong question detective. What do you want?'

'I want you and your crew inside, is what I want.'

'Not going to happen. Let me give you a clue who is sitting beside me right now. Short, greasy hair, dark skin and a fat nose. Are you outside looking for him?'

'Jacko? You've got Jacko? I'll fucking kill you Lamar.'

'*Tsk, tsk* Emma, such a temper. Have a listen to your man's sweet voice.'

'Emma, it's me. Do as he says or he'll kill me.'

'The boy's right, Emma,' Lamar said. 'Do as I say or you won't see him again. Now listen up.'

Chapter 47

Louise re-read the article she'd written on a spare laptop that Lisa allowed her to use. Before coming down to help Lisa make dinner, she called her editor, Kingsley Vincent. He gave her his usual line about her continued unauthorised absence and something about her feet being in deep water and anything else the idiot could think of. Vincent was a fine journalist and could edit and improve anything Louise put in front of him in a matter of minutes, but people-management was beyond him.

Tired of his excuses and accusations, she asked to be transferred to the head of news reporting. When she told him her story, he wanted to hear more and at one stage threatened to throw Kingsley from the roof of their building for treating her in such a cavalier fashion. She knew she couldn't reveal everything without compromising their position here at Windsor, but promised to write something soon and send it to him when she'd finished.

'Where's Chris?' Lisa asked, standing at the cooker and stirring the pasta sauce. 'The food's almost cooked.'

'Still in his room, I suspect. I gave him a knock when I went past about five minutes ago. He knows as well as anybody that you don't like him being late for dinner.'

'He seems to be spending more time in the Orangery. Maybe he's out there.'

'What the round, glass building in the woods?'

'Yes.'

'I think it's creepy out there, surrounded by all those trees.'

'It's not creepy at all. I used to play there as a child. Once I fell asleep and, unknown to me, Daddy and all the staff were out looking for me.'

'I wouldn't sleep out there if you paid me. If this is what happened to Chris, I'm not going down there to find out.'

Lisa turned the heat down on the sauce. 'I'm not going outside either as it's too cold, but I'll go up and check his room. Could you pour the water into glasses, please?'

Louise opened the large walk-in fridge and picked up the water jug. It was chilled and filtered with tap water flavoured with lemon and some herb whose name Lisa wouldn't reveal. It tasted wonderful and refreshing but Chris wouldn't touch it. She filled his glass straight from the tap instead.

She closed the fridge door and stopped when she heard a faint, but strange sounding noise outside. It sounded like metal scraping on metal, as if something had been dragged against the steel water collector that stood against the wall, close to the kitchen window. The kitchen was quiet as Lisa didn't like the radio or other music playing during dinner, the only sound being the occasional pop from the sauce. She leaned over to place the water jug on the table when she heard whispered voices.

She walked over and switched off the light and closed the door as if leaving the room. Instead, she crept over to the kitchen window and listened. The sound of movement outside was clearer now; people were out there. She lifted the side of the blind a little and looked out. Two figures were making their way towards the back of the house.

Louise fled from the kitchen and searched the hall table for her phone. She found it, but when she picked it up, it started to ring.

'Hello.'

'Louise it's Matt. Don't talk, listen. Men, I don't know how many, have been sent to Windsor by Dragon to recover Chris's laptop.'

'I know,' Louise said, 'I've just seen them outside.'

'What? Damn. I'm tempted to tell you to leave the bloody thing on the doorstep, but no, I won't give them the satisfaction. They've got Chris.'

'They've what! We thought he was down in the Orangery.'

'Where?'

'A place in the grounds; it doesn't matter. Did you see him? Is he all right?'

'Daniel Leppo, the Dragon Security guy, had been interrogating him and beat him up before we arrived. He drove off with Chris before we could stop him.'

'That's terrible.'

'Two of my team are on their way to Windsor and will be with you in about fifteen to twenty minutes. In the meantime, I want everyone to hide in the cellar.'

'I will, but first I need to go and find Lisa. Bye Matt, thanks for warning us.'

She was about to run upstairs when she saw Lisa walking down.

'Chris isn't in his room, but his laptop's still there, so he must have gone out for a walk. What's wrong with you, Louise? There aren't any ghosts in this house but you look like you've seen one.'

'Bad men are here; they're outside.'

'What are you talking about?'

'I've just been speaking to Matt. Dragon have sent two armed men to grab Chris's laptop. They're outside; I saw them sneaking around the back.'

David, Sir Raymond's personal assistant, appeared wiping his hands on a towel and looking flustered. 'What's going on? Did I hear you say something about armed men?'

'We've to move into the cellar, Matt says. He's sent a couple of his agents to help us, but they won't be here for another twenty minutes.'

'If Matt says we need to move to the cellar then move there we must. My wife's away at her sister's and the rest of the staff aren't here until the morning, so there's only we three and Chris. Where's Chris?'

'He's been kidnapped.'

'He's been what?' Lisa exclaimed. 'When?'

'I'll tell you later. First, we all need to get down to the cellar.'

They moved to a door in the hall which David opened with a key hanging nearby. Once opened, David bent down and picked up a torch. He handed it to Lisa.

'You two go on down and use the torch, not the main light. I'll be down in a second. I want to make sure all the main doors are locked.'

Using only the light of the torch they descended the stairs. Once at the bottom, Lisa walked towards the only window and covered it up. In some ways it was a futile gesture as the glass was grimy with years of dirt and Louise doubted if any light could escape. They sat on packing cases and waited.

'What's happened to Chris?' Lisa asked in a hushed voice. 'How did they kidnap him?'

'I don't know. Perhaps he went down to the Orangery and men were waiting for him. Matt said he'd been kidnapped and questioned by Daniel Leppo.'

'Oh my God!'

'Keep calm Lisa,' Louise said taking her hand. 'We'll get through this.'

Louise rubbed Lisa's hand for several moments although she felt just as scared as her companion.

'Who's Daniel Leppo?' Lisa asked.

'The security guy at Dragon.'

'This is terrible. Why didn't Chris take the laptop down to the Orangery with him? They could have taken it and left him alone.'

'I don't know. They must have caught him walking through the grounds.'

They sat without speaking for a couple of minutes, their ears straining for any unusual sound. The door to the cellar creaked making both girls jump, followed by the noise of the door being locked. David's feet then his legs appeared. When he reached the bottom, they could see he carried a double-barrelled shotgun.

He lifted it to show them. 'If they come anywhere near us, I'll give them a piece of this.'

Louise had grown up in a pacifist household, her father a member of CND, her mother a fund-raiser for Greenpeace. Even though she didn't like guns, she felt strangely comforted by its presence.

'We're pretty safe down here,' David said when he at last sat down. 'The staircase is the only way in and if the door at the top is locked, which it is now, it would take the strength of a bull to break it down.'

'That's reassuring,' Louise said.

'What's that noise?' Lisa hissed.

Louise listened and could hear an odd gurgling and tapping sound.

'Oh, it's only the water moving in the pipes,' David said, his face cheery and confident in contrast to the solemn faces of the two women. 'Don't worry about noises outside, you won't hear any. The walls are too thick.'

'So, how will we hear their approach?'

'We won't, unless they try to shoot out the lock or knock down the door. If they do, then they'll get a dose of this,' he said tapping the shotgun cradled in his lap.

'I hope it doesn't come to that,' Louise said. 'I want them to go upstairs, pick up Chris's laptop and go away.'

'Maybe they won't be able to find it,' Lisa said.

'Someone needs to go out there and tell them,' Louise said.

'Take it easy, Louise,' David said. 'None of us are moving from this cellar. Let's just deal with the situation in front of us, one step at a time.'

'I understand, David, but I'd rather it didn't end in bloodshed.'

'I don't mind, as long as it's their blood we're shedding.'

'Hear, hear,' Lisa said.

They said little for the next ten to fifteen minutes, the silence only punctuated by hushed snippets of conversation and the gurgling of water pipes as they fed the dishwasher operating upstairs. They all jumped at the sound of a loud knocking on the cellar door. Voices on the other side were saying something, but Louise couldn't make out the words.

'What do they want?' Louise asked.

'I don't know, I can't make it out,' David said.

'Couldn't you walk up to the door and listen.'

'No way. What if they start shooting at the door? They might blow my ear off. If they want to speak to us, they need to come down here.'

Seconds later, they heard a key turning in the lock and the staircase became illuminated by the soft light of the hallway.

'Damn!' David said. 'They must have found the spare in the hallway sideboard.' He stood and pointed the gun at the empty staircase. 'Cover your ears, girls if you don't want to be deafened. This thing makes one hell of a racket.'

'Is there anyone down there?' a voice said. It didn't sound American, nor was the tone aggressive. David repositioned the shotgun in his hand. Louise didn't know if he'd fired such a weapon before, although she knew he'd once served in Northern Ireland, but his hold did look solid and unflinching.

They heard fumbling and moments later the cellar filled with the light of several bare bulbs. If Louise didn't feel so scared, she would marvel at the huge space and let her imagination run riot at what it could be used for. For now, all her efforts were focussed on stopping her hands shaking and her knees trembling.

'Don't come any closer!' David shouted. 'I'm armed and I'll shoot!'

'That's all we need, bloody vigilantes!' a voice said. 'Is this what we get for trying to save you? It's Joseph and Jess from HSA. We've chased off the two guys who were outside. You can come out now if you like.'

Chapter 48

Matt was driving Rosie's replacement Seat hatchback. They were going around tight bends to the sound of squealing tyres and something rolling around in the boot. To his surprise, Rosie didn't protest.

The injured copper outside the cellar at Daniel Leppo's house didn't see the blow that felled him, but seconds before, he noted down the car's registration number. Using ANPR, they knew Daniel Leppo's Lexus GS was several miles further ahead. Rosie looked at the map, not an easy task for a confirmed satnav user. She was trying to find a straight bit of road for the police car in front of Leppo to lay a Stinger across the road or use their vehicle to block his path.

They were travelling along the Leighton Buzzard Road; Leppo had left the built-up areas behind, and they were now headed into the countryside. This was better all round. There would be fewer pedestrians to be mown down by speeding cars, and no one would have to take their lives in their hands as they overtook stationary traffic or rocketed through a succession of red lights.

'How are you feeling, Rosie?'

'About what?'

'Being back in the field again. Chasing a fugitive at high speed.'

'I told everybody, including the psychologist who picked my head apart, I feel fine. There's no need to treat me with kid gloves. Look, I'm not even holding on as you fling my lovely new car around these tight bends. I'm over it, all right?'

'No sleepless nights or flashbacks?'

'I'm not sleeping well, to be truthful, more a feature of the red wine I'm drinking than any fallout from the kidnap.'

Matt shot past a car that appeared to be stationary, more likely taking it easy following a visit to a local pub or restaurant.

'So, you're drinking more?' he said.

'Yes, Mr bloody settee-psychiatrist, I'm drinking more. I need help from somewhere and the booze does the trick. Now, concentrate on the road and not on me.'

Rosie's radio beeped.

'Agent Fox.'

'This is Tango Bravo. We can see the target vehicle coming towards us. Can't use the Stinger as there are other vehicles around. What do you want us to do?'

'When you see him, pull into his path to try to slow him down.'

'Roger, will do. Over and out.'

She put the radio down.

'If they can see the car,' Matt said, 'they can set the Stinger.'

'You heard him say, 'there are other vehicles around', or maybe it's a euphemism for, they couldn't be bothered. It's probably not much fun for the boys in blue doing our bidding.'

'To be honest, I don't have much faith in the Stinger. It's fine in a quiet country lane in the West Country or Yorkshire, but out here you're more likely to shred the tyres of half a dozen cars before the target vehicle gets there.'

'Do you think we're gaining on him?'

'You're the one with the map.'

'I'm useless with maps as you know.'

'Call the patrol car, ask them where they are.'

Rosie did as Matt suggested and a few minutes later laid the radio back in her lap. 'It sounds like the two cars are playing silly buggers. The police have Leppo right behind them and he's refusing all requests to stop. The cars are zigzagging down the road, the police car trying to block Leppo's car and him looking for a gap to overtake.'

'Shame the road isn't busier,' Matt said. 'With a few more cars coming the opposite way, the cops could bring Leppo to a stop and he wouldn't be able to overtake.'

'It'll get busier as we move closer to Leighton Buzzard.'

'Do you know their location?'

'I'm just checking it on the map.' A minute or so later she said, 'Hey, I reckon we're only about three kilometres behind.'

'You sure?'

'Yeah,' Rosie said. 'The cops must have slowed him down. In which case, we should be able to see his car in a few minutes. Maybe then we'll get a chance to box him in from the rear.'

'Would you like me doing this in your nice new motor? He might try to ram his way out.'

'I didn't think of that. The deal's off, okay?'

A few minutes later, Matt screeched around a bend and up ahead saw the dancing rear lights and bright glow of two pairs of frequently stabbed brake lights.

'Oh, ho,' Matt said. 'Do you see what I see?'

'I told you they weren't far off, you non-believer.'

Matt gritted his teeth. 'This time, no matter what happens, we're stopping him. He's not getting away. Agreed?'

'Agreed.'

'Check your weapon.'

They were about a hundred metres apart when Leppo's car braked hard, and disappeared off to the left on a road barely visible in the dark. It took the cop car a few seconds to realise they'd lost their follower. Matt made the turn before they did, heading towards a place called Ringshall. The car they were chasing was large and couldn't do the corners as fast as Rosie's nimble Seat and, in a matter of minutes, the HSA agents was right behind him. The road twisted and turned and gave them little room for mistakes with high hedgerows on either side of the narrow carriageway.

'When we reach a straight, take a shot. You know the drill, aim low at a tyre. If you miss you might put a hole in the fuel tank or the hydraulics.'

'No problem.' Rosie pushed the radio and map away and pulled out her gun, recovered from the floor of Leppo's cellar.

They soon reached a straight section of road. Matt edged the car towards the middle of the narrow carriageway to give Rosie a better view of the Lexus's left flank. She leaned out of the window and let off three shots in rapid succession. The effect was immediate and dramatic. Before the upcoming bend, Leppo's car swerved from side to side before crashing through the hedgerow, missing a telegraph pole by centimetres.

When Matt reached the spot, he brought the car to a halt. The Lexus wasn't bouncing across the field as he expected, but had stopped after smacking into something solid, maybe a thick tree stump or some abandoned farming equipment. Steam was pouring from the crumpled bonnet.

The HSA agents got out of the car, their guns held in a double grip on outstretched arms. He nodded for Rosie to approach the left side of the vehicle while he did the same on the right. When he reached touching distance of the car, he approached it slowly, his senses on the lookout for anything anomalous. Through the window he could see Chris slumped in the rear. Neither he nor Rosie would stop to attend to him. Leppo was the target. He needed to be neutralised first, either with the application of handcuffs or with a bullet.

The driver's door lay ajar, the spent airbags hanging limp and useless from the console. Matt peered into the gloom of the car's interior, no longer lit by a working light. As he turned to walk to the front of the car, a gunshot split the silence of the night.

Instead of a delighted whoop from Rosie in triumph, a hammer blow struck him on the shoulder, throwing him backward. He turned and slumped down in the open door of the Lexus, his vision clouded and his brain not registering the sights and sounds it had processed earlier with such ease.

Heavy footsteps crunched over damp grass and fallen twigs.

'You think someone like you can get the better of me, eh?' an American voice said. 'I'm a winner, always have been.'

Matt tried to focus and saw a figure standing over him, framed by weak moonlight at his back; Daniel Leppo.

'If you're the best you Brits can come up with, you need to spend more time with my buddies at the FBI.'

'You're a smug bastard, Leppo.'

'I am too. Well, I guess I better be off, can't stand talking here all day.'

Leppo raised his gun and pointed it at Matt's head. Matt heard two shots. His mind went blank.

Chapter 49

Emma left the Spice laboratory alone. If anyone took notice of Jacko not being with her, they didn't say. If they had, she would have given a ready-made excuse that he went back in one of the squad cars. If they weren't convinced, they would assume a colleague's tiff, or from the more twisted, a lover's quarrel. No one would dare to enquire further for fear of receiving a tongue lashing from her.

It didn't matter that everyone knew she loved Matt Flynn and he loved her. She would never let anyone, including her best friend in the force, Jacko, come between them. Police officers liked their conspiracy theories more than television script writers. It gave them something to talk about on late-night patrols, or hours spent on surveillance in a car with an individual who didn't bathe as often as they should.

She knew what she was about to do didn't make sense for a supposedly smart copper like herself. Lamar had given her strict instructions to come alone and not to mention this to anyone else. With her rational hat on, she knew she needed to turn back and hand the whole kidnapping thing over to the specialist teams set up for such a situation, but she believed Lamar. If she didn't do what he said, Jacko would die.

She told herself she would do the same thing for any other colleague, but deep inside she knew it to be a lie.

She and Jacko had worked together for over three years. In the claustrophobic world of the drug squad with weekends lost while holed up in a house or a van watching a suspect, and holidays spent observing crowds at outdoor markets looking for known faces, it felt more like ten years in a normal friendship. Jacko had become more than a colleague to her, more like a brother, but no way was there any sexual element or longing in their relationship.

She arrived in Romford, a place not unfamiliar to her as her aunt once lived in the town. Emma used to visit her two, sometimes three times a month before she died. The directions Lamar gave led her were to the north of the town, a place of large 1930s villas, most updated with doubled-glazed windows, paved driveways and garages.

In a road off Mashiters Walk, the familiar refrain of 'You have reached your destination' sounded from the car's satnav. The house was a sizeable detached place, brown-stained oak beams and leaded windows, but the giveaway for a nosey detective was the Audi A6 with black wheels, blackened windows and in-your-face murals on the bodywork. *Look at me*, it said, *I'm a successful drug dealer*.

She knew they wouldn't hand over Jacko without her giving them something in return; maybe an ear on the inside of the drug squad, or help at a forthcoming criminal trial. Whatever they wanted, she would consider giving it to them, as long as it didn't involve exposing any of her colleagues. She would need to do something to win Lamar's confidence. At the first opportunity, maybe in six weeks or six months' time, she would use the knowledge gleaned about their operations to destroy them.

Emma walked to the door of the house, but before reaching it a security light switched on, bathing the outside in a cold, white light. When she reached the top step, the front door opened and a gigantic black guy, who would find the weights in most gyms timid, ushered her inside.

'Turn around,' he said.

She did and he patted her down, avoiding groping her as the less experienced tended to do. Satisfied, he pointed to a closed door and said, 'In there.' The back room of this suburban house would be a dining room in neighbouring houses, but with the curtains drawn and the lights on, it had become the storage facility for a drug operation. If she could hazard a guess, a couple of million pounds' worth of Spice stacked in what she reckoned were one-kilogram bags. At the other end of the room, Jacko tied to a chair, Lamar in the chair beside him, a gun sticking out from his waistband.

'Ah, if it isn't Detective Davis. Come in Emma, don't stand at the door. And don't try to make a run for it. Tito breaks bones for breakfast.'

'I can believe it,' Emma said. 'How are you Jacko? How are they treating you?'

'How d'ya bloody think?' he snarled. 'I'm trussed up here like a fucking chicken.'

Lamar's big hand moved with the speed of an addict who had just scored his fix and slapped Jacko hard on the face.

'Whoa fuck, that hurt,' Jacko blurted out.

'No more insults, Harris, there's a lady present. Sit down Emma, we have a lot to discuss.'

Lamar wore a white t-shirt over loose-fitting chinos, his feet in loafers without socks. Give him a set of designer shades and he could be the stereotypical driver of the car outside.

'What do you want, Lamar?' she asked.

'I'll get to it in a minute. First of all, would you like a drink, Emma?' he said nodding towards a slim-line, glass-fronted wine cooler fridge she hadn't spotted earlier. 'I have all manner of beers, white wine and soft drinks. What'll you have?'

'I don't–'

'Now, don't say you won't take anything from me or I'll feel insulted. What'll you have?'

'You've twisted my arm. I'll take a beer.'

'Coming up.' He stood, tall and muscled, but slim. She assumed he used the bear in the hall to do any of the enforcing work and the gun for everything else. In her experience, drug dealers like him were willing and capable of using such a weapon, as the business they'd built was lucrative and worth fighting over.

He opened the bottle and handed it to Emma. When he resumed his seat, he lifted his bottle and said, 'Cheers.' With some reluctance, she did the same.

'Do you know where the intel for tonight's raid on the Grays operation came from?' Lamar asked.

Good question, she thought. She didn't. Superintendent Quigley said something about it coming from a good source but nobody thought to query it. 'No, I don't.'

'Me,' he said, tapping his chest.

In the process of taking a drink from the beer bottle, she spluttered out a mouthful over the floor.

'Not a good look, Emma.'

'Why the hell did you tell us about your own laboratory?'

'When your forensic boys examine the place, they will find the prints and DNA of people who work in Jamal Baqri's organisation. We broke into their place a few weeks back and nicked some of their kit and put it into the Grays warehouse.'

'Can't afford to buy the equipment now, you have to nick it from your competitors. Is this where you've ended up?'

He sneered. 'Don't be soft. Look behind you. There's about three and half mils' worth here and this is only one of a dozen places like this.'

Emma knew Simon Wood was making big money, but this big? It was hard for her to comprehend.

'Oh, I get it,' she said, 'you devised this little farce to put Baqri in the frame. So, why am I here?'

'Not Baqri. Think again.'

'You just wanted to bring me here?'

He nodded.

'Why?'

'Neat eh?'

She couldn't get her head around this. 'Why?'

'So, I could meet you face-to-face and we could have this conversation.'

He'd played her good style, and like a fool, she'd fallen for it.

'Why go to all this bother? What's so important about me?'

'My uncle, Simon Wood.'

She nodded, 'What do you want me to do?'

'Get him out.'

She let the comment hang, giving her time to think. Would she? 'It's not possible,' she said, finally. 'The case is out of my hands. It's with the CPS.'

'I dunno, you must be able to do something like hide the evidence, hide some statements, destroy a few photographs. You're the expert. You tell me.'

She smiled. 'Hide the evidence like what, fifty kilos of cocaine?'

'I meant the evidence against Simon.'

'He's in jail as part of the crew on the boat. Hang on, can he sail a boat like that?'

'Simon?'

'Yeah.'

''Course he can, it was his boat you raided.'

'Right. He could claim he was the captain, hired to bring the other guys over to the UK, and knew nothing about the cargo.'

'Yeah, sounds good, I like it.'

'Maybe it's a bit weak but I'm sure there's some other things I can do.'

'Listen Emma. I'm just testing the water like, see what else we can do if Plan A doesn't come off.'

'What's Plan A?'

'What I want you to do next week, is call him back to your nick for questioning. Then, all you have to do is give me the time and the route of the security van bringing him in from Wandsworth. We'll do the rest.'

Damn, she didn't realise their planning was so well advanced. 'I need some time to think about it.'

'No, you don't, not if you want him back anytime soon,' he said nudging Jacko with his elbow.

Emma shook her head. 'No deal. I said I need more time to think about what I can do. I'm agreeing to help you. In return, you need to release Jacko.'

'Don't talk to me about fucking deals,' Lamar said, raising his voice. 'I'm the one with all the cards, okay?'

She nodded.

'Don't leave me here, Emma. He'll kill me.'

Lamar turned to Jacko, 'Shut up you, I'm talking to your boss.' He turned back to her. 'Emma, I'm gonna need three days' notice before you call the security van back to your place. I need a date from you by Thursday next week, latest. Okay?'

'I can't just think up any old reason to bring him—'

'Why don't you question him about the Peterson case?' Jacko said.

'What's that about?' Lamar asked.

'Essex Police found the captain of a Baltic freighter, Olaf Peterson, dead in his cabin a day after it docked at Tilbury a month ago,' Emma said. 'Rumours were he was bringing in drugs from Russia.'

Intel suggested Peterson had crossed Simon Wood and paid for it with his life, but this wasn't what grabbed Emma's attention. Jacko was a ham actor, always had been, and the Peterson story rolled off his tongue too easily, like a bad actor trying to say his lines before quickly running off stage. Lamar couldn't act either as she could see he was feigning ignorance about a case involving his uncle. This could mean only one thing: Jacko and Lamar were in collusion with one another. This meeting was nothing but a charade.

Lamar looked at Emma. 'So, we're all set?'

'It's plausible.' She hesitated. 'I'll do it.'

'Hey, she agrees.' He turned to Jacko again. 'Man, you're not so dumb after all.'

A look of anger flashed across Jacko's eyes and it confused her at first, but she soon realised that Jacko was getting pissed at Lamar overplaying his role.

'Are we done?' she asked.

Lamar nodded.

She stood and walked to the door. She needed to get out and decide what to do. At least this time she wouldn't be hampered by thoughts of Jacko's kidnapping.

'Don't leave me here, Emma, they're vicious criminals,' he whined.

'Don't worry Jacko, I'll soon get you out.' She put her hand on the door handle. 'Be seeing you.'

'Christ, Lemmy, look at her face. She didn't ask when you're letting me out. She's got us sussed!' Jacko's pleading voice had gone to be replaced by a harder tone she'd never heard before. 'She'll tell the fucking world about me. Shoot her!'

She pulled open the door but before she could take a step and walk out, a gun fired. She slumped to the ground, life seeping away as her blood pooled over the tiled floor.

Chapter 50

Matt woke from a deep and groggy sleep, dreaming of his mother. They were walking along a beach in Suffolk together. They often went to Suffolk on holiday, but he couldn't recall ever walking along a beach with her. Sitting outside a pub, waiting for her and her latest 'squeeze' to finish boozing would be more like it. That said, he did appreciate the imagery, the first dream involving her for several months. He opened his eyes expecting it to be his bedroom in Ingatestone with Emma lying beside him. The inside of the hospital room took him by surprise. Rosie was seated in a chair close by, reading a book.

'What are you reading?'

'Oh, you're awake,' she said looking up. 'How are you feeling?'

'I don't know, I'm not awake yet.'

'I wouldn't advise you to move much as there's heavy strapping on your left shoulder.'

He shifted position but stopped when a sharp pain coursed through his shoulder, like hundreds of little needles stabbing him all at once. 'Christ! That's painful,' he said, sweat forming on his brow. 'What happened?'

'Leppo shot you.'

'Shot? When I fell, I thought he'd whacked me with something hard like a brick or a lump of wood.'

'No, he shot you. I assume due to the lack of light and his dazed state following the crash, he couldn't see you that well or the bullet might have been more accurate and killed you.'

'That guy's as cold as ice. Where is he?'

'In the morgue, where he belongs.'

'You?'

She nodded. 'He didn't know I was there as he seemed to dawdle a bit before deciding to finish you off. It gave me time to line him up.'

'Good job or I'd be in the morgue along with him. I assume your hands remained steady?'

'What? How did you know?' she said, her face quickly colouring.

'I looked for it. Often happens after a serious incident like the one you experienced. Don't worry, it's temporary.'

'So it seems. Luckily, it disappeared a few days before my unscheduled firearms test and didn't come back.'

'You've exorcised your demons.'

'I hope so. I'd be bloody useless as an HSA agent if I hadn't.'

'What's the story with Dragon?'

'Their toast. The scandal has hit the web and most newspapers and the US Stock Exchange has suspended trading in their shares. Sir Raymond will make a statement in the House today condemning their actions and Walter Ingham has been handed over to the Met. He'll be charged with a suite of things including conspiracy to murder.'

'Looking good.'

'Watch this space, but it's not all good news, Matt.'

'How do you mean?'

'I didn't want to be the one to tell you, but I'd hate for you to read it in a newspaper.'

'What?'

She hesitated, searching for the right words. 'There's no easy way to say this, Matt, but Emma's been killed.'

'How? When?'

'She was found with two bullet wounds by a dog-walker in Epping Forest. Initial forensics suggest she didn't die there but somewhere else, her body dumped. No one's been arrested yet. I'm sorry to be the bearer of such terrible news.'

Matt didn't hear the rest. Perhaps due to the drugs, the full impact of the words took several moments to penetrate his muzzy senses. When they did, he was hit with the force of an express train. He wailed and wailed, tears flowing freely. When he tried to move, to get out of the hospital and confirm Rosie's words for himself, the pain seared through his muscles and sinews, leaving him panting.

He heard some commotion at the edge of his bed, but what or who was causing it failed to penetrate his grief. A firm hand gripped his arm and he felt a small pinprick. Emma's face swam in front of his eyes, but then the picture faded, the pixels dissolving into the ether, before sleep lulled him back into its soft, comforting embrace.

Chapter 51

Over two hundred people attended the funeral service in the St. Edmund and St. Mary Church in Ingatestone. Matt came from a large Irish family and his many nieces, nephews and cousins were all there, but few from Emma's family. She only had her brother, Phillip, and her parents, Daniel and Cathy. The rest of the congregation was made up from officers from the Met and officers and admin staff from HSA. Eulogies were read by Emma's boss, Superintendent Tony Quigley, and her close working colleague, the newly promoted Detective Inspector Jack Harris.

No one had been arrested for her murder and now, almost two weeks after the event, Matt doubted they ever would. He'd heard rumours that with no real leads and no positive forensic data, the investigation was soon to be scaled back. The police would never forget a dead colleague, but he knew how frustrating it was without any sound intel to drive a case forward.

Outside in the churchyard, he shook many hands and comforted Emma's family. He liked her father, a nuclear engineer at Sellafield in Cumbria, and with Emma being a bit of a daddy's girl, he seemed to take her death hardest.

'I told her I didn't want her joining the police.'

'I know you did, but there are hundreds, maybe thousands of officers who suffer no more than a few bruises and broken bones in the course of their service.'

'Ach, we all have to die of something, I just wish it didn't happen so soon. However, I take comfort from knowing she died doing something she believed in. I must go and take care of her mother. See you later Matt.' He clapped Matt on his un-bandaged shoulder, dipped his head to hide his tears and headed towards the graveyard to join his wife and son.

Matt walked over to speak to the Director. Before he could, Jack Harris crossed his path.

'Matt,' he said shaking his hand. 'Good to see you. How are you bearing up?'

'Been walking around in a daze if I'm being truthful, not sure of the time or the day.'

'Are you back at work?'

'No, not yet. Before seeing you, I was on my way over there,' he said nodding towards Gill, now talking to Superintendent Quigley. 'I wanted to talk to the boss about the same thing.'

'Emma will be missed in our place for sure.'

'I'll bet.'

'Not only did we lose a good officer who played by the book and all that, but we could always rely on her.'

'I want to understand what happened on Emma's last job. You know what I'm saying, the drugs raid you guys did on the Spice lab at Grays.'

'Yeah.'

'Can I come and talk to you about it some time?'

'Sure thing, any time you like. Just give me a call.'

'Thanks Jacko, appreciated. Thanks for coming today.'

Matt walked towards Gill and the old feeling returned. Talking to Jacko always left Matt with a sense there was something shifty about him. He felt it moments before as he paid compliments to Matt's dead partner; they sounded hollow and insincere. He'd never mentioned it to Emma before as, to her, Jacko walked on water.

Matt noticed at previous funerals how some people would move away at the approach of the grief-stricken partner. Perhaps they were afraid of having nothing to say to provide comfort, or were scared of saying something that might cause offence. Whatever the reason, as Matt headed towards Templeton McGill, Superintendent Quigley walked away.

'Hello Matt. I won't ask you how you are as you told me yesterday.'

'And the day before.'

'True. I liked the service. Plenty of blue uniforms on display.'

'Quigley spoke well.'

'For a copper you mean, but that aside, I sense he's got a lot of respect for Emma. I've asked around her old colleagues and believe me, it's not bluster. He regarded her highly.'

'It's good to know,' Matt said.

'Do you want to know what happened to Dragon Technologies? You didn't yesterday.'

'Yeah. I'm much better now for seeing Emma off.'

'As you already know, Sir Raymond Deacon raised the subject in the House of Commons, Louise wrote a front-page story, and Walter Ingham and other senior people at Dragon in the UK and the US are now in custody. The UK and NATO orders for the Pulsar helicopter are suspended, awaiting the outcome of an investigation, and defence analysts expect them to be cancelled. The fallout has reached the US where shares in the parent company have been suspended on the New York Stock Exchange. Commentators say they could file for Chapter 11 in a matter of days.'

'Chapter 11?'

'It's a kind of quasi-bankruptcy, providing protection from creditors while they sort the mess.'

'How are Chris and Louise?'

'Louise returned to her flat and is back working at the newspaper where they are treating her as a hero. Chris is still living at his uncle's house and planning to return to university.'

'Excellent news,' Matt said. 'A successful end to a difficult case.'

'One last thing. Dejan Katić. Remember him?'

'How could I forget?'

'We found evidence on Leppo's laptop that he had hired Katić to shoot down the Anderson family balloon. It has all been passed to Interpol and I suspect Katić will never see the sky outside a prison courtyard ever again.'

'Best place for him.'

'I agree and it's great credit to you and Rosie for sticking with it to the end. Finding evidence that he'd been to the same field in Oxford was key to unlocking this whole case.'

'Cases like this often have significant turning points. For us, this was it.'

'What's bothering you, Matt? I can sense something isn't right. Are you hankering to come back?'

'Yeah, but when I do, I want to go after them.'

'By 'them' you mean the person or persons responsible for killing Emma?'

'Yep.'

'You're in no fit state to go after anybody. Setting aside the trauma of Emma's death, your shoulder is still in a sling and your doctors think you're suffering from PTSD.'

'The shoulder does hurt likes hell and I can't distinguish PTSD from grief, but when I'm able, I want to go after them.'

'What makes you think you could do a better job than Serious Crime?' Gill said, 'They threw a lot of weight behind the investigation, as you would expect for one of their own.'

'I don't need to tell you, how much more persuasive we can be than the Serious Crime boys.'

'Only when there are good suspects or witnesses in the frame, and in this instance, there aren't any. Matt, I need to counsel you against this sort of revenge thinking, even if we are talking about avenging the death of my niece. With the best will in the world, your judgement at the moment is clouded. Who knows how you'll react if you end up in a room with her killer or killers, or even those in possession of some information?'

'I know all this, but if I pass the psychology tests and I'm declared fit for service, I'm convinced my judgement will be clear. I'll be able to investigate the case without personal bias.'

'I'm afraid I cannot agree with you.'

'Gill, I'll investigate this either as an agent for HSA or freelance. I'm determined to see it through and get justice for Em.'

Matt took a deep breath; decision time. If he continued to work for HSA, he could legally question subjects and apply lethal force, but he wouldn't be allowed to investigate Emma's death. If he turned freelance, he could still be armed as he knew where he could buy a weapon, and he'd be free to pursue Emma's killers. However, if he overstepped the law, police and agents from HSA would hunt him down.

The Director sighed. 'I can understand your anger, Matt, but at the same time, I don't want to lose you. That said, I can't have you wasting your time on something the vast resources of the Met are finding difficult to solve.' He paused, thinking. 'This is the deal, take it or leave it, all right?'

Matt nodded.

'I want you working full-time on any case that comes into HSA that I deem to be a high priority. Any spare time this allows, you can use it to follow up on Emma's case. Don't think I'm being heartless Matt. I loved Emma too, and I want justice for her. Do we have a deal?'

The End

About the Author

Iain Cameron was born in Glasgow and moved to Brighton in the early eighties. He has worked as a management accountant, business consultant and a nursery goods retailer. He is now a full-time writer and lives in a village outside Horsham in West Sussex with his wife, two daughters and a lively Collie dog.

The Pulsar Files is the first book in the Matt Flynn thriller series. Find out about future releases using the links below.

Visit the website at: www.iain-cameron.com
Follow him on Twitter: @iainsbooks
Follow him on Facebook: @iaincameronauthor

Books by Iain Cameron

Iain is also the author of the successful DI Angus Henderson crime series. Check out the six books published so far.

One Last Lesson

The body of a popular university student is found on a golf course. DI Angus Henderson hasn't a clue as the killer did a thorough job. That is, until he finds out that she was once was a model on an adult web site run by two of her tutors.

Driving into Darkness

A gang of car thieves are smashing down doors and stealing the keys of expensive cars. Their violence is escalating and the DI is fearful they will soon kill someone. They do, but DI Henderson suspects it might be cover for something else.

Fear the Silence

A missing woman is not what DI Henderson needs right now. She is none other than Kelly Langton, once the glamour model 'Kelly,' and now an astute businesswoman. The investigation focuses on her husband, but then another woman goes missing.

Hunting for Crows

A man's body is recovered from the swollen River Arun, drowned in a vain attempt to save his dog. The story interests DI Angus Henderson as the man was once a member of an eighties rock band. When another band member dies, exercising in his home gym, Henderson can't ignore the coincidence.

Red Red Wine

A ruthless gang of wine fakers have already killed one man and will stop at nothing to protect a lucrative trade making them millions. Henderson suspects a London gangster, Daniel Perry, is behind the gang. He knows to tread carefully, but no one warned him to safeguard those closest to him.

Night of Fire

A man is found burned to death. DI Henderson is forced to trawl through the victim's life as the fire left few clues. The case is about to be shelved due to lack of evidence when new information is uncovered. This leads the DI to confront the real murderer, but this psychopath will kill anyone that gets in their way.

For information about characters, Q&A and more:
www.iain-cameron.com

All my books are available from Amazon in Kindle and paperback format.

Printed in Great Britain
by Amazon